ACCLAIM FOR ROBIN T. POPP'S PREVIOUS NOVELS

SEDUCED BY THE NIGHT

"Entertaining . . . Popp spins a suspenseful yarn and many will enjoy this take on vampire romance."

—*Publishers Weekly*

"Thrilling and enthralling . . . If you're looking for a great paranormal romance, allow yourself to be *Seduced by the Night*."

—RomRevToday.com

"I definitely recommend reading [this book]."

—FreshFiction.com

OUT OF THE NIGHT

"Wonderful . . . a fabulous supernatural romance."

—*Midwest Book Review*

"A paranormal masterpiece . . . it captured my heart from the very beginning."

—*Rendezvous*

"Top pick! Four-and-a-half stars . . . Popp does a stellar job combining intriguing characterization with gritty suspense, adding up to a major thrill ride."

—*Romantic Times BOOKclub Magazine*

"Four hearts! Pulls the reader right into the story . . . the action is fast-paced . . . [the] romance heats up nicely, and the ending is a doozy . . . Ms. Popp delivers a surprise or two."

—*Romance Reader*

"Thrilling all through its action-packed pages. You will be desperately turning pages just to see what is going to happen next."

—TheRomanceReadersConnection.com

"Fascinating . . . reimagines old legends and puts a new 'spin' on them."

—*Huntress Magazine*

"A new twist makes this story unique and I was thrilled to see that there will be a sequel."

—ARomanceReview.com

Also by Robin T. Popp

Out of the Night

Seduced by the Night

TEMPTED IN THE NIGHT

ROBIN T. POPP

WARNER FOREVER

NEW YORK BOSTON

Warner Forever is an imprint of Warner Books, Inc.

Cover design by Diane Luger
Book design by Stratford Publishing Services, Inc.

Warner Forever
Hachette Book Group USA
1271 Avenue of the Americas
New York, NY 10020
ISBN-13: 978-0-7394-7760-1

Printed in the United States of America

To my friends—
you make my world a happier place.

Acknowledgments

A special thank you to:

Marlaine Loftin, for the endless hours she spent with me brainstorming the action scenes and plot twists that eventually became this story. Getting there without her would have been much harder and not nearly as much fun.

Fellow authors Donna Grant, Mary O'Connor, and Georgia Ward, for their daily support in the trenches, whether it was by chatting, brainstorming, reading chapters, or just letting me vent.

Adam Popp, whose love and support get me through each day. He really came through for me when times got tough.

Tandy LaCour, for being able to discuss, in analytical terms, exactly what makes a story great. I appreciate our discussions of story premise, plot development, and character arcs on the many stories we've both read, but especially as related to TEMPTED IN THE NIGHT. I know for a fact that this story is better as a result of our discussions.

Sgt. Clarence "Turk" Marthet of the Louisville Metropolitan Police Department, for sharing his technical expertise and opinions with me. It has been a great pleasure getting to know him. Any errors the reader might find in this story pertaining to homicide/criminal investigations and judicial process are wholly my fault.

Cathy Grant, for e-mails that made me smile, enthusiasm for my stories, and for introducing me to Turk.

Patricia Reid, who provided me with Max Caine's name. With luck, we'll be running into this villain again.

Corkey Sandman, for always being my greatest fan.

All the wonderful people who have read and enjoyed my books—in the end, it's all about you.

TEMPTED IN THE NIGHT

Chapter 1

"Tell me something, Boehler, just what the fuck were you thinking?" Assistant Chief Gamble's voice was loud enough to rattle the windows in his small office.

"I'm sorry, was that a rhetorical question?" Veteran homicide detective John Boehler remained unfazed as he faced his boss across the desk.

"What the fuck do you think?" Gamble bit out sharply.

Another rhetorical question, John thought but this time said nothing. He was too tired to sit through much more of this ass-chewing, not that he had any hope of getting to bed soon.

"Why in the hell would you even approach Simon Brody after the trial, much less threaten him in front of every reporter in the greater D.C. metro area?"

"I didn't threaten him," John said with as little inflection as he could.

Gamble picked up the TV remote on his desk and aimed it at the small television sitting on a nearby bookcase. Soon, the news footage outside the courthouse was rolling across the screen. John didn't bother to watch. He didn't want to see Simon Brody strolling down the steps of the courthouse with that smug, self-satisfied grin plastered across his face.

It was harder to ignore the little cocksucker voicing his seemingly heartfelt reaffirmation of innocence, especially when Gamble turned up the volume. As it had before, both Brody's tone and his words ignited a slow, white-hot burn of rage deep inside of Boehler. Today, justice had not been served. The jury may have found Brody innocent, but John knew the truth.

"Don't get too comfortable, Brody. You're going to hell—if I have to drag your sorry ass there myself." John found himself silently reciting the words as his televised voice echoed across the room.

Gamble shut off the television and the silence that followed was deafening, if brief. "Sounded like a threat to me, and the media's having a field day with it."

John didn't bother to respond. When he'd uttered his threat, the media had been the least of his concerns. Five long months of hard, by-the-book investigative work flushed down the proverbial toilet because someone in the department had managed to "lose" a critical piece of evidence. John had no doubt that Franklin Brody and his millions were somehow involved.

Daddy might have saved his spoiled son from death by lethal injection, but who was going to save the young women of the Washington, D.C., area? Now that Simon Brody was free, it was just a matter of time before he killed again.

"I want to know what's bothering you, Boehler," the assistant chief continued in a surprisingly sympathetic tone. "You haven't been yourself lately. You used to be one of the best detectives I had. I never had to worry about you. Lately, though . . . I don't know." He studied John's face closely in a fair imitation of the department's psychiatrist trying to see inside his head. "Are you having problems at home? With your wife?"

John wanted to laugh at the absurdity of the question. "I'm not married." He had been once, fifteen years ago, if one could call a drunken night, a quick trip to Vegas, and eleven months of sheer hell a marriage. John didn't.

"Then maybe you need to find someone; settle down; start a family."

Yeah, John thought, because it had worked so well the first time. Gamble's attempt to counsel him was pissing him off. "I'm fine. Just a little tired." He didn't want to continue this particular line of conversation, so he changed the subject. "Sir, I'd like permission to look into how that evidence against Brody disappeared."

"That's not your job."

"I realize that. However—"

Gamble waved him to silence. "Forget that. You've got bigger problems to deal with."

"Sir?"

"First, you practically accuse the late Miles Van Horne of being involved with terrorists. Now, you've publicly threatened the son of Washington's *second* most influential man. Is it the rich you hate, Boehler, or are you just tired of being a cop? Because I assure you, you're well on your way to committing career suicide."

John felt himself grow very still. "Van Horne wasn't a random target. The Exsanguinators killed him because he tried to double-cross them. I'd call that being 'involved.'"

Gamble heaved a frustrated sigh. "Well, his mother disagrees. Now Marcie Van Horne has got the D.A. breathing down my neck to reopen the case. I have to bring in someone from Internal Affairs to take a second look."

John wasn't stupid. He read between the lines. Gamble was bringing in IA to investigate *him* as much as the circumstances of Miles Van Horne's death. And if they got too close . . .

John wondered how much time he had to "clean up" his files and was about to make his excuse to leave when Gamble pressed the button on his intercom. "Gail? I want to know when Dresden gets here. He is? Good, send him in."

A moment later, the door to the office opened and a short, stocky man walked in wearing a pressed suit, polished shoes, and an attitude that said his shit didn't stink. John hated him instantly.

"John, meet Richard Dresden, with Internal Affairs. He'll be handling the investigation into the Exsanguinator cases. I expect you to show him the same respect you'd show me—and give him your full cooperation."

Yeah, John thought, he'd show *Dick* some respect. Count on it. He managed to keep his mouth shut and his face expressionless.

At his boss's dismissive gesture, he stood and headed for the door. He was seconds from freedom when the assistant chief dropped the last bomb on him. "Don't let me catch you anywhere near Simon Brody or anything having to do with him, got it? Right now, you've got two strikes against you. One more and you'll be so far out, not even God will be able to get you back in the game."

A couple of hours later, instead of being at home in bed relaxing, John was driving around town, scanning the dark streets for . . . he wasn't sure what, exactly. If anyone had asked, he would have told them he was looking for members of a fanatical group of serial killers—a group he had dubbed the Exsanguinators because of the way they drained their victims' bodies of blood.

Of course, he was more likely to find one of their victims than the actual killers. In over a year of searching, that's all he'd ever found.

His first exposure to the Exsanguinators had come when several Navy SEALs disappeared under violent and mysterious circumstances. Days later, one of them was found dead in an abandoned building. There had been no obvious wounds and yet, the body had been drained of blood. Later victims would be found also drained of blood, each having two puncture wounds in the neck that were to become the group's signature mark.

That case had been a first for John, and in his search for answers he had called in the dead SEALs' commanding officer, Admiral Charles Winslow. John had met the older man years earlier when the admiral had been a guest lecturer for one of John's college classes. They'd instantly struck up a friendship that had survived the years.

To his surprise, the admiral had claimed to be familiar with both the modus operandi and the group responsible, leading John to believe that the problem was something the government was handling. This wasn't the first time the police and the government had worked on the same case, so John started calling the admiral or one of the members of his security team whenever he found another victim, hoping the collaboration would help him solve the cases.

The admiral and his team, however, had not exactly been forthcoming with information, John reflected as he found a place to park his car. He'd been left to draw his own conclusions, which were as disturbing—and bizarre—as the killings themselves.

Then, a couple of months ago, the case had taken an interesting turn in a new direction as the victim demographics changed. Instead of killing average citizens, the Exsanguinators were targeting criminals; scum of the earth who had, through power, money, or the negligence of the legal system, managed to escape justice. In one sense, the Exsanguinators were now performing a community service. John wasn't so sure he wanted that to end.

Getting out of the car, John started walking. The park loomed before him like a graveyard, silent and eerie, the shadows of trees obstructing his view. A chill raced down his spine and he pulled his coat tighter to keep out the stiff February breeze and continued on, wondering if his purpose tonight would still make sense in the morning.

Last week's snowfall lay in dirty piles of slush along the edges of the street, and he had to step over several small puddles to avoid getting his shoes wet. When he reached the park, he stepped onto the paved path. His senses were hyperextended as he strained to pick up even the slightest sound, and though he heard nothing, he sensed he wasn't alone.

Walking as silently as he could, he continued on, eyeing the large grouping of bushes ahead to his right. He was less than twenty yards away when a figure suddenly appeared ahead of him.

Time stood still as John stopped to study the man whose features were too shadowed to see clearly. It wasn't unusual for there to be someone in the park at this late hour and the man could be anyone. He didn't have to be a killer. Yet, when he lifted his head, John noticed that his eyes glowed with an unnatural red light.

Before John could decide if what he saw was more than a trick of the moonlight, the sound of running feet caught his attention. He turned just as the lithe figure of a woman came racing out of the darkness, long black hair flapping wildly in the wind behind her. The exact details of her other features were lost in deference to the sword, which she wielded with apparent confidence and purpose.

Screaming like a banshee, she raced toward him, showing no signs of slowing.

"Police—stop right there!" John shouted, pulling his badge from one pocket at the same time he reached for his gun. The woman merely glanced at him as she continued to run. He realized then that her target was the dark stranger, who seemed to come to the same conclusion, because he turned and raced off, the banshee hot on his trail.

Knowing he couldn't shoot her in the back, John shoved his badge into his coat pocket and raced after her. He was almost close enough to tackle her when she suddenly whirled around, slashing her sword through the air.

"What the fu—" John stopped short, arching his body into the shape of a *C* so the sword barely missed slicing open his midsection.

"Stay out of this," she yelled at him, turning again to race off.

John shot after her and, praying she didn't turn around, launched himself through the air and tackled her to the ground before she could race past the next stand of bushes. They landed with a painful jolt that should have knocked the wind out of her, especially with his added weight on top of her. She recovered quickly and immediately began trying to buck him off, all the while shouting at the top of her lungs.

"I'll kill you, you bloodsucking—"

"Settle down," John ordered, noting the British accent even as he ripped the sword from her hand and tossed it a safe distance away. "Don't make me hurt you."

She continued to struggle, bucking her hips to throw him off balance. Her efforts were distracting, drawing his attention to the gentle swell of her hips and her pert, round butt as it came in repeated contact with his groin. It'd been too damn long since he'd been with a woman, he thought, almost groaning aloud.

Get a grip, Boehler. Cuff her, read her her rights, and haul her hot ass to jail.

She bucked again, and a part of his anatomy stirred to life. Reacting like he'd been hit with a hot brand, he shifted his body enough to be able to shove a knee into her back, pinning her to the ground.

"Oompf! Bloody hell," she swore. Her long hair spilled about her head as she twisted this way and that, trying to look at him. "What are you doing?"

"I would think it's obvious." Trying to remain professionally detached, he ran his hands along her body, searching for hidden weapons, enjoying the feel of her even as he resisted the urge to take advantage of the situation.

"You're letting him get away! Let me up now before it's too late!" she demanded, breaking into his thoughts.

John glanced up and saw that the other man had, in fact, disappeared. "Who was that? Your boyfriend?"

She huffed at him in anger. "Not bloody likely."

Yeah, right. Not anymore, he thought. A woman like this—hot body, spirited, probably great in bed—there was always a catch. In this case, the poor bastard had gotten involved with a woman who thought nothing of racing through the park at night with a sword, no doubt intending to execute her own "Bobbitt" maneuver. She was clearly psychotic, and the man was lucky to have gotten away.

Pulling handcuffs from his belt, John secured her wrists behind her back. Then he flipped her over and helped her to sit. "You want to tell me why you're running around the park at night with a sword?"

When she glared at him, he got his first good look at her face. She was stunning. It was too dark to see the color of her eyes, but her lashes were long and full. Her eyebrows were like dark accent marks above her eyes, and her oval face tapered to a delicate but firm chin. A slender nose with a slightly rounded end gave her an impish look, and her full lips, slightly parted now, were a temptation all their own.

John cleared his throat. "Look, you're in serious trouble. A little cooperation would go a long way. Who are you?"

Still, she refused to answer him.

He tried to read her expression as she looked up at him through disheveled hair. When she spoke, her words were soft and beseeching. "Please, you have to help me. People are going to die if we don't stop him. You have to let me go."

She sounded so sincere, he almost found himself believing her; wanting to help her. Almost. "I don't think so."

She immediately renewed her struggles to break free, cursing and issuing threats of violence. John stood and picked up her sword. Then he reached down to grip her arm and hauled her to her feet. This was a deeply disturbed, possibly psychotic woman in desperate need of a seventy-two-hour lockdown and a Thorazine drip—and John knew a judge who owed him a favor. He'd get Zorro checked in and then would go home where, if he was lucky, he might still grab a couple of hours of sleep.

Hours later, John was jerked from a deep sleep by the sound of his home phone ringing. As he lay there debating whether or not to answer it, the ringing stopped. He held his breath, waiting to see if it started up again, and when it actually seemed that it wouldn't, he closed his eyes and let his mind drift . . .

He came awake at the sound of his cell phone ringing.

Glancing at the clock on the bedside table, he saw that it was almost noon, which meant he'd had maybe two hours of sleep. Throwing back the covers, he half-rolled, half-fell out of bed, still fully clothed in yesterday's wrinkled outfit, and stumbled across the room to where his coat lay draped over the back of a chair.

Hauling it up, he dug in the pocket for his phone and answered it just before it rolled over to voice mail.

"Boehler here." His voice sounded like wet gravel under rolling tires.

"I want to see you in my office. Now," Gamble ordered.

"Yes, si—" The line went dead. John stared at the phone in dumb fascination for a minute. "Good morning to you, too," he mumbled, wondering what he'd done wrong this time.

The events of the prior evening came racing back—the dark figure in the park, the sword-wielding, screaming banshee—whose name he still didn't know because she'd had no ID on her and had refused to talk to him, even when he'd checked her into the psych facility for observation.

John remembered the look of hate and betrayal on her face when he'd dropped her off—it had bothered him. It shouldn't have. His rational side argued that she was just another psychotic criminal, no matter how attractive a package she came in. Yet, even now, he remembered the details of that package much too vividly—the curve of her waist, the flare of her hips. And that ass. He felt a groan building deep inside and quickly reined in his thoughts.

He'd hated leaving her in lockdown, but told himself, again, that leaving her in lockdown was better than the alternative—jail. But what was he to do with her? Unbidden, another memory rose, this time of him straddling her at the park; of her ass, round and firm. He imagined her on all fours while he knelt behind, naked from the waist down and burying himself in her, time and again.

He shook his head and remembered her last lover—the man he'd seen in the park; the one who'd barely escaped with his body parts. No, he needed to keep this situation strictly professional, which meant that in seventy-two hours, he had three options: file charges against her and throw her in jail, have her committed for a full psych-eval, or let her go.

He was hoping her short stay in lockdown would make her more forthcoming with information about herself so he could make the right decision. His plan to pay her a little visit as soon as he woke up today would have to wait, though, and he felt an inexplicable twinge of disappointment.

Not bothering to change clothes, John ran his fingers through his hair and put on his shoes. His holster was slung over the bedpost, so he shrugged into it and then, out of habit, checked the gun to make sure the safety was on. As he left the bedroom, he grabbed his coat and pulled it on as he walked. He was almost to the front door when he shoved his hand into his coat pocket and it slipped through to the other side. Wondering how it could possibly have a hole in it, he remembered the sword slicing the air and just missing him. The blade must have caught the inside of his coat instead. He tried to remember what had been in that pocket and suddenly recalled shoving his badge in there just before racing after the woman.

Swearing, he checked his other pockets, but the badge wasn't there. On the chance that he'd lost it after getting home, he retraced his steps from the front door to the bedroom, even going so far as to examine the bed. Next, he ran out to his car and searched it. No luck.

Heaving a sigh, he started the car and headed for the station. As he drove, he pulled out his cell phone and called the main desk. "Hi, Joyce. I need to report a lost ID. Yeah—mine."

The call took about ten minutes and by the time he clicked off, he was already halfway to the station. Traffic wasn't a problem and fifteen minutes later, he was walking through the building, headed for Gamble's office.

His cell phone rang again and he recognized Joyce's number. Hoping someone had turned in his badge, he answered the call. "Tell me you have good news."

"Sorry, John, not the kind you're hoping for," she replied sympathetically. "Billy, over at Impound, called. He said to tell you they just brought in a car you might be interested in—a rental."

John knew that his sword-wielding Jane Doe hadn't materialized out of thin air. He figured she'd left her car close enough to the park to have walked there—or run there, as the case might be—so he'd asked to be notified of any cars towed in from inside a two-mile radius of Thompson Park.

He glanced at his watch and saw that it was almost one. "Joyce, Gamble's expecting me to walk in the door any second. Can you call Billy back and tell him I'll be there as soon as I can?"

"Will do."

"Okay, thanks. I owe you."

Once he reached Gamble's office, he took a bracing breath and then knocked on the closed door.

Gamble's voice erupted from the other side. "Come in."

John hadn't even made it to the chair in front of Gamble's desk before the assistant chief started in on him. "Were you in Thompson Park last night? South side?"

Warning bells started pealing inside his head. "Yes."

"What were you doing there?"

"Walking."

Gamble stared at him, his hard glare boring through him. After a second, he opened his middle desk drawer, reached in to grab something, and then tossed it onto the desk.

John stared down at his badge. Resisting the urge to snatch it up, he raised his gaze to meet Gamble's.

"We found that at the park last night," the assistant chief said. "It was under a bush, less than a foot away from Simon Brody's dead body."

Chapter 2

Simon Brody was dead? John's threat in front of the courthouse echoed in his head. He was in big trouble. "How'd he die?"

The assistant chief's expression was both suspicious and doubtful. "You telling me you don't know?"

John wanted to send his fist through the other man's face, but carefully schooled his expression to reveal none of his thoughts. He started to reach inside his jacket for his gun, but froze when Gamble raised the hand previously resting in his lap and placed it on the desk, aiming the .40-caliber Glock at him. "I suggest you move real slow," Gamble advised.

Resentment welled up inside as John used his fingertips to pull his own department-issued weapon from its shoulder holster and place it on the desk. Raising both hands so the assistant chief could see them, he unhurriedly raised his leg and rested it on the seat of the chair in front of the desk. Then, slowly, he lowered one hand and used it to pull his S&W Airweight from his ankle holster. He laid it on the desk beside the Glock.

"Since you obviously consider me a suspect," he said, "here are my guns for testing. Ballistics will verify that neither gun has been cleaned or fired in at least a week, since I was at the practice range last Tuesday."

Gamble made no move to take either weapon. "Brody wasn't shot." He stared at John like he would a specimen under a microscope, but John ignored him and waited patiently for him to continue. The wait wasn't long. "He was found with two small holes in the side of his neck, over the carotid artery. The M.E.'s report said he was missing a lot of blood—emphasis on *a lot.*"

Exsanguinators. It fit the MO. Immediately the image of the figure from the night before sprang to mind. It *had* been the killer he'd been searching for—and the man had escaped, thanks to that crazy bitch. John's irritation with her ratcheted up a notch. He knew he needed to do something about her, but first he had to find out exactly how much trouble he was in.

"Let's cut to the chase, sir. Are you arresting me?"

"Are you confessing?"

"No. For the record, I didn't kill Brody." John fought to keep his patience. "I didn't even know he was there."

Gamble stared at him, his expression unreadable. Finally, he heaved a small sigh. "Let's just say that right now, you're a 'person of interest.' Pending further investigation, you're relieved of all duties except one—helping Dresden."

John didn't like it, but knew better than to argue. He reached for his badge, but Gamble palmed it and moved it out of his reach. "I'll hang on to this for a while. The gun, too," he added when John reached for the weapon.

The Glock was department issue, but . . .

"The Airweight is mine," he said, picking it up and tucking it into his ankle holster. "Is there anything else you wanted?"

"No. That'll be all."

John left, managing not to slam the door after him, and headed for his desk. There were papers and files there he needed to get. Some distance behind him, he heard the sound of Gamble's door opening.

"I'm going to lunch," he heard the assistant chief grumble to his secretary.

John flipped through a stack of folders on his desk and pulled out the ones he wanted: all the Exsanguinator files. Glancing around, he noticed the bullpen was nearly empty. Only a few cops remained at their desks on the far side of the room. Picking up his files, he was about to leave when a thought occurred to him. Setting his files down, he grabbed an empty folder off his desk and walked to Gamble's office. As he passed the secretary, he held up the folder.

"Gamble wanted this on his desk before he got back from lunch," he said, barely glancing at her as he headed for the door.

She nodded, reaching into her lower desk drawer to pull out her purse. "Just set it anywhere," she told him. "I'm going to lunch now, too, unless you need something."

He shook his head. "No, I'm good. Enjoy lunch."

He stepped inside the office and slowly eased the door shut behind him.

Gamble's desk was a mess, but it didn't take long to find the file on Brody. He picked it up and scanned the contents. There wasn't much there.

Closing the folder, he carried it to the door and peeked out. The secretary was gone. Behind her desk, the copy machine beckoned. What he was about to do would no doubt be the nail in his coffin if anyone found out, but John figured his career was already over, so what did it matter?

Ten minutes later, he'd copied the contents of the folder, returned it to Gamble's office, placing it exactly where he'd found it, and was back at his desk, gathering his things. With a final look around, he left. He was almost to the elevators when the doors opened and Dresden stepped out.

"Detective Boehler? Are you leaving?" Dresden asked, his superior tone instantly grating on John's nerves.

John didn't slow down as he passed the shorter man, wanting only to be in that elevator when the doors closed, preferably with Dresden on the other side.

"Where are you going?" Dresden demanded, taking a step to follow him just as John hurried onto the elevator. "You're supposed to help me today."

"Just delivering a few files, Dick." John held them up with one hand as he punched the lobby button with his other and watched the doors close.

He spent the rest of the afternoon at home, reading the file on Brody's murder and reviewing the other Exsanguinator cases.

John couldn't find any reason why Brody would be involved with the Exsanguinators as Miles Van Horne had been. More likely, Brody was a victim because he matched the latest victim profile—he was a killer who'd escaped justice. Further reason to believe the man he'd seen in the park that night was an Exsanguinator.

John tried to remember the man's face, but instead saw only the image of a raven-haired beauty with brilliant emerald green eyes that had scorched him last night when he'd left her. He rubbed his temples, trying to wipe her face from his mind, and turned his thoughts to the Exsanguinator once more. It seemed unlikely that he would find the man in Thompson Park a second night in a row, but he had to look.

The night was alive with screams of pain and death. Fear kept her frozen in place. She wanted to shut her eyes, but couldn't. The creatures were everywhere, looking human except for their talon-like fangs and fiery red eyes. There were so many of them. Too many.

She huddled closer to her mother's side. Felt her mother tremble. Then, in a flash, her mother was gone and she was alone.

She looked around—desperate, terrified—and saw her mother lying on the ground. So still. Unmoving.

"Momma, wake up." She crawled to her, frightened at the sight of blood covering her mother's neck and body.

Feeling a cold trickle of fear lance down her spine, she turned and fell back. One of the creatures was coming toward her. His mouth was covered in blood; her mother's blood. When he smiled, his fangs dripped a crimson red.

She scrambled back, pumping her childlike legs as hard as she could, knowing she could never move fast enough. Never get away.

Heart slamming against her chest, Jessica pulled herself from the nightmare only to feel hands holding her down. Immediately, she struggled, knowing she was fighting for her very life.

"Hold her," a disembodied voice ordered.

"I'm trying," a second voice grumbled. Another set of hands joined the first, pinning her to the bed as she struggled against the captivity. She felt a sharp pain in her thigh and, in her mind, saw fangs sinking deep into her flesh. She cried out in frustration and fear.

The sharp pain seemed unending, and she felt her body grow sluggish from the loss of blood. She continued to fight, but her efforts seemed ineffectual. After a few minutes, the hands holding her eased their painful grip and finally let go. She tried to jump out of bed, to escape, but her body was too heavy to even move. She should have been terrified, but she wasn't. She lay still, strangely calm in the face of her own death.

From somewhere in the darkness, the voices spoke again.

"What do you think?"

"I don't know. Maybe a psychotic episode or maybe just a nightmare." The voices grew fainter.

"That must have been one hell of a nightmare . . ."

The ringing of the phone dragged John from his sleep with an eerie feeling of déjà vu. After hours of wandering around the park in vain the night before, he'd finally dragged himself to bed at four in the morning.

"Hello?" he barked into his cell phone.

"Yo, Johnny. I can't hang on to the car forever. You want to see what's in it or not?"

Shit, he'd forgotten. "Sorry, Billy. Thanks for calling. I'm on my way."

After shaving, showering, and putting on a fresh change of clothes, John felt almost human as he headed for the impound yard.

"Found it over by Thompson Park," Billy said a little later, leading John across an almost filled parking lot and stopping at a white, midsized Buick. "Here it is."

John peered through the windows and spotted a purse on the floor of the front passenger seat, with a silver-and-onyx sword scabbard propped next to it.

"Thanks, Billy. Looks like you were right." He straightened and pulled out the keys that he'd confiscated from the woman the night before. He pressed the button on the automatic opener and heard the satisfying click of the lock bolts opening on the doors. Now, he thought with anticipation, it was time to find out exactly who this Jane Doe was.

It was almost 4:00 P.M. when John pressed the buzzer on the door to the lockdown wing of the psych facility. The paperwork had taken longer than he'd anticipated, not that he'd hurried.

He turned his face to the camera so the guard inside would have a good view of him and waited. Seconds later, John was given instructions over the intercom to enter, followed by the mechanical grind of the heavy-duty door sliding back. John stepped past it and stopped at the next set of doors, which didn't open until the outer door closed behind him. Once inside the facility, he crossed the open seating area, quickly scanning the faces of the dozen or so "guests" sitting there, searching for one in particular but not finding it.

He made a brief stop at the nurses' front desk before heading to the room where he expected to find Jane Doe. Jessica, he quickly amended as he knocked on the door and waited for a response.

He was met with silence, and though courtesy dictated that he should knock a second time and wait, after what he'd discovered digging through her purse he wasn't feeling particularly inclined toward courtesy.

He pushed open the door and found her sitting on the bed, leaning against the headboard. She was wearing a pair of unisex institutional coveralls; the makeup around her eyes was smudged and her hair hung in snarls about her face.

She looked up when he walked in and relief briefly flickered across her face before she masked it.

"I see you're availing yourself of the amenities," he criticized, even though her appearance did nothing to diminish her attractiveness.

She put a hand to her hair and then let it fall as she barely glanced at him. "I was not provided with amenities. It would seem you forgot to approve them. No doubt you thought I'd try to drown myself in the shower or slit my wrist with the comb."

He felt momentarily guilty. "I'm sorry. I forgot."

"What are you doing here?" she asked, sounding sullen, but he thought he detected a note of hope.

"Time to go." He tossed the bag he'd picked up at the front desk onto the bed. It held the clothes she'd been wearing the day before. "Put these on. I'm leaving in ten minutes, with or without you."

He left her staring off into space, showing no sign that she'd heard a word he'd said. A dull ache in his jaw told him he was grinding his back teeth again, so he forced himself to relax. He'd read the report from the night before and knew they'd had to sedate her. It bothered him that no one had tried to talk to her before resorting to the use of drugs, but he supposed that in this facility they had their reasons.

Exactly nine minutes and fifty seconds later, her door opened.

"Cutting it a little close, aren't you?" He fought his irritation as he stepped out of her way. She gave him a disdainful look as she walked past, carrying herself with a regal air as if she were the queen of England. As soon as she was in front of him, however, John saw the reason why.

"Hold it." He was half-surprised when she stopped and turned back to face him. Taking her by the shoulders, he turned her around and stared at the dark hair caught in the buttons on the back of her shirt. "Problems?"

"Don't touch me," she ordered, trying to move away from him, but it was a halfhearted attempt.

"Hold still." He tried not to notice the silken feel of her hair as he unhooked it from around the buttons. In his imagination, he saw the combed strands flowing between his fingers like a cool stream of water on a hot day. *Get a grip, Boehler*, he chastised himself.

"Okay," he said, his voice sounding a little huskier than normal as he lowered his hands and took a step back. "All done."

"Thank you."

The words, even the tone, were lost on him as soon as he lowered his gaze to hers. Suddenly, the air between them seemed electrically charged as those emerald green eyes held him momentarily mesmerized. It was ludicrous, he told himself, and yet he had the hardest time breaking the spell. That bothered him a lot more than he wanted to admit.

"Come on," he growled at her. The sooner they left, the sooner he could be rid of her.

"Am I under arrest?" Jessica asked, trying to ease the tension in her shoulders without the detective noticing. The drugs they'd injected into her the night before hadn't entirely left her body, but they were nothing compared to the lingering images of the nightmare. It hadn't felt that real in a long time, but she knew why last night had been different.

She cast a surreptitious glance at the detective. It was hard to judge his age, but she guessed him to be in his late thirties or early forties, which made him a good ten to fifteen years older than herself. His dark hair was overly long, but she thought it was because he had put off getting it cut more so than because that was the intended style. His jaw was covered in a layer of dark whiskers, giving him a slightly rugged appearance. Physically, he was an attractive man, but the thing Jess noticed most about him was his presence. This man exuded quiet confidence, in a take-charge kind of way. She thought he probably had a hard time working undercover because this was not a man one could easily overlook.

Her gaze was drawn to his hands on the steering

wheel. They were large, square hands, with nails that had never been manicured. Strong hands, she mused, remembering how they'd felt stroking her body the other night.

She suppressed the slight tremor of reaction and reminded herself that she had unfinished business. "Are you letting me go?"

"No."

She stifled her frustration. "Then where are you taking me?"

"You'll see."

"I have rights, you know."

"Not tonight you don't."

She gave him a disgusted look and then turned her attention to the passing landscape, absently rubbing her arm.

"What's the matter?"

She eyed him disdainfully. "My arm hurts."

"What'd you do to it?"

"Me?" Was he kidding? "You body-slammed me to the ground last night. Or have you forgotten?"

He took his eyes off the road long enough to glance at her, giving her a raised eyebrow. "What I remember is you trying to cut off my head with a sword."

She glared at him. "I wasn't after you."

He laughed. "Yeah, that makes me feel better."

They drove on in silence, leaving the city limits, going God only knew where. As he drove, the detective reached behind his seat. "Here, I have something of yours." He dumped her purse into her lap.

The significance of his having it made her uneasy. "Where'd you get it?"

"A patrol unit found your rental car and towed it to the impound yard."

"What about my suitcases?"

"In the trunk."

"—and my sword?"

"It, too."

She opened her bag and searched its contents.

"They're not there," he told her.

"What?" She tried to sound innocent, though she supposed it was too late.

She knew she was right when he gave her a look that said "nice try." "That nasty-looking dagger and odd assortment of—what were those? Wooden stakes?"

"You searched my purse," she accused him, feeling violated.

"No shit. That's my job, Jessica. Jessica Winslow, from Hocksley, England." He reached into his front jacket pocket and pulled her passport up far enough for her to see it. She held out her hand, but he ignored it.

"You have my things. I want them back—all of them."

He shot her a dark look. "Yeah, I don't think so. I'll hold on to them."

"For how long?"

"Until I'm ready to give them back," he snapped. "How the hell did you get through airport security with all that hardware anyway? Never mind," he grumbled when she opened her mouth. "I don't think I want to know. I might have to arrest you again."

John watched her fall quiet and remembered the moment he'd found out who she was. Somehow it had seemed only fitting that she turn out to be a Winslow.

Lately, it seemed all of his problems were related to Admiral Winslow and his security team. And right now, the woman sitting beside him was the personification of all those problems, albeit wrapped in a very appealing package.

As the object of his current frustration retrieved a brush from her purse and started to work through the tangles in her hair, John focused his attention on the area through which they were driving. On one side of the road were open fields, and on the other were trees so thick and tall, it was hard to see what lay beyond them. Somewhere in those trees was a driveway, and John slowed the car so he wouldn't miss it.

In the past year, John had been to Admiral Winslow's mansion only once—and he'd been expected. This time, however, he didn't want to give anyone a chance to prepare for his visit. The time for secrets was well past.

Taking the turnoff, John drove up the long driveway. The trees on either side thinned, and it was possible to make out the large two-story mansion up ahead. The setting sun shone like a bright orange ball, backlighting the home so that the front was cast into dark shadows broken only by the warm glow coming through the front windows.

Even before he pulled to a stop and shut off the engine, the door opened and two men, one with dark hair, the other with blond, stepped outside.

If John hadn't already known that Mac Knight and Dirk Adams were once Navy SEALs, it would have been an easy guess. Both were in peak physical condition and carried themselves with the air of quiet confidence and controlled power only years of stringent military training can give a man.

"Hey, John. What's up?" Dirk came forward to shake John's hand as he stepped from the car.

"Dirk. Mac. Hope I'm not catching you at a bad time." John walked around the car to open the passenger door, pausing once along the way to shake Mac's outstretched hand. "Let's go," he said quietly to Jessica.

"No, we're good," Mac assured him, his gaze drifting to the car door.

"Is the admiral home?" John asked Mac while wondering what was taking his passenger so long to get out of the car. He glanced at her and saw the stubborn set of her jaw. She clearly had no intention of getting out, so he leaned inside, putting his face close to hers. "Get out of the damn car, now," he growled softly. "If you don't, I promise that I will haul you out."

Just a few more minutes, he told himself, leashing in his temper. If he was right about her being related to the admiral, then it was only a matter of minutes before he was free of her. He saw her gaze shift to the mansion and, behind the defiance, flashed a spark of something else. Fear? Uncertainty? John tried to be sympathetic. "This isn't another mental institution."

Her gaze cut to him. "And I should trust you because . . . ?"

His sympathy evaporated. "I can always take you back if that's what you prefer."

"John, this is a surprise." Admiral Winslow's loud voice interrupted from the doorway of the mansion.

"Hello, Admiral. I brought someone to meet you. Jessica, say hello to Admiral Charles Winslow."

John saw the minute the name registered with her. "Charles?" She gave John a curious look and then slid out of the car, ignoring his proffered hand as she moved past him.

"Jessica?" The admiral sounded both pleased and surprised. "We were expecting you two nights ago. I tried calling Gerard when you didn't arrive, but he wasn't home." He hurried forward, glancing at John as he enfolded Jessica in his arms. "We've been worried."

"I take it you *do* know her?" John asked, watching them.

"Yes; she's my cousin's daughter from England," the admiral replied before turning to Jessica. "Are you all right? You look a mess. What's going on here?"

Standing tucked against the admiral's side, she glared at John. "I would have been here sooner, but for the last two days, I've been locked in a hospital for the criminally insane—compliments of Detective Boehler."

"What?" The admiral sounded aghast and three sets of protective male eyes turned on John.

He reluctantly gave her credit for twisting the story in such a way that he came out the bad guy. "I think you should tell them the rest of it."

She opened her eyes a little wider, all innocence and sweetness. "Oh, you mean the part about how you threw me to the ground, roughed me up, cuffed me, and then interrogated me?"

John clenched his fists in an effort not to strangle her, but couldn't help his involuntary step toward her. "Back off," he muttered to Mac and Dirk when they moved to intercept him. "If I haven't killed her by now, I'm not going to."

Mac and Dirk stopped in their tracks, but their expressions said they were clearly concerned.

"Is this true, John?" the admiral asked sharply.

"Technically? Yes." John shook his head in exasperation. "But do you really think I'd do something like that without having a damn good reason?"

Charles's tone was almost frosty. "I think I'd like to hear what reason you have for treating my cousin that way."

"How about attempted murder?"

"What?" Now all the attention turned to Jessica, and John was glad to see her squirm beneath it.

Taking advantage of the moment, he reached into his pocket and pulled out his car keys, which he tossed to Dirk. "There's something in the trunk that you'll want to see."

Dirk moved to the trunk and opened it. Seconds later, he lifted out the ornate sword.

"I remember seeing that in the admiral's study once," John explained.

"Not this one," Dirk said, sounding awed as he pulled the sword from its scabbard and sliced the air a couple of times with it. In the fading outdoor light, his eyes gleamed with an unnatural reddish hue, which gave John a start. He'd only seen that trick of the lighting once before—on the man in the park.

"My cousin in England forges these swords," Charles explained. "That's why Jessica came to the States. She's delivering the sword to me."

"Well, I guess she took a slight detour because I found her running through Thompson Park the other night, waving that thing in the air, looking like she meant business. Since she was headed my way, I felt compelled to protect myself. When she resisted, things got a little rough and because she refused to tell me who she was, I had her placed under protective observation. It wasn't until her car was brought into the station with her purse and ID that I discovered her name."

The admiral shifted so he could pin her under his glare. "Jessica? Am I to understand that you were running through a public place with *that* particular sword?"

Jessica wasn't looking too happy. "There were extenuating circumstances," she said with enough emphasis that John felt certain the admiral and the others understood what she meant. After seeing their quick exchange of glances, he decided it was time to call a spade a spade.

"Extenuating circumstances," he repeated. "That would be the vampire."

Suddenly the focus of everyone's full attention, John pressed his point. "Yeah, I know about vampires. So, if you don't mind, I've got questions and I'd appreciate honest answers; no more bullshit about terrorists, okay?"

Chapter 3

Jessica felt Charles tense beside her as she stared at the detective, feelings of shock and dread washing over her. She shouldn't have gone after a vampire while there were witnesses around, but at the time she'd thought he was one of them. When she realized he was human, she knew she had to save him. What she hadn't expected was for him to tackle her and lock her up in an institution.

To make matters worse, as a member of the Winslow family, charged for centuries with the responsibility of hunting down and destroying vampires, she was supposed to guard the secret of their existence from others, not broadcast it. One rare moment of spontaneity had thrust her into an unending nightmare of one disaster after another.

She quickly glanced at the other men, trying to read their thoughts, watching the play of emotions across their faces. Mac's and Dirk's expressions were guarded as they studied the detective, who looked like he'd just received confirmation of something he'd rather not have known. She almost felt sorry for him, but not quite. After all, she was in much bigger trouble than he was.

"Why don't we all go inside," Charles suggested, gesturing toward the house. "Knowing Julia, she's got a pot of coffee ready, and we might as well talk someplace comfortable."

"We'll get Jessica's bags and join you as soon as we put them in her room," Mac said, joining Dirk at the back of the car where the two exchanged comments too soft to overhear.

Alone with Charles and John, Jess felt ill at ease. She might be family, but that was merely a technicality. The reality was that she and Charles were practically strangers. And the only thing she had in common with the detective was this mutual hate thing they had going on.

She watched him now, walking with Charles. He was almost the same height as her cousin, which meant he was only slightly taller than she was, and he moved with an easy, masculine gait. She could well imagine women everywhere falling over themselves vying for his attention. It wasn't because he was drop-dead gorgeous, because he wasn't. His dark hair was prematurely streaked with gray and it seemed that the dark stubble across his jaw that she'd noticed the other night was a permanent feature. The combination should have made him look old and unkempt. Instead, it gave him character. Beneath his long coat, she knew he was lean, hard muscle, though she tried not to dwell on the memory of the way his body felt when he'd tackled her. In a totally objective light, she thought, there was nothing special about his looks. The thing was, he commanded such presence that no one could be around him and stay objective for long.

Feeling uncomfortable, she stepped through the mansion's front door and into a vaulted foyer that was surprisingly warm and cozy despite its size. Looking around, she was impressed with the quiet elegance that surrounded her. It was much lighter and friendlier than the decor of the old English castle where she'd grown up.

"Lanie, I want you to meet Jessica," Charles said as a woman about her own age walked in, giving her a friendly smile that was hard to resist.

"It's nice to finally meet you," she said, ignoring Jess's outstretched hand to hug her instead. "I'm Mac's wife. And this is Bethany Stavinoski." She stepped back and gestured to a second, shorter woman.

Bethany came forward and also embraced Jess warmly. "I'm Dirk's fiancée. We're so glad you made it. I hope you're planning to stay for a while. Dirk and I are getting married next week, and we'd love to have you there."

It was the first Jess had heard about the wedding, and she wasn't sure what to say. "Well, I—"

"Of course she'll stay," Charles interrupted. "We haven't seen each other in, what? Thirteen years? Goodness, has it really been that long?"

She smiled and nodded at the sudden flood of memories. "Yes. I was twelve, and you thought you would teach me and Kacie how to use a sword."

"Ah, yes. That was certainly a mistake." Charles laughed, shaking his head. "I think that by the time the lesson was over, you two had taught me a trick or two." He gave her a fond smile. "Ah, the memories. Please say you'll stay. If nothing else, we should catch up on all that's happened."

Jess made a noncommittal noise. She hadn't flown all the way to the States just to deliver a sword, but now was probably not the time to mention the photo.

At that moment, an attractive older woman with auburn hair appeared. "Hello, everyone."

"Julia, there you are," Charles said, moving forward to draw the woman into the foyer. "Jessica has finally arrived, and we also have John Boehler here—you've heard us mention him."

Jess made a mental note that Charles hadn't exactly explained who this woman was in relation to the rest of the group as she watched Julia extend her hand to the detective.

"We've spoken on the phone several times," she said warmly. "It's very nice to finally meet you."

"And this is Jessica."

Julia turned that warm smile her way. "Welcome, Jessica," she said. "I've heard so much about you."

"Thank you. But please, call me Jess."

Julia dipped her head briefly to acknowledge the request and then turned to address the group in general. "I've taken the liberty of making coffee, and there are cookies left over from earlier."

"Excellent," Charles said, beaming. "Let's take our conversation into the kitchen. I hope you won't mind," he said to John. "It's my favorite room in the house, and I think we'll be more comfortable there."

Jess moved with the others into the kitchen and immediately saw why Charles loved the room. Painted in shades of buttery yellow, with accents in green and tangerine, it reminded Jess of an open field of flowers on a cool morning just after sunrise.

She moved toward the table and was disconcerted to find the only available seat was next to the detective, who looked equally thrilled to be stuck next to her. After Julia finished pouring coffee for everyone, she placed sweetener, cream, and a tray of cookies in the center of the table and then took her seat beside Charles.

"Now," Charles began. "No more bullshit." He looked at John, letting him know that his choice of words had been an intentional echo of the ones John had used earlier. "John, you are correct. Vampires do exist, and you can appreciate why that's not something we wanted made public. When you first got involved with this, I admit that I purposely misled you. I believed that you would be safer, the less you knew."

John didn't look convinced. "So, for *my* protection, you lied to me?"

"It wasn't a complete lie," Mac jumped in. "We might have omitted a small detail, like the killers weren't human, but they *were* terrorists. After all, Burton—the first vampire—did put together a team of vampires to kill the president."

John shot Mac a disdainful look, before turning back to the admiral. "I don't get it. Where'd they come from?"

"Originally?" Charles asked with a smile. "Have you ever heard of *El Chupacabra*?"

John shook his head.

"Literally translated, *El Chupacabra* means 'the goatsucker.' For most people, these creatures exist only in legend, like Bigfoot. But they are very real. They survive on blood and typically feed off of livestock. However, they do, on occasion, attack and kill a human—when that happens, the venom they inject into the body while feeding turns the corpse into a vampire."

Jessica watched the detective's face as Charles spoke. A confused look came to his eyes. Knowing what was to come, she knew that confusion was about to get worse.

"There are two types of vampires—Primes and Progeny. When a chupacabra kills a human, the vampire that rises up is a Prime. When a Prime kills a human, the vampire that results is a Progeny.

"The Primes, having received the pure chupacabra venom, are more completely converted into the living dead; they retain their human intelligence. Their Progeny, on the other hand, get only diluted chupacabra venom and so their conversion is 'flawed,' for lack of a better term. They retain their intelligence for only a short while and then it deteriorates. In the end, all that's left is a primitive bloodsucking creature obsessed with finding its next meal."

"Miles Van Horne was a Progeny," Dirk added.

"Miles Van Horne was a vampire?" The detective sounded shocked, and Jess wondered who they were talking about.

"Not at first," Mac hurried to explain. "But there at the end, Patterson—the Prime who was responsible for all those attacks on Bethany?—killed Miles and turned him into a vampire." Jessica saw Mac turn and look specifically at Dirk. "That's why Miles Van Horne had to die. It was just a matter of time before he started killing."

There was some unspoken exchange taking place between Mac and Dirk that Jessica couldn't figure out, but before she could wonder any more about it, John spoke up.

"Who the hell is Patterson? How many vampires are there?"

Jess saw Mac and Dirk exchange looks and could practically hear their thoughts, debating how much to admit. "Patterson was behind the attacks on Bethany last month, but don't worry—he's dead now. As for how many vampires are out there now, I don't know. There for a while, we were killing three or four a night, but it's slowed down some."

John stared at them, openmouthed. "Three or four a *night*? Why haven't you called me?"

"John, the last thing you—and your career—needed was to be involved in this city's vampire problem. So, as much for your protection as anything else, we haven't called you every time we destroyed a vampire."

"If it makes you feel better," Lanie put in, "we keep a list of names and addresses of all the vampires killed—at least, those who are still carrying IDs. Uncle Charles sends their families a small anonymous donation to help them out a bit. They think they've won a contest their loved one entered before they disappeared. It doesn't bring the loved one back, but the money helps them a little while they adjust."

The detective rubbed his jaw, shaking his head.

"John, I'm sorry," Charles said. "We did what we thought was necessary."

"If you don't mind my asking," Bethany asked when the group fell silent, "how did you figure out the truth?"

Jess found herself leaning closer, wanting to hear the answer. She prayed that maybe his revelation hadn't been entirely her fault.

"Until tonight, I didn't know for sure," he admitted,

dashing her hopes. "I've spent so much time trying to fit the facts of the Exsanguinator cases into a logical pattern—a pattern in keeping with human terrorists—yet there was always some part of each case that wouldn't gel with the rest. Finally, it occurred to me that maybe the answer was right in front of me if I would open my eyes and see it. So I tried to come at it from a completely objective angle, but the answer I got was ludicrous—or so I thought at the time. Still, the more I thought about it, the less crazy it seemed until eventually, I found myself taking long midnight strolls around town, looking for vampires."

"Which is why you were in Thompson Park the other night?" Mac asked. "You were looking for vampires?"

"Yeah."

"And you found one," Charles concluded.

"I don't know. I ran into a man while I was in the park, but I didn't have time to speak to him." John glanced at Jessica and she felt her face heat up. "We were interrupted."

"Jessica?" Charles turned to her with a questioning look.

"It was a vampire," she confirmed, holding Charles's gaze. She wasn't about to let him intimidate her when there was a good reason for what she'd done. "It was dark by the time I reached D.C. As I was driving through town, the eyes on the pommel of the sword began to glow." She spared John a look. "It does that whenever a vampire is in the area." She fixed first Charles, then Mac, and finally Dirk, with a level gaze. "So I did what any one of you would have done under the same circumstances. And I would have succeeded if Detective Boehler hadn't stopped me." She turned to the detective, silently daring him to refute her.

Mac, who'd been taking a drink of his coffee, set down his cup and turned to face John. "If that was a vampire you ran into, you're lucky he didn't attack you."

"I had my gun," John assured him.

Mac snorted. "In a year of hunting, I've only stopped one vampire with a gun before and it took eight closely grouped rounds to his head to bring him down."

John cast a quick glance at Jess and she knew he was remembering the dagger and stakes he'd found in her purse. Now that he understood, maybe she'd get them back.

"If the vampire didn't attack you," Lanie said, sounding like she was working out a logic problem, "then he must not have been hungry. That would mean he'd recently fed. Did you find a body?"

Only because she was studying the faces around her did Jess spot the subtle shift in John's expression when he answered. "No, I didn't see a body."

She was trying to decide whether or not he was lying when Dirk looked at his watch.

"Speaking of vampires," he said, pushing back from the table, "if you'll excuse us, it's time for our patrol." He held his hand out to John and they shook hands. "Welcome to the inner circle." Then he turned to Jess and his expression softened a bit as a twinkle came to his eye. "It's nice to finally meet you. We'll have to exchange hunting tips." Then he reached out a hand to Bethany and helped her to her feet. "Come say good-bye to me."

Together, they disappeared through the door.

"I've got to go, too," Mac added as he and Lanie also rose from the table. "I know you have more questions, John. We'll try to answer them later." He turned to

Charles. "To be safe, we'll take a spin through Thompson Park tonight."

Charles looked at his watch and gave a small exclamation. "Julia, if we don't hurry, we'll be late for the reception downtown." He turned to Jessica with an apologetic frown. "I'm sorry, my dear. This function has been scheduled for months and I can't get out of it. Julia and I will be gone for a couple of hours, but Lanie and Beth will be here. They can get you anything you need, and I promise that we'll catch up tomorrow."

"I guess I'd better be going as well," the detective said, rising to his feet.

The more Jess watched him, the more convinced she was that he was hiding something, so when he walked outside to his car, she followed him.

"What do you want?" he asked when he opened the driver's-side door and saw her coming up behind him. "The thought of being separated from me got your panties in a knot?"

"Don't flatter yourself. I wanted to talk to you, alone."

"What about?"

She hesitated as two dark-colored SUVs emerged from behind the house and drove past them. Mac and Dirk were going out on patrol. She watched them disappear down the drive and then turned to see the detective watching her, clearly not trusting her intentions.

"You lied in there."

If possible, his expression became even more guarded. "Is that right?"

"Yes, it is. I was there that night, remember? Before you knocked me to the ground, I got a good look at that vampire. I saw the blood staining his lips and teeth. There was a body, wasn't there?" She held her breath, waiting for his response. She hadn't been close enough to really notice if there'd been blood or not, but hopefully he wouldn't know that.

He stared at her as if he was deciding whether or not to tell her the truth. "Yes," he finally said.

"Where was it?"

"Behind the bush."

She eyed him suspiciously, afraid she already knew the answer to her next question. "Did you stake it?"

"Stake it? No, I never even saw it."

She stared at him in shock. "This is important. Do you know if it was staked? Because if it wasn't staked through the heart or decapitated, it's going to rise up." She quickly did the math in her head. "Tonight. It's going to rise tonight, unless we stop it. Do you know where the body is? Can you take me to it?"

He was staring at her like she'd lost her mind. "Are you suggesting I take you to the funeral home and let you defile the deceased?"

"Fine. Then you do it, but you need to hurry. You'll need a sword—damn. Mac and Dirk probably took both swords with them, but that's all right." A plan was coming together. "Do you still have my dagger and stakes?"

"You really are nuts, aren't you?" He reached into his pocket and pulled out his cell phone. "I'll call Mac and Dirk."

"No, wait." She snatched the phone from his hand and closed it. "We can do this ourselves. It's our fault this situation exists, but we can make it right."

He studied her and she held her breath, waiting for his

decision. Then he grabbed his phone out of her hand. "Go back inside, Jessica. I'm not taking you anywhere."

She shot him a scathing look. "Fine, but when this body rises up and starts killing innocent people, it'll be your fault, because I tried to prevent it." She turned on her heel and headed for the door, almost reaching it before John called her name.

She stopped and turned to glare at him. "What?"

"You stake 'em through the heart, right?"

She hurried back to the car. "Yes, but there's a trick." She opened the passenger-side door and climbed in.

"Get out, Jessica. I'm not taking you with me. Just tell me what the trick is."

She crossed her arms over her chest and stared at him defiantly as he leaned into the car. "I'm not getting out and you're wasting time."

He glared at her, but she refused to budge. Then, muttering something vulgar under his breath, he climbed into the driver's seat, started the car, and they drove off.

Chapter 4

John called himself all sorts of a fool for allowing Jessica to go with him, but there wasn't time to argue with her. He hesitated only a moment before pulling out the emergency light he was no longer authorized to use and placing it on the roof where the magnetic bottom kept it in place. With the blue-and-red colored strobe lights piercing the night, he stepped down harder on the accelerator and felt the power of the car as it surged forward.

"Where are we going?" she asked him.

"Rest Haven Funeral Home. That's where Simon Brody's body was sent today."

"How do you know?"

"I saw the police report. His father is wealthy—practically owns the town. He didn't want his son being autopsied, no matter what the law says, so he arranged to have it delivered to Rest Haven earlier today. I don't think they've had a chance to bury him yet, so that's where we're headed."

* * *

Simon Brody woke with the worst hangover imaginable. Not only did his head hurt, but his entire body ached. He was in so much pain that all he wanted to do was slip back into sweet oblivion, but he knew he wouldn't. He was starving; it felt like he hadn't eaten in weeks instead of hours. He wasn't exactly sure whose bed he'd ended up in, but he hoped she had food in her kitchen—although he wasn't sure he could stomach just anything. Even the thought of eggs and bacon made him ill.

The sound of muffled voices filtered past the sleepy fog covering his brain, adding another irritant to his list of complaints. He couldn't help but half-listen to them as he tried to fall back sleep.

"I appreciate you letting me in here tonight . . . Fred, is it?" Simon recognized his father's voice and congratulated himself. Apparently, though he'd been too drunk last night to remember anything that happened, he hadn't been too drunk to find his way home. That was a bonus.

"Sure thing, Mr. Brody," a second male voice said with a considerable amount of subservient awe. "I understand."

Understand what? Brody wondered, still not bothering to open his eyes. Not even caring why his father and Fred were in his room, he only wanted them to go away and leave him in peace. He was starting to feel worse than he had when he first awakened, if that was possible. The hunger was turning into actual, physical pain that couldn't be ignored.

"Right this way, Mr. Brody," Fred said, his voice growing louder as if they were getting closer.

"Have you worked here long?" the senior Brody asked politely.

"About twelve years."

"That's a long time. Don't you find it depressing?"

"Oh, I suppose so at times," Fred admitted.

From the sound of it, the two men had to be practically standing next to his bed, Simon thought, infuriated. Why wouldn't they go away?

"But it's also interesting," Fred continued. "I've seen shit . . . uh, pardon my language."

Simon heard his father's indulgent reassurance for the man to continue, which, to Simon's great annoyance, Fred did.

"I've seen stuff happen that just plain scared the bejeebers out of me."

"Really?" His father's voice came from directly above him, like he was standing over him; lording over him, just like he always did. Hovering, watching. Criticizing.

"Yes, sir," Fred went on. "There was one time, I was helping another guy prep a body, and it just sat straight up."

"No." His father sounded dismayed.

"Yep, straight up. Damnedest thing I ever saw, but it happens. Don't mean the person ain't dead. Just a delayed reaction of the nerves and muscles. Like a camera's flash, all charged up and ready to go, but then you don't take another picture. That flash sits on the camera until something sets it off and then it discharges. That's all the muscles are doing—discharging, so to speak."

The story was ludicrous, but Simon could tell from the way his father's breath hitched and his heart started beating faster that the old man believed it. Simon wanted to laugh but then wondered how it was possible for him to hear his father's beating heart—or the way his father's pulse raced, sounding like an underground current of rushing water.

The pain now was crippling, and unable to ignore it any longer, Simon opened his eyes and stared into the shocked face of his father, who for once was speechless.

"Oh, shit," Fred said from elsewhere in the room, his voice little more than a muffled noise beneath the sound of hearts beating too fast.

Brody's vision faded to red and he became aware of nothing more than the hunger driving him.

Pulling to a stop in the front drive of the funeral home, John turned off the car and studied the building, noticing how too few outside lights and too many shrubs and trees cast dark shadows around the sides and front of the building. The cemetery, with its aboveground tombs, stretched out to the right while undeveloped acreage intended for future expansion was to the left.

John had replaced his confiscated Glock with an S&W .44 mag, which he now pulled from his holster. He flipped open the cylinder and checked the six chambers to make sure they were loaded.

"Stay here," he told her as he reached for the door handle.

"Absolutely not," she protested, starting to open her door. "You brought me along to help. Give me my dagger and let's go stake a vampire."

He grabbed her arm and forcefully held her in place. "I said, stay here. If I need your help, I'll come get you."

"If you need my help," she countered, "you won't have the chance to ask for it."

He knew she was right, but he didn't really have a choice. "I don't have your dagger or stakes here, okay? All I have is this gun, so stay in the car, lock the doors and let me check things out first by myself." He was growing all too familiar with the stubborn set of her jaw and seeing it again wasn't helping his mood. "I mean it, Jessica. Stay in the car." He got out before she could protest further and pocketed the keys.

Walking to the front entrance, he wondered how he would get inside. As it turned out, the door was unlocked, which he found odd at this time of night.

He listened for a few seconds, but heard no sounds coming from inside. Moving forward as silently as he could, his senses alert, he began checking out each room as he came to it. The first two visitation rooms were empty. Standing in the doorway of the third, John took in the room's appearance at a glance. The soft glow from electric wall sconces lit the scene. Black drapes hung across the windows, providing a backdrop for the black-and-gold casket set before it. The lid was up and from where he stood, John saw that the casket was empty. Off to one side was a table with Simon Brody's framed picture on top. Beside it were several candles that had been left burning.

Chairs, covered in black cloth, stood in neat rows in the back half of the room. The chairs in the first couple of rows, closest to the casket, had been pushed aside and some had been knocked over—and lying in their midst was Franklin Brody.

John rushed to the old man's side. He was pretty sure the man was dead, but went through the motions of double-checking. When he went to press his fingers against the man's neck he spotted the two puncture holes. They appeared to be fresh—the blood was just starting to congeal.

Movement drew John's glance to the door, even as he trained his gun on the figure standing there. "Damn it—I told you to stay in the car."

"I don't like being out there alone," Jessica whispered, coming forward to kneel beside him. "Is he . . . ?"

"Yes."

"What about the other guy?"

John looked to where she pointed and saw a second body. He went over to it and knew just by looking that the man was dead. Still, he checked for a pulse. "Nothing."

"They'll have to be staked," she said, sounding all business.

He stared up at her in disbelief. "These men just died here. Do you mind?"

She narrowed her eyes. "You think I'm insensitive? Well, I'm sorry that they died, but frankly, I'm more interested in making sure that no one else dies because we didn't do what needed to be done." She walked over to one of the chairs, picked it up and smashed it against the doorframe, causing parts of it to break off. Selecting two of the longer leg segments, she carried them over to where John crouched beside the body.

Kneeling across from him, she stared at the body. "You might not want to watch this."

He reached for her arm as she lifted it and took the chair leg from her. "I'll do it. In the heart, right?" Staring down at the body, he couldn't remember ever looking forward to anything less than what he was about to do.

"I don't mind doing it," she offered, now sounding sympathetic.

"No."

"Okay," she conceded, reaching for the man's shirt. "It'll be easier if you don't have to go through the cloth as well," she explained, undoing the buttons and pulling back the left side. "Wait. What's that?" A bloodied piece of wood protruded out of the man's chest directly over where the heart would be. "Who would have done that?"

Jessica got up and went back to Franklin Brody's body, quickly undoing the shirt and pulling it back. "This one's been staked as well."

"We should get out of here," he said, taking her hand and leading her to the front door, where he paused long enough to look outside. Seeing nothing suspicious, he led her to the car and opened the door while she climbed inside. "I'm going to take a quick look around the grounds," he told her. "Lock the doors and please, this time, don't get out."

He slammed the door shut before she could protest and walked off, not bothering to see if she obeyed him.

Around the side of the building, everything looked normal, so he continued toward the back. He'd just turned the corner when the hairs on the back of his neck started to prickle. The shadows were thick, and John didn't see the figure until it stepped out into the open.

"You! What are you doing here?"

"I came to finish the job that you interrupted the other night," the man from Thompson Park said conversationally.

"You mean, stake Simon Brody before he turns into a vampire?"

"So, you figured it out." He sounded like a teacher pleased with a favorite pupil.

"What? That you're a vampire?" John made it sound like an accusation. "Did you think I wouldn't?"

"I was beginning to wonder." The man smiled, revealing the tips of his white fangs.

John grimaced at the implied insult, trying to ignore how surreal it felt to be carrying on a conversation with a real vampire. "What now? You try to kill me?"

"Try?" There was a rumble of laughter. "No. I have no interest in killing you."

John didn't know if he believed that. "Did you kill Franklin Brody and the other man?"

"No. They were dead when I arrived."

A new thought occurred to John. "But you staked them, didn't you?" The vampire didn't have to answer for him to know the truth. "You did. In fact, you've been staking all of them, haven't you? All the other criminals you killed. That's why they never became vampires."

John knew it was true. Someone had to have been doing it because he'd stopped calling Mac and Dirk, who had presumably done it before. The vampire, he noticed, didn't try to deny it. Then, belatedly, something the vampire said registered. "How did you know Brody was here? It wasn't public knowledge."

"I went to the morgue earlier tonight and discovered that the body wasn't there." The vampire shrugged his shoulders in a very human gesture. "The Brodys have been burying their dead in this cemetery for almost a century—it seemed like the next logical place to look."

"And did you find Simon?" That was what John really wanted to know.

"Not yet."

* * *

Jess sat in the car waiting for the detective to finish his search of the grounds. It wasn't the waiting that bothered her so much as her total lack of defense. She felt too much like the proverbial sitting duck.

A shift in the shadows off to the side caught her attention and she watched a figure emerge. Expecting it to be John, she was surprised to discover it wasn't. Her first thought was that this could be the vampire and she squinted to bring his features into focus, but he was too far away. He moved away from the funeral home in a stumbling gait that was too slow to be a vampire's, and she allowed herself to relax a little as she watched him start across the driveway, passing about ten feet in front of the car.

As he moved under the glow of the driveway light, Jess saw that he was about her age, mid-twenties. He had a serious case of bed head, with his sandy blond hair mashed flat against the back of his head. His suit, by contrast, looked pressed and neat, although the patterned shirt looked out of place.

His attention seemed focused on the ground as he ambled along, almost as if he were drunk. The last thing they needed was a drunk wandering around with a vampire on the loose. Concerned for his safety, she considered getting out to warn him. Doubt made her hesitate.

Just then, he stopped walking and slowly turned to face her.

His eyes took on a reddish glow and when he smiled, she saw the two bloodstained fangs.

Alarm slammed through her and she reached for the driver's-side master door locks as he rushed the car. She heard the sound of all four locks snapping into place just as he threw himself against the door. Instinctively, she lurched backward, trying to get as far away from him as the car would allow.

He lowered his head to the window and stared at her, devouring her with his hungry gaze. From this close range, she saw that the decorative pattern across his shirt was actually a pattern of bloodstains.

It unnerved her to be this close without a stake or other weapon. She sat there, her fingers nervously fingering the locket about her neck as she prayed that the locks held under the vampire's efforts to get the door open. It seemed that the pounding against the door lasted forever, but then it stopped. Instead of going away, however, the vampire stared at her through the window. When their eyes met, he started to laugh.

John heard the blaring of his car's horn and swore. The damn woman was going to wake the dead with her impatience, he thought, trying to focus on what the vampire before him was saying. He tried to block the noise from his thoughts, but it wouldn't stop. Then he caught the pattern of horn blows—three long, three short, three long: S-O-S.

Trepidation shot through him and he took off running.

The first thing he saw when he rounded the corner of the funeral home was Simon Brody, looking as alive and well as he had the day his trial had ended, looming over the car. He was smashing his fist against the window, clearly intent on breaking it. John worried that he wouldn't get there in time to stop him.

Then the Thompson Park vampire raced past him so

fast that by comparison, John felt like he was barely moving. Brody froze in the middle of smashing the window and looked up. Then he turned and quickly disappeared into the night, with the Thompson Park vampire still chasing him.

Knowing there was no way to catch either of them, John went to the car instead. He pulled the keys from his pocket as he ran and pressed the auto-unlock. When he reached the car, he found Jessica sitting unusually still, with the locket around her neck clutched in her fist. He worried she was in a state of deep shock.

"Are you hurt?" he asked as soon as he had the door open.

She didn't answer, so he ran his hands up and down her arms and legs dispassionately, searching for signs of injury. He even tipped her head from side to side, checking her neck. He didn't think Brody had reached her, but he had to make sure.

"I'm taking you back to the admiral's," he said finally, closing her door and going around to the driver's side. He climbed in, started the car and headed down the driveway, glancing over at her occasionally as he drove. He didn't like her ashen pallor. "You don't look so good—I thought you fought vampires all the time. You should be used to this."

She turned to him slowly and he saw sparks of anger. "I usually have a weapon."

Sheldon Harris raced after Brody until he lost him in the woods. There, he stopped and stood very still as he stretched his range of awareness, using his vampire senses to pick up clues from his surroundings. From the direction of the main road he heard the sound of traffic, and from the direction of the funeral home came the sound of the detective's car driving off. Harris hoped he hadn't made a mistake by revealing himself to the detective back at the funeral home, but they were bound to run into each other eventually. The detective had been looking for him, specifically, for weeks now, and Harris had to admit a certain curiosity about the man who seemed to be unusually tolerant of his latest kills, which had all been individuals deserving of death. It might not have been his place to make that determination, but a year and a half ago, Harris had been forced to the harsh conclusion that life wasn't fair.

Harris brought his thoughts back to the present and scanned his surroundings with the trained eye of a former SEAL. Brody had been this way, headed for the main highway. Once he reached it, Harris knew the trail would end, so he turned his thoughts inward, searching the psychic link he shared with Brody, who was his Progeny; the vampire that he, Harris, had created.

He brushed across Brody's mind. Chaos reigned as the new vampire struggled to make sense of what had happened to him, yet Harris caught the distinct thread of delight over having killed. It was disturbing.

With dawn so close, Harris knew he had to abandon his search for tonight. He hoped Brody would get caught out in the sunlight, turn to a fragile type of stone that would blow away with the first good breeze, but knew he wouldn't get that lucky.

Tomorrow night he'd start his search all over again, but for now he headed back the way he'd come. The body of the night security guard still waited for him behind the funeral home where Brody had left him. Harris had to finish what the detective had interrupted before he could go home to his hidden chamber inside the sewer. He supposed he could find a nicer place to sleep during the day, but this place was secure—and sadly apropos to his current life.

Chapter 5

Mac swore. "You should have told us earlier."

"I know," John admitted. He and Jess were back at the mansion with the others, sitting in the living room where John had just finished telling them what happened at the funeral home, carefully omitting the part about his personal conversation with the Thompson Park vampire. He wasn't sure why, but he wasn't ready to share that just yet.

"It's too close to dawn for us to go searching for him now," Dirk said. "We'll start again tonight."

"What time should we meet?" Jessica asked, drawing everyone's attention to her.

"*We?*" Dirk asked, looking pointedly at first Jess and then John. "Mac and I will take care of this. You two stay out of it."

"No way. I'm going with you," John argued, hurrying to make his case before either of them could tell him otherwise. “I know this guy better than anyone. I’ve been studying him for over a year.”

“You think you know where he’ll go hunting for food?” Mac asked.

“Yeah, I do.” He didn’t even have to stop to think about it. “The university.” He quickly explained Brody’s penchant for female college students, and the two men agreed that the university sounded like the most likely spot.

“I don’t believe this,” Jessica said heatedly, looking at each man in turn. “I’ve been hunting vampires longer than any of you and yet not only will you not let me go, but you’ll take him?” She pointed a finger at John. “He’s never hunted a vampire before in his life.”

“I never said he was going,” Mac pointed out.

John started to argue, but Mac and Dirk rose as one, cutting him off. “This is nonnegotiable,” Mac said. “I think you’ve seen enough to realize just how dangerous vampires can be. We’ll handle this.”

John left the mansion, frustrated and angry. He might not have been a SEAL, but being a homicide detective wasn’t exactly a “cush” job; he understood the dangers involved with tracking a killer—especially this killer. Mac and Dirk might not want him to go along, but there was no reason he couldn’t conduct his own investigation.

That evening, John arrived at the university a few minutes before nine o’clock, pulling into a parking space across the street from an off-campus bar. He was lucky to find a spot, considering it was Friday night.

He felt tired, having finally fallen into bed just after dawn. Waking up six hours later, he’d briefly considered going into the office, but the thought of facing “Dick” was more than he wanted to deal with, so instead he'd called in sick. He was pretty sure word of his suspension had already spread throughout the station, so his absence wouldn't be totally unexpected.

Opening his car door, John got out and looked around, hoping to catch a glimpse of Mac or Dirk. He'd called the admiral's house and talked to Lanie. She'd told him that the men were patrolling the campus, and though he hadn't asked, she'd told him that Jessica had retired early after Mac and Dirk refused, again, to let her go with them.

John slowly headed for the quadrangle around which the majority of the dorms were located. If he were trying to find a woman out alone at night, the quad would be the perfect place.

He received a few curious looks from the students he passed along the way and had to accept that he no longer looked like one of them. At thirty-eight, the passage of time and stress had taken its toll on him.

He reached the quad and found it alive with student activity. Unsure where or how to conduct his search for Brody, he had just started a slow walk around the perimeter when he was suddenly grabbed and pulled behind a stand of trees.

John's hand shot out, trying to land one good punch at his attacker—instead, it struck a man's open palm, which closed around his fist and didn't let go.

Then he saw his attacker's face. "Jesus—don't you guys ever do anything normal? A simple 'Hey, we're here behind the bush' would have worked. Or better yet, you could have called me and told me where to meet you."

Mac frowned. "Sorry, John. What were we thinking?

Oh, yeah. I remember now. We were thinking that *we didn't want you here.*"

John ignored him. "Any sign of Brody?"

Dirk shook his head. "Nothing so far. Now that you're here, you might as well help us look."

Together, the three waited, scanning every face that passed.

A couple of hours later, just as John was wondering if he'd been mistaken about Brody, Dirk suddenly grew very still. Concerned, John turned to Mac only to notice that he, too, appeared to be listening.

Before John could ask what was up, Dirk raced off across the quad. Not wanting to be left behind, John took off after him with Mac by his side. It was impossible to keep up, and shortly after losing sight of Dirk around a corner, John had to stop and catch his breath.

"Where'd he go?" he gasped.

"The park, up ahead," Mac said, not sounding winded at all. "You know where it is?"

John nodded.

"Meet us there." Then Mac raced off, leaving John to follow at a slower pace. He reached the park a few minutes later.

Several of the overhead halogen lights had been broken, leaving the park in shadowy darkness. At first, it was hard to see anything, but then John spotted a shape moving just beyond a small cropping of bushes. He headed over to it, and when he reached the small clearing where Mac and Dirk stood, he saw what commanded their attention.

Steeling himself as he did every time he had to view another homicide, John took a closer look. "Damn," he muttered. Death was always ugly, but some deaths were worse than others.

She couldn't have been more than nineteen or twenty, he guessed. Pretty and blonde, just like the others Brody had killed. Her clothes hung in shreds about her body and from the markings on her, John was left with no doubts about whether vampires were capable of sex—or rape.

Though she'd clearly fought for her life, she hadn't died from being beaten. The two puncture wounds on the side of her pale neck shone like ugly dark beacons; harbingers of death.

John placed his fingers against her throat, searching for a pulse. It was done more out of habit than because he thought there was a chance she was still alive. There wasn't.

He spotted her small purse tossed off to the side and picked it up. Unzipping the main compartment, he reached in and found her wallet. Inside was her student ID; she'd only been a freshman. Behind that was a family picture.

Dirk slipped beside him, putting a hand on his shoulder. "You should come with me."

John looked at him, confused, until he heard Mac draw his sword from the sheath strapped across his back.

"Wait," he protested, shrugging off Dirk's hand and moving forward to intercept Mac. "You can't do that. She's not a vampire. She's just a kid."

"If I don't do this, in two nights she's not going to be a kid anymore. She'll be a bloodsucking monster."

John held up the picture of her with her parents. "She's got a family," he argued.

"They all do, John," Mac shot back. "That's what

makes what we have to do so goddamn hard. But it still has to be done. If you don't like it, then help us find the vampire who did this. We have to kill him so he never does this to anyone else."

Drawing a deep breath, John nodded. He knew Mac was right. He didn't have to like it, but he was playing a whole new game—*their* game—and he had to learn the rules.

He stepped back but didn't turn around. It wasn't his nature to hide from the truth, no matter how ugly.

The blade slid cleanly through. There was no blood.

"Now what?" John asked after swallowing hard.

"Now, I go get the truck so we can haul the body back to the admiral's place," Mac said.

"We have a dumping ground there," Dirk explained.

"You stay here and make sure no one comes by," Mac said just before he walked off.

John turned to Dirk and noticed the other man's expression. "You don't look so hot," he observed.

Dirk gave him a wry, humorless smile. "We've had to behead a lot of bodies in the last year, and it's never easy to do. But this is the first time we've had to do a woman. And this one looked a lot like Mac's little sister did when she was this age. That had to have been hard for him to do."

John felt his admiration for Mac grow. He suspected that Mac had made a good leader in the military, never asking others to do what he himself was not willing to do.

John heard giggling and looked across the quad to see two female students walking, their heads bowed together as they talked. They were leaning into each other and from the way they kept stepping off the edge of the sidewalk, John thought maybe they'd started their evening's festivities several hours earlier. They were well on their way to a serious hangover the next morning.

"If I were Brody," John said thoughtfully, "those two would be next on my list."

"You stay here while I follow them," Dirk said, causing John to glance at him sharply. "No offense, John, but Brody would make short work of you."

John inwardly flinched. "Ouch. I think you just dented my ego. I'm not exactly helpless, you know."

Dirk clapped him on the back. "Yeah, well, just remember what Mac said—it takes a hell of a lot of bullets to stop one vampire."

"Fine, I understand, but what about you? You can't just walk up to those women and tell them a vampire is after them. They'll think you're nuts."

Dirk gave him a bemused look. "Relax. They won't even know I'm there. Stay here and wait for Mac. I doubt Brody'll come back to this site, so you'll be safe. I gotta go—we'll talk more later."

And then, with a speed that seemed inhuman, Dirk left him and hurried across the park to follow the girls. John watched them disappear and then looked around. Even for someone who was not easily spooked, the darkness in this particular section of the park was unusually disquieting. When he heard the snap of a twig behind him, he whirled around, pulling his gun.

"Easy, Detective," a familiar voice said as a shadow moved behind the tree. "It's me, Sheldon Harris, aka the vampire. We met last night, remember?"

"What are you doing here?" John asked, not bothering to hide his suspicion. He wondered how much longer Mac was going to be, not sure whether he wanted the man to hurry or take his time.

"I'm here for the same reason you are. We're both looking for Simon Brody." John saw the vampire's gaze flicker to the body on the ground; saw his eyes glow red and heard him swear under his breath.

"Yeah," John empathized. "We didn't get here in time—again."

"At least you severed the head to keep her from rising."

"I didn't do—"

"Hold it right there. Campus Security."

Shit. A beam of light hit John's face. "You'd better go," he said as quietly as he could, hoping the vampire would hear him. So far the security guard had seen only him, but as soon as he spotted the body lying at John's feet, things were going to get ugly.

As the guard moved closer, John saw Harris fade back into the shadows.

"Do you want me to kill him?"

The offer floated on a breeze and caught John by such surprise that at first, he wasn't sure how to respond. Then he saw the shadows move, as if Harris was coming back, and hurried to prevent further disaster. "No."

The shadow receded again, but John heard a soft chuckle and belatedly realized the vampire was joking with him. John, however, wasn't amused, and vowed that the next time he saw the man—vampire—he would tell him just how funny he hadn't found the joke. Then he forgot all about the vampire because the security guard finally noticed the body at John's feet and the proverbial shit hit the fan.

Not wanting to be accidentally shot, John allowed

himself to be searched, allowed his gun to be confiscated and his hands cuffed. As he waited for the local police to arrive, he caught sight of a familiar Expedition. Mac looked at him from the front seat, a concerned expression on his face. He made a gesture with his hand, but John shook his head slightly in response. He felt reasonably certain that after being questioned, he'd be released.

At least, he hoped he would be.

Harris watched as the detective was hauled off and found himself grudgingly admiring the man. There was absolutely no reason why John Boehler should have protected him, and yet he had—for the second time now. Maybe it was just a part of the detective's personality. That same quality that made him want to be a detective also had him protecting those who were innocent. Not that Harris was exactly innocent. He'd been responsible for many deaths—including that young woman's at the park, indirectly.

The irony of the situation haunted him. His effort to rid the world of a psychotic killer had resulted in an even worse threat being loosed on the community. Harris felt the responsibility of it like another black mark on his eternally damned soul; another spiritual weight around his neck dragging him farther into the fiery pits of hell. Already the flames were licking at his heels; driving the air from his lungs.

Taking a deep breath to prove he still could, Harris picked a direction at random and began to walk, not consciously aware that he was headed toward St. Magnus Cathedral until the building loomed before him.

Harris stood staring at it, feeling almost lost. Moisture

collected in his eyes, no doubt from the bite of the wind, and he blinked it back.

As if drawn, he moved toward the front doors. It was time to test another myth, he thought resolutely. Reaching out, he grabbed the handle of the front door, almost sagging in relief when all he felt was the cool metal against his palm.

Pulling the door open, he placed a foot across the threshold. Nothing happened, so he stepped all the way inside and found himself standing in an elegant foyer. The building was old, and the odor of the ages wrapped around him in a welcome embrace.

He continued forward, pushing open the chapel doors to glance inside where he saw lit candles glowing on the altar, flickering and casting shadows across the walls and ceiling. The place was mostly empty with only a few late-night worshippers sitting alone in the pews, absorbed in their worries and thoughts.

When he was younger, he'd attended church with his mother, but that had been so long ago.

Now, Harris moved toward a pew near the back and sat down. For several minutes, he sat there, tense, as if waiting for the heavens to open up or lightning to strike him down. The sanctuary was filled with an overwhelming yet reverent silence. For the first time in over a year, Harris felt an easy peace come over him. He breathed deep, wanting it to last forever.

As the events of the past year intruded, he braced his hands against the pew in front of him and leaned his head down against them, letting the guilt and horror of the things he'd done beat at him.

"No matter what your sins, God loves you," a kindly voice said beside him, causing him to look up.

"I don't think so, Father," Harris replied, feeling suddenly very uncomfortable. "In fact, given my current situation, I must conclude that He hates me." He stood and the priest moved aside to let him pass.

"God has all manner of tests to prove our worthiness. Though yours may seem unusually difficult, His purpose will be revealed—in time."

Harris stopped and turned back to the priest. "Well, Father, I hope He hurries, because I'm not sure how much more I can take."

"Sometimes, living is the ultimate test."

Harris left the church, the priest's words echoing in his head.

Jessica sat on the bar stool in one of the local college hangouts, nursing a Long Island Tea.

She'd had a difficult time sneaking out of the mansion with Beth and Lanie sitting downstairs, but she'd done it, even managing to steal the keys to someone's car so she'd have a way to get into town. Mac and Dirk might have experience killing vampires, but she'd been hunting them practically since birth and was willing to stack her twenty-five years against their twelve months any day.

The key to vampire hunting, she knew, was to make the creature come to the hunter. That was why she was at the bar. She was in its territory, offering herself up as bait by being alone and pretending to be drunk. From what little she'd read in the old newspapers Charles kept stacked in his library, someone like Brody wouldn't be able to resist the opportunity of a vulnerable female college student out all alone.

She took another swallow of her drink and pretended to sway a bit on the stool as she leaned forward to rub her knee, which really did hurt. The second-story balcony of the mansion ran all the way around the outside of the house, but there had been no good place to jump down. Not to mention that the short skirt she wore was not the best for such gymnastics.

In the end, she'd misjudged her landing and ended up on her knees in the gravel, where several tiny stones bit into the unprotected flesh. The wound hadn't been bad enough to change her plans, though.

She checked her watch again. It was almost two in the morning. She had no doubt that by now, she had been missed and the note she'd left explaining her absence had been found. Charles and the others would be worried, but she hoped that when they found out she'd killed the vampire, they'd understand.

Now, if Brody would just cooperate, she thought, looking at her watch—again.

"I don't think he's going to show."

A young man, looking big enough to play on the university football team, sidled up to her, his drunken smile overly friendly.

"He'll show." She turned back to her drink, but he didn't take the hint.

"I could keep you company," he suggested, coming to stand by the empty stool beside her.

"Really, don't feel you must."

He smiled as he sat down and motioned to the bartender to bring him another drink. Jessica tried to ignore him and glanced around the room, still not seeing Brody. It wasn't that she expected him to attack her right there in the bar, but she was counting on him doing exactly what she was doing—surveying the landscape and locating the next target for attack.

A hand at her elbow interrupted her thoughts and she turned to face the man beside her, the odor of stale beer hitting her in the face as he leaned close enough to speak to her over the noise. "Say, baby," he drawled, "how 'bout you and me having some fun."

Fighting off humans was harder than fighting off vampires. It wasn't as easy as pulling out a dagger and sinking it into their chest to be rid of them. That made her current situation a real predicament. Jess wasn't exactly sure how to get herself out of it without hurting someone.

Mistaking her silence as interest, he shifted his body closer to hers. She was about to use a Judo move to make her intentions clear, when someone grabbed the man's arm and roughly twisted it, causing him to release her and double over the counter in pain. Turning, she saw Detective Boehler, looking like he'd had a rough night, holding on to the young man's arm.

"You're in my seat," he growled, yanking the man off the stool and shoving him off to the side. "Beat it."

"Hey, I saw her first," the drunk protested loudly.

"Don't make me hurt you." John turned his back on the man, effectively dismissing him, and gave Jess his full attention. "What the hell are you doing here?"

"I *was* enjoying a bit of peace and solitude," she said.

"Not anymore." He reached out, took the glass from her hand, downed its contents, and set it on the counter.

Then he took her elbow and pulled her to her feet. "I'm taking you home."

"Thanks, but I'm not ready to go," she said forcefully, pulling her arm from his grasp with a quick jerk. "Don't let that stop *you* from leaving."

They were drawing attention from the other patrons, though John didn't seem to care.

"Does Charles know you're out all alone?"

"I don't have to account for my whereabouts to anyone," she informed him.

He shook his head. "Lady, you are one piece of work."

The football player chose that moment to return. He charged at John, who barely had time to brace himself before being shoved halfway across the room. He quickly regained his footing, though, and grabbing the other man's hand, used his forward momentum to send him toppling into the crowd. The jock, however, recovered more quickly this time, and came back swinging his fist, catching John in the jaw.

John's head snapped to the side, but he didn't go down. Instead, he stood there, rubbing his jaw until Jess wondered if it was broken. Things were getting out of hand. She was about to get off her stool and go to him when suddenly he exploded into action. It was almost like he'd been waiting for the young man to throw the first punch and now that he had, John was free to retaliate. He threw several fast jabs at his opponent's face and belly, hitting him so hard that Jess worried he might have broken the bones of his hand in addition to whatever damage he'd inflicted on her unwanted admirer.

She was relieved when the bouncers arrived to break up the fight.

"Not in the bar," one shouted, grabbing the football player and roughly maneuvering him out the door. "Take it outside."

John straightened his shirt, grabbed a napkin off the bar to dab at the blood from his split lip and stared at her, his expression dark and angry. She knew she was about to catch an earful, but then the bouncer put a hand on John's shoulder. "You, too, buddy."

He nodded once. "All right. Come on," he said to her.

"I think not," she said, sounding outraged for the sake of the bouncer. "I hardly even know you and I'm certainly not leaving with you."

John's jaw dropped. "What the hell . . . ?"

"That's it, buddy. You're outta here. Lady doesn't want to go."

The bouncer put his hand on John's shoulder to escort him out, and for a second, Jess thought he might balk. He certainly looked mad enough.

Instead, with more dignity than she would have given him credit for, he straightened his shoulders and nodded to the man. "You and I are going to have a nice long talk—later," he promised her and then walked out of the bar without looking back.

Jessica felt a shiver of apprehension race down her spine, but the emotion was quickly replaced with guilt. She knew the detective had only been trying to protect her, but when would he learn that she didn't need his protection?

Outside, John crossed the street to his parked car. He was in a foul mood. It was bad enough that he'd had to go to the station and be grilled about the young woman's death, but then Dick from Internal Affairs had shown up. John had barely succeeded in convincing the man that he wasn't working a new case, arguing that he'd been following up on an Exsanguinator lead that had, unfortunately, led to the most recent victim.

Dick had demanded to be told everything and John had promised to bring him up to speed, just as soon as he got a cup of coffee. He'd walked out of the debriefing room and straight out the front door, bumming a ride from one of the other homicide detectives back to his car.

Seeing the bar open, he'd only wanted one small drink to take the edge off yet another bizarre night. Instead, he'd walked in to find Jessica Winslow, looking entirely too good in a figure-hugging top and a skirt so short that her mile-long legs were on display to every male eye in the place. Dressed like that, she was bound to attract trouble.

It was on par with his luck tonight to get thrown out of a bar for trying to protect her. He dabbed the napkin against his lip again and saw that the bleeding had slowed considerably. Crumpling the napkin in his hand, he tossed it onto the dash where it landed next to other wadded-up pieces of trash.

He glanced at his watch again and saw that it was almost three. Hell, he didn't even know why he was sitting here, waiting for her to come out. She sure as hell wouldn't appreciate it.

He heaved a sigh and settled in for a long wait because while he might not know *why* he was waiting, he knew he wasn't leaving until he saw her again.

At three o'clock, the doors to the bar opened and patrons began stumbling out. John sat a little straighter in his seat as he watched for Jessica. When she didn't appear, he grew concerned.

He reached for the handle of his car, about to go search for her, when the door opened again. He stayed where he was and waited. Like watching a movie in slow motion, the first thing he saw was a slim foot with painted toenails clad in a black high-heeled sandal. His gaze traveled up the slender ankle, past a toned calf to a shapely thigh that seemed to go on forever before the hem of the skirt blocked further view.

Her hips were slim, he noted, but shapely, and they curved into a narrow waist. The formfitting red top was just visible beneath the black leather jacket she now wore, but he already knew what lay beneath. Her breasts weren't large, but to his eyes, they were the perfect size and shape for her toned body.

As he watched, Jessica started walking down the sidewalk, but stopped after taking only a few steps. She pulled her purse in front of her, opened it and seemed to be searching it for something.

"Come on, Jess," John muttered to himself, growing anxious. He didn't like her being out there all alone. "You should always have the keys in your hand before you leave the bar," he lectured her, practically holding his breath until she pulled the keys out.

Then she scanned the street in both directions, probably trying to remember where she'd parked. If she couldn't remember that, then she was definitely too drunk to drive.

He reached for the door handle again, but then he saw her smile at something. Curious, he turned his head and saw someone walking toward her. From where he sat,

John couldn't see the man's face, but the thought that it was the jock who'd accosted her before was more than a little irritating.

With his jaw still aching, and remembering the man's size and mass, John decided a show of force was in order. He reached for the baseball bat he kept on the floor behind the driver's seat and then opened the door and got out. About to walk across the street, he was forced to stop and wait for a car to drive by. It temporarily blocked his view until it passed and then John saw a sight that made his blood boil.

The jock had Jess pressed up against the side of the building, his body pinning her in place while his hands groped beneath her jacket.

"Hey! Get your fucking hands off her," he shouted, racing across the street. His grip on the bat tightened and suddenly it seemed less like a defensive weapon as his hands itched to smash it against the man's head.

The man seemed unaware of John as he ripped the jacket off Jessica and lowered his head as if to kiss her. John grabbed him by the collar and jerked him around, not caring if he choked the man. "I said, get your—"

The words died in his throat as the man turned and John found himself staring into Brody's face. Then recognition lit up Brody's eyes and the vampire smiled, baring his fangs.

Chapter 6

John snapped out of his trance and swung the bat. Brody put up an arm to block the blow and the bat snapped in two. Shaken, John stared at the splintered piece of wood still clutched in his hand.

Brody, on the other hand, seemed unfazed and shoved John, sending him crashing into the side of the building. The impact knocked the breath out of him. How could he fight an opponent with superhuman strength?

John shook his head, trying to rid his vision of the white sparkling lights blinking behind his eyelids, and saw Brody lower his head once more to Jess's neck. She did nothing to defend herself and John thought she must be in shock. John knew he had to stop Brody before he killed her.

Scrambling to his feet, he reached for his gun. Then he remembered what Mac had said about guns and vampires. He looked around for a better weapon and with a start, realized he was still clutching the broken half of the baseball bat. Changing his grip so he held it like a dagger, he brought his arm down, stabbing Brody through the back where the heart would be. It was much harder to do than he anticipated and instead of crumbling to the ground, Brody howled in rage and lurched back, twisting his arm and torso in an effort to reach the bat and remove it.

John didn't wait to see if he succeeded. "Run," he shouted at Jess, who was scraping the spilled contents back into her purse. He grabbed her by the hand and practically dragged her to his car. When they reached it, he pulled open the driver's-side door and unceremoniously shoved her inside.

A bellow of rage echoed in the night and John risked another look back. Brody was glaring at them with such feral anger and hunger that John was afraid they might not survive after all.

"Move over." He shoved Jess aside as he climbed in and pulled the door shut, locking it just as Brody reached them. With the vampire pounding on the window, John started the car and put it in gear. He hated leaving Brody alive, but his first priority had to be getting Jess to safety.

For the next ten minutes, John drove with one eye on the road ahead of them and the other on the rearview mirror, searching for signs that Brody was following them. He didn't think it was possible, but he couldn't be sure. Though he hated to admit it, even to himself, tonight had seriously spooked him.

Once he was sure they were safe, he slowed the car and let his attention turn to Jessica, sitting quietly beside him. There was blood on her neck, but he didn't think Brody had done more than scratch the surface. Still, the experience must have been horrifying. Wanting to offer her comfort and reassurance, he reached out and tried to lay his hand over hers. "I'm sorry I didn't get there sooner. Are you all right?"

At his touch, she pulled away. "All right?" she echoed, finally turning to pierce him with an icy stare. "Are you daft? No, I'm not all right. I'm absolutely furious."

John actually felt his jaw drop open and quickly closed it. "You know? I find your lack of gratitude a little shocking."

"You want gratitude? Well, thank you very much—for letting him get away, *again*."

Her reaction was not what he'd expected. "Are you telling me that you went out tonight specifically looking to find Brody?"

"Of course. I lured him to me and in another minute, he would have been dead. It was a brilliant plan, until you ruined it with your compulsive need to play the hero."

"What was I supposed to do? Stand by and let him drink you dry?" John gripped the steering wheel so tightly it was in danger of snapping.

"That wouldn't have happened." She heaved a sigh, like *she* was the one forced to tap into her last reserves of patience. "Centuries ago," she finally began, "my family developed an herb that is toxic to vampires, but not to humans. We brew it into a tea and drink it. For twenty-four hours, the herb resides in our bloodstream and if, in that time, a vampire attacks and drinks our blood, it will kill him." She paused before going on. "I had several cups of that tea tonight with dinner. All I had to do was let Brody drink enough of my blood and he'd drop dead; problem solved."

John felt the shock of her statement run all the way

through him. "Jesus Christ," he swore, tearing his eyes away from the road to stare at her. "You really are a psycho." His tone wasn't gentle and she had no way of knowing that he was as furious with himself as with her. If what she'd told him was true, it *had* been a brilliant plan, but damn, she was taking risks.

Her eyes shot fire bolts back at him. "Maybe if you'd lost your mother to a vampire, then you'd understand why I hate them so much. You'd understand why I'll do whatever it takes to hunt them down and kill them."

"Even at the risk of your own life?"

There was nothing but grim determination in her expression as she held his gaze. "*Whatever* it takes."

Fifteen minutes later, the car pulled to a stop in front of the mansion and Jessica braced herself for the lecture she was sure to get as soon as Charles and the others discovered what she'd done. She had no doubt that the detective would love being the one to tell on her. When he shut off the engine, she made no attempt to open the door.

"What's the matter?" he asked.

She glanced at the house. "Nothing." She wasn't in that much of a hurry to go inside, but didn't expect him to understand.

"Look," he said. "I'm sorry I screwed up your plans this evening. Mac, Dirk, and I spent the earlier part of this evening dealing with Brody's latest victim, a young woman not much younger than you, so when I saw you being mauled by what I thought at the time was a drunk—well, I didn't want you to be a victim either."

"I knew what I was doing," she said again, sounding petulant. "Why won't you people trust me?"

He studied her. "By 'you people,' I'm assuming you mean me?"

She waved a hand to generally encompass the mansion. "You, Charles, Mac, Dirk—none of you seem to trust that I know what I'm doing."

"Maybe that's because everything you've done so far has been reckless—and seemingly psychotic," he said heatedly.

She glared at him. "That's only because you *assumed* that I was a helpless female in need of rescuing, when, in point of fact, I'm not." When would she learn that men everywhere were the same? She might not be as athletic as Kacie, or as good a swordswoman, but she *was* a vampire slayer, capable of taking care of herself, and she would prove it to everyone—the detective, Mac, Dirk, Cousin Charles—and, most especially, to her father.

Frustration, old and new, made her feel more tired than usual. "Tell me something. This evening, when you, Mac, and Dirk went out hunting for Brody, did you even see him?" His silence was answer enough. Her plan had been the better of the two.

"I have to ask," John said, sounding worried. "Are you going to turn into a vampire now? You know, since Brody bit you."

"No, it doesn't work that way." She held his gaze, willing him to understand. "When a chupacabra or a vampire feeds on a human, a venom—for lack of a better term—is injected into the victim's body through the fangs as blood is being sucked out. It's the venom that turns that person into a vampire, and it's no small amount. For there to be enough venom, essentially all of the blood must be drawn out of the body—and then, of course, the victim has to die. The conversion takes about forty-eight hours."

"Will you suffer any side effects from the bite itself?"

She frowned. "I don't know," she replied honestly. "I've never been bitten before, but I don't think so. Besides, the wound's not that serious."

He leaned toward her and used his hand to gently turn her head so he could get a better look at her neck. "It looks pretty bad to me."

His touch sent electric shocks sizzling through her, making her breathless. "I feel fine," she assured him, forcing herself not to look away.

With the light from the mansion spilling in through the windows, she noticed the golden flecks in his rich brown eyes. His nose, on another face, might have been called beakish, but in combination with his angular face, shadowed jaw, and rumpled hair, he was ruggedly handsome in a "real" way, not like any brushstroked Adonis she'd seen in magazines.

Her anger and frustration with the detective faded as her awareness of the man took over. She was entering unfamiliar waters. Her heart sped up a beat or two, and her mouth seemed to have suddenly gone dry. The space inside the car grew smaller, more intimate. She tried to look away, needing to break the sudden tension humming between them, but failed.

When the detective leaned closer, she didn't know whether to meet him halfway or run screaming from the car, not that it mattered either way. She couldn't move.

She thought she heard him whisper her name, but couldn't be sure with the sound of her pulse thundering in her head. She found herself holding her breath, certain that he was going to kiss her and she was going to let him.

At that moment, the front door of the mansion opened and Charles, followed by the others, came rushing out. John reluctantly sat back and reached for the door handle. He climbed out of the car just as Charles opened her door.

"Jessica? Are you all right?" Charles offered his hand to help her alight. Then his eyes widened. "Good Lord, your neck. What happened?" There was obvious worry in his tone.

"I'm fine, really."

"But your neck—"

"A scratch. Nothing serious."

He studied her face and she refused to look away. Finally he nodded. "Okay, a scratch. Still, it might be a good idea to have Julia take a look at it."

"I will," she promised, grateful for any excuse to go inside. She'd just started to walk toward the mansion again when Mac reached out a hand and grabbed her arm, pulling her to a stop.

"I don't give a rat's ass who you're related to or how long you've been hunting vampires. The way I see it, our current problems are largely your fault. Now, if you want to stay and help, then fine. We'll let you help, but you'll have to follow our rules, and number one is that no *human* goes hunting alone. Got it?"

"Mac, back off. She's had a hard night," John warned, surprising her by coming to her defense. Not that she needed it. Used to hunting vampires, she was not going to let a *half*-vampire like Mac intimidate her.

"If you had let me go with you—"

"No," Mac cut her off. "Not now, not ever. You're reckless and you don't follow orders. That puts everyone in danger."

Jessica felt her face heat up with anger and embarrassment. No one had ever accused her of being reckless before. Now, in one evening, she'd been accused of it twice. If anyone in her family was reckless, it was Kacie. Jess, by comparison, had always been the thinker, the planner; every action analyzed for all contingencies before execution. Granted, grabbing the sword and racing through the park the other night hadn't been either well thought out or planned, but everyone was entitled to break the rules at least once.

Lost in thought, she didn't notice immediately that Mac had let go of her arm until she was moving once again toward the front door and had to stop because Dirk stepped into her path.

"No more borrowing cars that don't belong to you," he said. "A car which, by the way, we're going to want back, so if it's been towed, you get to pay the fine to have it released. Understood?"

Jessica nodded and then pushed past him to get inside. She knew she should say something to the women; assure them that she was all right—apologize for what she'd done—but at the moment, all she wanted was to go upstairs.

Fortunately, she reached her room without running into anyone. Once there, she closed the bedroom door and felt a little of the night's tension ease. Despite how everything had turned out, she had succeeded in luring Brody to her. That alone was a huge success. No one could accuse her now of not being a real vampire hunter—not even her father. Though, to be fair, he hadn't meant to be insulting. Her father loved her. The problem was that while she could use a sword, she wasn't what one would call "accomplished." Not like Kacie was.

When her father had adopted Kacie after her parents had been killed, Jess had been thrilled that her best friend had become her sister. And though she begrudged Kacie nothing, she resented that Kacie seemed more worthy of the Winslow name than she was. It left her feeling inadequate and wanting to prove herself—if she could only figure out how. Finding the photograph of the old plantation home in Louisiana had been like Fate offering her a unique opportunity. The magazine article had been about the aftermath of Hurricane Katrina, and the photograph had been of just one of the many homes in the New Orleans area.

What had piqued her interest were the gargoyle figures perched on the corners of the plantation home. Others might think they were part of the architectural design, but she recognized them for what they were—chupacabras. And where there were chupacabras, there were vampires.

With the current population of vampires at home in England seemingly under control, there wasn't much opportunity for Jess to hone her skills. That's why she'd volunteered to deliver the sword to Charles for her father. It was an excuse to come to the States, and if for some reason the two changelings living with Charles wouldn't let her hunt with them, then she'd fly on to New Orleans, find the house in that photo and hunt the vampires that were sure to be there. She would prove to everyone that she was just as much a vampire slayer as any other Winslow.

With the drying blood on her neck pulling the skin tight, she went into the bathroom to clean up. She carefully avoided looking into the mirror while she wet a facecloth. Then, inevitably, morbid curiosity drew her gaze to the reflection in the mirror.

It was a mistake. Her neck was covered in blood.

Just the sight of it set her heart pounding in her chest. She struggled to catch her breath as a cold sweat broke out across her forehead. Darkness crept along the edges of her vision, gradually expanding until she was looking through a long, narrow tunnel.

When the ringing started in her ears, she knew she was going to pass out.

She let her legs fold and sat where she was, pressing the cool cloth to her forehead as she forced herself to take deep, steadying breaths. Some vampire hunter she was, she thought derisively, if she passed out every time she saw blood.

Unavoidably, her thoughts raced back to the time she'd been five years old, to the vampire attack on her home. The nightmares that plagued her weren't fabrications; they were actual memories, and they played out in her mind's eye much as they had in real life. There was fighting all around her as she crouched beside her mother's prone and lifeless body. Blood, dark red at night, coated her neck and chest, standing out in stark contrast against her mother's pale skin.

A shudder ran through her as she tried to stop the memory and failed. Phantom screaming filled her head as she remembered watching her father and Kacie's parents fighting for their lives. Then she saw nothing but the face of the vampire who stood before her, reaching for her. At the time, she'd leaped to her feet, wanting to flee but tripping instead over her mother's body. Her feet had kept working as she used them to avoid the arms reaching for her.

Then the vampire had stopped moving. A gaping hole had appeared in his chest and blood had spewed over her as the giant creature toppled and fell, pinning her to the ground.

Shaken, Jess pulled herself from the memory and drew a deep breath of air, proof that she wasn't being suffocated.

She reached up blindly and felt along the countertop until her fingers touched the small necklace she'd left there earlier. She'd taken it off, not wanting to risk it getting broken or lost, but now she needed the comfort it brought her. The small heart-shaped locket wasn't of great monetary value, but to Jess it was priceless because it had been a gift from her mother. Over the years, no matter to what extent the memories of her early life had faded, she had only to open this locket to see her mother's loving face. When she was younger, she would imagine that the locket was actually a window to heaven and her mother was just on the other side, watching her.

After a minute, Jess felt better. She set the locket aside and cleaned as much of her neck as she could without actually being able to see what she was doing. Then she stood up and risked another look in the mirror. This time, with most of the blood wiped off, the sight wasn't nearly as grisly and she was able to take a closer look at the wounds, which, as she'd suspected, were minor.

Brody hadn't had enough time to do much damage. *Thank you very much, Detective Boehler.*

Jess rinsed out the cloth and returned to the bedroom, intent on changing clothes and going to bed. She had just crossed to the dresser when a scratching sound beneath the bed caused her to pause and listen. It sounded like an animal, and she tried to remember if she'd seen a dog or cat around the place. She didn't think she had.

Was it a mouse? A shudder ran through her, putting another dent in her tough vampire-slayer facade. Maybe she really was a fraud.

Tiptoeing backward, she crossed the room to the dresser where she'd left her small dagger. She stared at it, belatedly wondering exactly what she intended to do. She couldn't really see herself chasing the mouse around the room trying to stab it.

Still, she couldn't bring herself to lay it aside. It made her feel better.

Placing each foot carefully on the carpet, she moved toward the bed. When she was close enough to step up on the mattress but not so close that whatever was under the bed could grab her toes, she did, causing the bed to creak under her weight. The scratching stopped.

Jess listened for several seconds, not daring to breathe. Finally, unable to take the anticipation any longer, she lay on her stomach and, pulling up the bed skirt with one hand, leaned over to look under the bed.

Two glowing red orbs shone in the darkness and Jess was so stunned to see them that at first, she couldn't react. Then the creature—she had no idea what kind—shuffled closer to her. She immediately lurched back on the bed and waited.

Seconds later, a gray shape emerged and stopped several feet away. It was the strangest animal she'd ever seen, with a round head, large glowing oval eyes, and an elongated muzzle with two overly long front fangs. When it rose up on its two large hind legs and moved toward her, she leaped to her feet, her dagger held out in front, ready.

About the size of a large Labrador retriever puppy, the animal stopped and stared up at her as intently as she watched it. With its hairless gray skin, fins running from the top of its head and down its back, and the sharp, three-toed claws, it looked exactly like a gargoyle. A living gargoyle.

Jess remembered her father telling her that Charles had a real-life chupacabra at his house, but she had assumed he kept it safely locked outside in a metal cage. Not running loose inside where it could attack at will.

Her fear escalating tenfold, Jess watched the chupacabra warily. They were reported to have great strength and speed. At any minute it could attack, and she'd be dead before she could defend herself.

Oddly enough, however, the small chupacabra was simply staring at her, a seemingly bemused expression on its face. Maybe it wasn't going to attack after all.

As her fear ebbed, rational thought returned. Of course Charles wouldn't allow a dangerous creature to run loose in his house and, given its size, this one must be rather young.

Fascinated now that she was certain her life wasn't in danger, she sat quietly, waiting to see what the creature would do. Surprisingly, it emitted a noise that sounded very much like a deep rumble and came toward her. Tentatively, she reached out a hand to touch it and when she did, the rumbling grew louder.

Feeling braver, she stroked its head, still keeping her dagger in the other hand. "Where did you come from?" As the minutes passed, Jess grew more comfortable with the creature. When Lanie knocked on her door a short time later, she found Jess with the chupacabra in her lap. It was making a deep, contented rumbling noise.

"Well, I see you've met Gem," Lanie said gently as she moved into the room and sat on the edge of the bed, reaching out a hand to stroke the creature. "I hope she didn't frighten you too much."

Jess smiled. "Maybe a little at first," she admitted. "I expected her to attack me."

"Chupacabras aren't really like that. I mean, they'll attack if they sense a threat to themselves or to their young, but otherwise, they'd just as soon leave humans alone."

"Really?" Jess knew she sounded skeptical.

Lanie smiled. "I know it's hard to believe. I didn't believe it myself, at first, but after taking care of Gem for the past year or so, I know they're not the evil creatures we thought they were."

"I find that a little surprising," Jess said, "given they are responsible for making vampires."

"But I would think you, of all people, would know that not all vampires are evil. I mean, don't you have a vampire living at the castle where you grew up?"

"You're talking about Erik, Charles and my father's great-great-great-uncle. I might be missing one or two greats in there." She smiled. "Erik keeps to himself a lot, but it's true, I wouldn't call him evil."

"Neither is my father—who I guess you've heard is also a vampire. Before he left for the Amazon jungle, he had a chance to study the chupacabra venom and found it to have remarkable healing powers. And I'm living proof of it. I would have died if Gem hadn't injected me with some of her venom."

Jess remembered the story that her father had shared with her about how Lanie had been kidnapped, attacked by a vampire, and almost died.

She understood Mac's anger a little better now; his fear that something might happen to the wife he loved—or the people he cared about. Suddenly, guilt hit her full force. "I'm so sorry that I snuck out of the house without telling you. I was afraid you would try to stop me."

Lanie gave a soft laugh. "Well, we probably would have tried, but maybe not as hard as you think. Beth and I can certainly empathize with not liking how the men always seem to think they're the only ones who can fight vampires. If Mac and Dirk had their way, we'd probably be locked away in a safe room until the last vampire on earth had been eliminated."

Jess gave her a grateful smile. "Thank you for understanding, but I *am* sorry that I wasn't honest with you about it."

Lanie patted her leg and gave her a smile. "Don't worry about it." She got to her feet and looked down as Jess stroked Gem along her fins. "Do you want me to take her with me so you can get some rest?"

"Would you mind terribly leaving her here?" Jess countered.

Lanie laughed. "Truthfully, I'm not sure I could keep her away." She walked to the door and opened it. "Just be sure you get some sleep, all right?"

The rest of the week passed quickly, and despite the fact that Mac, Dirk, and John went out every night looking for Brody, he remained elusive. They did, however, find two more victims. But by the third night, it was as if Brody had stopped killing—or had left the area.

Though she longed to go hunting herself, Mac, Dirk, and John refused to let her go. In truth, as Beth and Dirk's wedding drew nearer, Jess's desire to prove herself worthy as a Winslow took a backseat to her excitement over the last-minute preparations—including finding something appropriate to wear.

Beth went with Jess to the stores to help her shop. Jess felt a little guilty for pulling her away from both the wedding plans and the research she was conducting in the mansion's basement, which had been recently remodeled into a working research lab. Beth waved aside her concerns, claiming that only so many hours a day could be spent searching for a vampirism cure.

"Are you trying to find a cure for Dirk?" Jess asked her, thinking she understood why the changeling might not like being half vampire.

"Oh, no," Beth hurried to assure her. "Dirk doesn't mind being a changeling. I'm doing it in part because I'm curious, but mainly I'm doing it to help a friend."

"You have a friend who's a vampire? You mean Dr. Weber? Lanie's father?" Jess was confused.

"No, I've never met Dr. Weber. I meant someone else. Maybe friend is too strong a word. Let me explain. Last month, Dirk and I were kidnapped by a vampire named Patterson. This was after several weeks of being stalked by him. We would have died if another vampire, Sheldon Harris, hadn't helped us to escape. I really feel like we owe him our lives, so while I'm looking for a cure for all of them, I'm also doing it for Harris. Just don't tell the others."

"Why not? I'd think they'd be glad to know you're trying to help, especially if Harris saved your life."

Beth's smiled faltered. "Unfortunately, it's a little more complicated than that. You see, Harris is also a former teammate of Mac and Dirk. They think he was involved in an incident a couple of years ago that resulted in the death of several of their fellow SEALs. They don't exactly trust Harris, especially after he helped kidnap and almost kill both Lanie and Mac. That was a year ago, right after he'd turned, and I think he was confused about what had happened to him."

With this new information, Jess could understand why Mac and Dirk might not trust the vampire. In fact, she was a little surprised that one of them hadn't just staked the guy under the heading of "better safe than sorry." The dynamics of the vampire's relationship with the changelings were none of her concern, however, and she pushed him out of her mind.

Later that evening, she sat on the bed petting Gem, thinking about her plans for after the wedding. There was no reason for her to stay here any longer. Now more than ever, after spending so much time with Gem, she wanted to find that home in New Orleans. Maybe she could find a young chupacabra of her own.

All she had to do was capture one during the daytime and keep it caged until she had domesticated it. How hard could that be?

The night of the wedding arrived, and Jess sat with Charles and Julia in the pew traditionally reserved for the groom's family, since Dirk's parents were dead. Beside her sat several of Dirk's closer SEAL friends, in full military dress.

Jess was forced to admit that there really was something about a man in uniform.

The man beside her was particularly attractive, and Jess found him more than eager to engage in casual conversation while they waited for the rest of the guests to arrive. She was thinking that the evening was full of promise when she saw the man's eyes flicker to something on the other side of her. She turned and was shocked to see John Boehler shaking hands with Charles.

"So glad you could make it," Charles said.

"I wouldn't have missed it for the world," John replied, glancing up long enough to wink at her.

Nonplussed, Jess could only stare at him as he next greeted Julia. For a change, his face was clean shaven and his dark hair was neatly combed back; his usual rumpled suit had been replaced with a much nicer one. The change in appearance made him seem a completely different person, one who could even pose for the cover of *GQ*—or maybe a policeman's calendar, given his wide shoulders and trim hips.

He definitely cleaned up well, and she suddenly wondered if he would think the same of her. She'd chosen to wear a simple, sleeveless black cocktail-length dress, with a V-neckline and simple lines that showed off her figure to good advantage. She'd pulled her hair back in a loose bun, letting a few tendrils hang down. Up until now, she'd thought the gown was perfect for the evening. Now, as John came to her, she felt scantily clad.

"Excuse me, do you mind?" he said to the man beside her, pointing to the spot between them. "I was hoping to sit next to my date tonight."

Before Jess could say a word, the man shot her a look that let her know he didn't approve of her flirting with him when she was clearly involved with someone else, and scooted down. John immediately took his place.

"I trust I'm not interrupting," he said softly, leaning toward her in what had to look like an intimate gesture. "I really don't think he's your type, though."

"I guess we'll never know, thanks to you—again." She spoke with saccharine sweetness, but John laughed, seeming to be genuinely amused. That made her mad, so she decided to ignore him through the rest of the evening and turned her attention to the front of the church, even though the only thing to see there were the large bouquets of white roses sitting atop each of two pedestals.

Clearly not taking her hint, John leaned close again to whisper in her ear. "You look very nice tonight." His breath fanned across her neck, sending a small shiver racing along her body.

Jess continued to stare at the roses, not wanting to encourage him to speak to her.

"Great dress," he whispered again, and she practically felt the heat of his gaze on her plunging neckline. "Although you probably should have worn something warmer," he continued, his voice caressing her. "Do you want to wear my coat?"

Was he daft? It felt like someone had turned the heater on full blast. "No, thank you," she said in a hushed tone. "I'm not cold."

"Ah."

Up until now, she'd been staring straight ahead, but that simple response drew her attention. When their gazes met, she saw that his eyes were shining with amusement—and something more; something heated. He broke eye contact and his gaze dropped to her breasts and lingered too long to be polite before he brought his gaze back to hers and winked. "I'm flattered."

Immediately, she felt her breasts swell and knew, without looking, that her nipples were distended; a fact that must have also been obvious to him through the fabric of her dress.

Mortified, she had an overwhelming urge to cross her arms, but resisted, not wanting him to know he'd embarrassed her. Instead, she gave him a frosty look. "You flatter yourself." Then she leaned forward a bit more and graced the man on the detective's other side with a seductive smile.

John frowned and she turned her attention back to the front, a smug smile spreading across her face.

"What I want to know," John whispered, moving close enough that she felt his body heat warming her, and his breath against her neck stirring the small hairs, "is where you're hiding your sword."

Before she could say anything, the blaring of the Trumpet March announced the bride's appearance, and Jess found herself lost in the moment. Jess had seen Beth several times before in her wedding gown, but she'd never seen her looking lovelier than she did at that moment. Walking beside her father, it was clear to all present that the sole object of her attention and love was the man who waited for her at the end of the aisle.

Jess felt her breath catch, and despite previous vows to not get too emotional, her eyes filled with tears. The thought that a vampire slayer shouldn't be this emotional raced through her head, and she tried to discreetly wipe the moisture from her eyes.

Beth reached the front, and the look in Dirk's eyes was hot and hungry. It was the kind of expression every woman deserved to see in her husband's eyes, especially on their wedding day. Reaching up to dab at her eyes again, Jess was surprised when a tissue suddenly appeared before her. Even more surprising was the source, but there was nothing in John's expression to lead her to think that he was about to tease her for crying or in any other way belittle her.

"Thank you," she said softly, taking it from him. Maybe he wasn't so bad after all, she thought. Then her attention was fully focused on the ceremony for the next twenty minutes.

Afterward, as Charles, Julia, and most of the guests left the church to head over to Charles's mansion for the reception, Jess waited patiently for Mac and Lanie to finish with the photographer who was taking pictures of the wedding party. For a while, she stood and watched the pictures being taken, but eventually she had to find the ladies' restroom.

When she returned to the chapel a few minutes later, she found it completely empty. Thinking the party had moved outdoors to take a few moonlight photos, she hurried outside to find the yard dismally empty and the last of the guests just driving off.

"There you are." John's voice came from behind her, giving her a start.

"It appears that my ride has left without me." She gave him a baleful glance.

"No, it hasn't." Standing beside her, he gestured to the lone vehicle in the parking lot. "Your chariot awaits."

He put his hand at the small of her back and ushered her toward his car.

"Thank you." She walked beside him, feeling ill at ease. "I guess Mac and Lanie forgot me." She tried to sound like it didn't bother her, but it did.

"They didn't forget you," he said as they stopped at his car and he unlocked the passenger door.

"Are you trying to imply that they left me on purpose?" She knew that she shouldn't let anything he said affect her, and yet—

He smiled. "What I meant is that you're not that forgettable."

"So you're suggesting that they left me intentionally? Because I'm a nuisance to be with?" she accused as she got into the car.

"You? A nuisance? Don't be ridiculous," he said in mock protest, closing the door and walking around to the other side to get in. "I know that I enjoy being with you, but then, I like dodging sword blades and getting the crap beat out of me by vampires."

"Sorry," she muttered as he started the car. "You getting beat up wasn't supposed to be part of the plan."

She fell quiet as he maneuvered the car out of the parking lot and onto the street. They arrived at the mansion several minutes later and John parked his car in the back, where Mac had parked Charles's Humvee. Together they went inside. Seeing how many people had shown up for the reception, Jess was absurdly grateful not to be arriving by herself.

The mansion was filled to capacity, and the admiral had opened up the west wing for the occasion. There was a ballroom on this side of the house where tables had been set up for the meal. A small band was playing off to the side where an area had been cleared for dancing. At the front of the room, on a low dais, was the wedding party's table. Already, Dirk, Beth, Mac, and Lanie were sitting down.

"There you are," Charles said, coming toward them. "We saved you a spot at the family's table, so if you two will come with me."

Charles led them across the room to where the wedding party waited. Jess saw that there were two seats, side by side, left open. She and John each took one.

"I'm sorry we had to leave the church so quickly." Lanie, who was sitting on Jess's other side, gave her an apologetic smile.

"That's okay," Jess said graciously.

Lanie looked relieved. "I knew, once you heard the problem, you'd understand."

Now Jess was confused. "Problem?"

Lanie looked past her to John. "You didn't give her my message?"

John looked embarrassed, though Jess suspected it was an act. "I guess I forgot."

Jess shot him a look before turning back to Lanie. "What problem?"

Lanie leaned in conspiratorially. "Gem. I thought that Mac had locked her in her carrier before leaving for the church, and he thought I had. When we realized that neither of us had, we knew we had to get back here as quickly as we could before she either scared the caterers or ate the cake."

Jess looked around to see if she spotted anyone serving the food. When she did, her gaze flew to the cake. "She has a sweet tooth, does she?"

Lanie grimaced. "Let's hope that no one else notices that we're one tier short."

When Lanie looked away to respond to something Mac said, Jess turned to John. "You let me think they forgot me," she accused him.

"No, I specifically said you were not forgettable. I'm not responsible for any conclusions you drew after that. Besides, as your escort this evening, I am responsible for your safe conduct from the church to the reception, and"—he gestured around the room—"mission accomplished."

Jess didn't understand him at all. One minute, he was dashing and charming and the next, he was irritating to the point where she wanted to scream. To make matters worse, she suspected that he knew the effect he had on her and did it intentionally.

In an effort to thwart him, she purposely avoided further conversation with him, choosing instead to chat with Lanie. Then all too soon the meal was over and Jess could hear Charles, farther down the long table, addressing the newlyweds.

"I believe it's traditional for the bride and groom to have the first dance."

Jess looked over and saw Beth's smile as she turned to Dirk expectantly. He didn't look too excited about the prospect of getting up in front of everyone, but after a rueful glance at the dance floor, he turned to his new bride. "Come on, but I'm warning you now that if I hold you close for too long, I'm going to have to drag you upstairs for some privacy."

Beth leaned close to whisper something in his ear that had him hurrying her to the dance floor.

"They look so nice together, don't they?" Lanie asked on a soft sigh as everyone watched the couple dance. Midway through the number, the newlyweds motioned for the others to join them.

"Come on," Mac said resignedly to Lanie, standing up and extending his hand to her. "I'm not about to let Dirk show me up."

Lanie pretended to be affronted. "Is that the only reason you want to dance with me?"

His suggestive smile made her blush. "Come with me and I'll tell you exactly why I want to dance with you."

Lanie rose and Jess watched the pair join Dirk and Beth on the dance floor.

"My dear," Charles said a moment later to Julia, "shall we show these adolescents how it's done?"

Julia's eyes beamed as she smiled and placed her hand in his. "Why yes, that's a marvelous idea."

Jess watched Charles and Julia walk to the dance floor, realizing that she and John were now alone at the table. She felt horribly conspicuous sitting there, as if every eye in the room was staring at them, waiting for them to join the others.

"Shall we?" John finally asked, sounding hesitant.

"Oh, that's all right. We don't have to." Just as she said the words, however, Charles pinned them each with a look.

She gave John an apologetic smile as he stood and pulled back her chair. "I'm sorry," she whispered as they walked out to the dance floor. "Perhaps we could make one quick circuit and then sneak out the back doors—no one would know we'd left."

He raised an eyebrow at her as he pulled her into his arms. "Maybe find a dark corner outside where you can have your evil way with me? Tempting, very tempting."

Startled, she looked up into his face. "What?"

"I don't usually take a woman to bed on the first date, but I'm not about to turn down your offer." He guided them around another couple. "In fact, let's skip the subterfuge and go upstairs to your room right now."

"How dare you!" she sputtered, trying to pull away. His arm around her waist was iron tight, and she was all too aware of the way his body moved against hers as he guided them around the dance floor. She was as embarrassed as she was mad. "I wouldn't . . . make love to you if you were the last man available."

He lowered his head until he could whisper in her ear. "Then why did you suggest it?"

"I didn't suggest it," she bit out indignantly.

"Careful, Jess. People are starting to stare."

She cast a look around and saw that he was right. Several pairs of eyes had turned to them in blatant curiosity, and Jess snapped her mouth shut on the rest of what she wanted to say.

They continued to dance in silence for several minutes, and she felt his chest rumble with quiet laughter. It made her all the more furious with him. He was just baiting her, trying to get her riled up, and damn it, it was working. It was her own bad luck that she actually found him attractive. Otherwise, she could have brushed off his suggestions like lint from a cheap suit.

She reined in her emotions by focusing on their dancing. She was surprised at how well the detective moved about the floor. "Where did you learn how to dance?" she asked, unable to stop herself. "Is ballroom dancing a hobby of yours?" She had trouble meshing the rough cop image with this *GQ* Fred Astaire.

"No," he said, sounding insulted. "Ballroom dancing is *not* a hobby of mine. However, it is something that my wife wanted to learn, so we took a few lessons."

Wife? She nearly tripped. "I didn't know you were married."

"That's *married*, as in past tense," he said. "It was a mistake that we rectified a long time ago."

"Any children?"

"No, thank God."

For some reason, the way he said that bothered her. "You don't want children?"

"Maybe one day—with the right woman. Liz definitely wasn't the right woman."

They'd been dancing a waltz and when the number ended, the band started another slower dance. As much as she tried not to let being so physically close to John affect her, she was all too aware of him. She fought the temptation to lean into him by holding herself more erect in his arms. She didn't care if she was being rude. She would not let herself be attracted to this man.

"What's the matter?" he asked.

"Nothing."

He gave her a curious look. "Well, try to relax. You're acting like a virgin on her wedding night."

She gaped at him, embarrassment causing her face to heat. "Excuse me? Did it occur to you that maybe I don't like being held so tightly?" She shoved at his chest to give herself more room and created a four-inch gap of space between them.

"It's a slow dance," he bit out, pulling her close again. "You're not supposed to be able to drive a bus between us."

Fighting hard to control her rising temper, she shoved at him again a little harder, only to find that his arms were, once again, like iron bands holding her in place. "We're too close," she said between clenched teeth.

"We are *not* too close." He sounded like he was fighting to keep his temper.

"Please," she scoffed. "If you were any closer, you'd be inside me." Looking up to see why they'd suddenly stopped dancing, she found John staring at her so intently that the heat from his gaze nearly scorched her. Then her words registered in her brain and she prayed for the earth to open and swallow her whole.

Chapter 7

John was barely aware of Jess's obvious mortification or the expression of horror spreading across her face. His mind was firmly locked on acting out the very thing she'd suggested. He couldn't remember a time he'd wanted a woman this badly, and, instinctively, he pulled her closer, the room full of people forgotten as he leaned forward, intent on tasting her sweet lips.

He heard her gasp right before she shoved him, struggling to break free of his embrace. He released her so fast she would have fallen if he hadn't reached out a hand to steady her, but as soon as she regained her balance, she jerked her arm from his grasp and stormed off.

He watched her leave, wondering who was more psychotic—the reckless female who went around trying to kill vampires—or him, for finding her attractive?

Needing solitude, he headed out the French doors opening onto the back patio of the mansion and stopped long enough to take a deep breath of cool night air. It helped calm him, but not enough. He knew he should just find Dirk and Beth, congratulate them and leave, but he wasn't quite ready to call it a night.

The door to the patio opened and several other guests emerged, so John headed around to the side of the house where he could think in private.

He wasn't sure exactly when he noticed he had company. He even knew who was there before he turned around and confirmed it with his eyes.

"Hello, Detective Boehler," Harris said, stepping forward so the light from the house would fall on him.

"If you're going to keep sneaking up on me like that, Vlad, I'd appreciate it if you'd wear a bell."

The vampire smiled—a small lifting of the lips that showed the tips of his fangs. John worked to keep his heartbeat at a slow, steady rhythm. Just because this vampire had passed up several previous opportunities to kill him didn't mean he might not still try. "At the risk of sounding rude, why are you here?" Then a sudden thought had him reaching for his gun as he searched the darkness. "Is Brody—"

"No, he's not here," the vampire said. "I came for another reason."

John caught the muted sound of a footstep just as the vampire's gaze shifted to something behind him. John whirled and saw Mac and Dirk approaching. As they drew near, John made a decision.

"Run," he said to the vampire, stepping forward so he was blocking Dirk and Mac from seeing the creature.

"What's going on here?" Mac asked, glaring at him with an ice-cold, piercing stare.

Glancing behind him, John saw the vampire hadn't moved. "I can explain . . ."

"Harris, what brings you out tonight?"

"I wanted to talk to Bethany."

John stepped away from the group and stared at them in stunned surprise. "You know each other?"

"We have a history," Dirk said cryptically. Then to Harris, "She's a little busy right now."

Harris looked back at the mansion as the sound of music and laughter filled the night.

"Yes, I can see that," Harris said.

"Beth and I were married today," Dirk explained. "This is the reception."

John thought he saw a pained expression cross the vampire's face, but it was quickly gone. "Congratulations to you both."

Dirk nodded but didn't smile. "Thanks."

There was an uncomfortable pause and then Harris reached into his pocket and pulled out a vial. "Please give this to her," Harris said. "It's filled with the adult chupacabra venom." He held the vial out until Dirk took it from him. "Tell her if she wants more, I can get it. You know how to get in touch with me."

Dirk extended his other hand and John saw that he held a sealed blue envelope. When Harris looked surprised, Dirk shrugged. "This is from Beth. I don't know what it says, but it's been sitting by the door for a couple of days. She thought you might stop by."

"Thank you." Harris took it from him. There was an uncomfortable shift in their stances and John simply stared at them all in surprise.

"How's the chupa?" Mac asked after a moment.

Harris smiled. “She’s fine.” He turned his head to look off into the distance. “She’s developed a taste for the deer in these woods.”

Mac nodded. “I’ll tell Lanie. She was worried.”

An awkward silence fell as John tried to figure out what was going on. Then Dirk looked at his watch. “We’d better get back inside. John, are you coming?” They turned to him.

“Not just yet,” he said.

Mac and Dirk gave Harris a hard look as if they weren’t sure if they trusted him not to kill John as soon as they turned their backs.

Harris sighed. “I’ve already fed tonight. I won’t hurt the detective.”

“Damn right, you won’t,” John said, affronted. “And I promise not to stake your ass.” Mac and Dirk studied them carefully, like parents trying to decide if it was safe to leave two kids by themselves.

“All right,” Dirk said, then he and Mac turned and walked off.

John watched them leave and then looked back at the vampire. “I’m guessing you three have a connection beyond the obvious?”

“Old Navy buddies. It’s a long story.”

“I’d like to hear it.”

“Some other time, Detective. I have only a few hours before dawn and I need to look for Brody.”

“Do you know where he is?”

“Not yet. Good night.” He walked off and was soon swallowed by the night. “Oh. Detective?” The vampire’s voice drifted out of the darkness. “Thank you.”

“For what?” John asked, confused.

"For stepping in to save my life—again," Harris said, inadvertently raising an issue that had been bothering John.

"I'll be honest," he found himself saying. "I'm not sure I did the right thing."

There was a moment of silence. "I understand," Harris said quietly. Then John was alone once more.

"Detective Boehler, are you listening to me?" The sharp tone of Richard Dresden's voice pierced John's eardrums and set his back teeth on edge.

"Yes, I'm listening." All afternoon, he'd done nothing but listen to theories and answer questions. Like a kid stuck in class, he glanced at the clock on the wall and wondered how much longer he'd have to suffer through this interrogation.

"Then tell me how these five Exsanguinator cases—the ones where the victims have rap sheets—are related to the others."

"I don't know," John said, not trying to be a smartass. "I was never able to determine a connection other than that they were all killed by the same person or group." Now he knew more—that all the victims had been killed by a vampire.

It was clear that Dick didn't like John's response because he paced back and forth twice more, holding the files in his hand as if the physical contact would somehow help him understand them better. John could have told him it wouldn't work. He'd spent hours searching for an answer that wouldn't make him sound like a candidate for a padded cell.

For a brief moment, watching the man pace, John was

tempted to tell him about the vampires, just to see his reaction. Finally, Dresden stopped pacing and sat down. His coat had come off two hours ago, and now his tie hung loose and the top button of his shirt was undone. He was on a fast downhill slide into slovenliness and John almost felt sorry for the prick; the operative word being "almost."

Afraid Dick was settling in for another round, John abruptly stood up, grabbed his coat, and put it on. "I don't know about you, but I've had all I can take for today. I'm done." He put his hand into his one good pocket and found the folded note that Joyce had slipped him earlier.

"Wait, I've got a few more questions," Dresden said as he started to walk off.

"Sorry, but I'm fresh out of answers," John shot back, stopping long enough to give the man his full attention. "As far as I'm concerned, you're as current on the cases as I am. There's nothing more I can tell you. My suggestion, at this point, is to let your brain stew on it while you do something else. When you come back to it, maybe you'll see something we both missed. Hell, maybe you'll even solve the cases."

"Do you really think so?" Dresden asked, sounding hopeful and appearing so much younger than John felt at that moment.

"I don't know," he said truthfully. "But rule number one, kid, is that sane, logical people don't commit murder, so don't expect their crimes to make sense. Now, go home or go meet friends or stay here if you must, but I'm leaving." With that, he turned and left, not once glancing back.

Minutes later, in his car and driving from the station, he pulled out the note with the address written on it. John had asked Joyce to let him know if she learned of anything unusual, no matter how trivial she might think it was. That morning, she'd told him about a complaint they'd received from a homeless man, who had clearly been drunk. There was too much noise coming from the abandoned building behind which he slept and he wanted a patrol unit to swing by and make the building be quiet. A patrol car had driven by, but the officers had heard and seen nothing to concern them.

John, however, wasn't as convinced that there was nothing more to the story, and he wanted to check out the place himself.

The sun was just going down by the time he reached the abandoned building and parked. Before getting out of the car, he removed the small dagger he had placed in the glovebox earlier and slipped it into the new sheath on his holster strap.

Grabbing a flashlight, he exited the car and walked around to the alley running behind the building, spotting one large cardboard box propped against it.

He went over to the box and glanced inside, but found it empty. Newspaper lined the bottom and several more pages were pushed off to the side. In one corner, there were a couple of empty cans of food and a candy bar wrapper; obvious signs that someone had been living there, but John got the impression that whoever it was hadn't been there in at least a day.

Taking a look around, he didn't see any more shelters. There was no one around to answer questions, so John headed for the nearest entrance into the building. With the last of the sun about to disappear beneath the horizon, it was getting too dark to see, so John flipped on his flashlight. He shone it along the back of the building, looking for a door. When he found it, he pulled his gun from its holster and, aiming the light ahead of him, went inside.

He found himself standing in a hallway that was too narrow to be comfortable, should he be attacked. He moved down it quickly and quietly, his gaze darting all around. When he reached an open door, he stopped to listen before inspecting the room with the beam of his light. Seeing nothing, he moved farther down the hallway to the next room and checked it out. Again, nothing. He was halfway down the hall when he caught the tinkling of a small bell coming from behind him.

Whirling around, he almost shot Harris, easing up on the trigger at the last second. "What the—?"

"I did wear a bell this time—as requested." Harris's calm tone was irritating.

"You almost got yourself shot," John pointed out. "What are you doing here?"

"I suspect the same thing you are—looking for Brody."

"What makes you think he's here?" John asked.

The vampire looked at him as if trying to figure out how much to tell him. "All the vampires with the same chupacabra venom in them—whether they got it from the creature directly or indirectly through a vampire the chupacabra created—share a psychic link. Since I created Brody, I share a link with him. It's not a strong link, which makes it hard to follow, but I got a strong enough impression of this building that I was able to find it." He paused and then gave John a curious look. "How'd you find this place?"

John shrugged. "Old-fashioned detective work." At the vampire's skeptical look, John elaborated. "I followed up on a lead from a homeless man complaining of noise. Thought that maybe I'd find Brody."

"He's not here," the vampire said, pushing past him to continue down the hallway. "But he was."

"How do you know?" John asked, falling into step behind him.

"I don't sense that he's close by—however, there is something here." Harris stopped and looked back at John. "It might be safer if you left."

John frowned. "I'm good, thanks. Let's keep going."

Harris shrugged. "Suit yourself. I think the room he was staying in is just ahead."

"How can you tell?"

"Odor."

John followed the vampire down the hall until they stopped outside a room. This close, John smelled the stench of human waste mixed with rotting flesh.

The door was closed. John exchanged looks with the vampire before opening it.

At first, John saw nothing. The windows were boarded up, preventing any light from the streetlamps from filtering inside, so he played the beam of the flashlight across the room. It was dirty, filled with old newspapers, long-empty food containers that had been picked clean by rodents, rodent droppings in the corners, and a lot of dust that had been recently disturbed by human footprints, but nothing to account for the smell.

"You'd better go," Harris said again, his attention focused on the door at the back of the room.

"Why?"

"In about five seconds, this place is going to be crawling with Brody's meals, coming to life. I need to stake them, and I don't want to have to worry about you while I'm doing it."

"Don't worry about me," John said, putting up his gun and pulling out the dagger. "Just make sure you don't get staked by mistake."

Harris smiled, his fangs gleaming in the flashlight's beam. "In that case, heads up—four o'clock. I'll get the two on the right."

John whirled around just as three creatures came hurtling through the back door so fast that John barely had time to react. He raised his dagger and didn't so much stab the creature as held his dagger at exactly the right height while the creature, carried by his own momentum, impaled himself through the heart.

John wasn't sure what he'd expected to happen, but he felt a combination of surprise and shock when the vampire didn't poof into dust like in the movies. Easing the body to the ground, he turned to see how Harris was doing and discovered that the vampire had already dispatched his two and was watching him.

Harris smiled at the expression on John's face. "What? Did you expect them to explode into a cloud of dust? Sorry to disappoint you."

John fought to keep his expression straight. "How do we know they're really dead?"

Harris and John both looked at the bodies. "Trust me," Harris said, "they're dead. Come on, we'd better check out the rest of this place. I don't think there are any more waiting to attack, but I could be wrong."

They left that room and continued along the first level,

checking out each room as they got to it. It was in the second to last room that John realized the search for Brody had just taken on a new level of complexity.

If there had simply been bodies, John might have coped with it better. Even the blood on the walls wasn't something new. It was seeing Jessica's name spelled out in that blood that unnerved him. And it wasn't just written once. It was splashed across every wall, several times, both large and small.

"Brody is one sick fuck," Harris commented.

"How old do you think that writing is?"

He felt Harris glance at him. "A day, maybe two at the most. Why?"

"That's her name."

"Whose?"

"Jessica Winslow's. She's Admiral Winslow's cousin." He tried to put it into a context Harris would better understand. "The woman from the park. And she was in the car that night when I went to the funeral home; the one Brody went after."

Harris shook his head. "It has to be coincidence. When would Brody have met Winslow's cousin?"

He was right, John thought. Then he remembered. "No coincidence. She set a trap for him the next night—at a bar. He attacked her; even bit her, but I got there before he could do more than break the skin."

Harris frowned. "Still—two encounters doesn't seem like enough for Brody to have formed any kind of infatuation. Like you said, how would he even know her name?"

"Unless he's been stalking her?"

Harris shook his head. "No. I would have sensed him close to the mansion when I was there, and I didn't."

John tried to shake off his feeling of doom. "You're right." He gestured to the short hallway leading to a couple of back rooms. "Let's see if there's anything else in here."

John went into the first room while Harris continued down the hall to the second.

"Shit." Harris's voice seemed unusually loud in the surrounding quiet of the room.

"What?" John hurried to where he was and came to a sudden stop in the doorway. The walls here were also covered with "Jessica" spelled in blood, but this time, the body of a woman with long dark hair, lying facedown in the corner, caused John's heart to nearly stop beating.

Chapter 8

"Oh, God." John rushed to the figure and gently rolled her over, brushing long strands of hair away so he could see her face.

"Is it—?"

"No," he said. "It's not her." His relief was so great, he felt guilty. But the dead woman was beyond his help now—almost. "She has to be staked."

Stabbing a dead body shouldn't be hard, he thought, and yet . . . he took a deep breath, instantly regretting it as the putrid smell of death filled his lungs.

"I'll do it," Harris said.

John wanted to argue with him, prove he was up to the task, but instead he nodded and stepped aside. The chaotic tangle of his thoughts shared one common theme: Simon Brody—psychotic killer of women—vampire—obsessed with Jessica Winslow. Needing the distraction of physical movement, he wandered around the room, playing the beam of his flashlight over the floor and into the corners. When he reached the closet doors, he peered inside. A small dark shadow on the floor caught his attention.

Taking a closer look, he discovered that it was a black leather jacket. He bent down to retrieve it and when he held it up, saw only half a jacket. The other half still lay on the floor.

His gaze fell on the small decorative dragonfly pinned to the lapel. He'd seen it before and it didn't take long to remember where. His memory of the evening outside the bar came rushing back and he knew that this was the jacket Brody had ripped off Jessica when he attacked her.

Not sure what he intended to do with the garment, he leaned over to pick up the other half. As he did, several things fell from the folds and landed on the floor. Using the beam of his flashlight, he saw a tube of lipstick, two writing pens and a small notebook—all things that could have spilled out of her purse that night Brody attacked her.

Bending over, he picked up the notebook.

"What's that?" Harris asked, coming to stand beside him.

"I don't know." John shoved the jacket halves under his arm so he could open the book. "Looks like Jessica's day planner. I found her jacket in the closet."

Harris looked over his shoulder as he flipped through the pages. "She likes to write."

"Understatement of the year," John said, scanning the detailed comments, notes, names, addresses, and phone numbers scribbled across the pages.

"Oh, look," Harris said in what sounded like a teasing tone to John. "She even wrote something about you. I didn't know your parents weren't married when you were born."

"She meant it as a term of endearment."

"Yeah, I'm sure."

John smiled, but it soon faded. "Someone ripped out the page for this week." He flipped the pages back and forth, hoping they were just stuck together. His first thought was that Brody had ripped it out. The question was—why?

He hadn't seen Jessica since the wedding and wondered what she had planned for this week. Whatever it was, she needed to change her plans. He absently handed the book to Harris as he pulled out his cell phone and quickly keyed in a number.

"Julia?" he said a moment later. "This is John. Is Jessica there? It's important."

"Why, no she's not, John," Julia replied. "I thought she would have told you. She went back to England yesterday. Is there a problem?"

"She did?" He tried to ignore the unexpected stab of disappointment he felt that she had left without saying good-bye. It wasn't like they were friends or anything, he reminded himself. Julia said something on the other end, but his mind was too muddled to follow along. Then he heard the admiral's worried voice on the line.

"John, what's going on?"

"Admiral, I have reason to believe that Brody is after Jess, but if she's in England, then she's probably okay."

"I'll call her anyway, just to make sure she arrived safely."

"Thank you."

"I don't think she's headed to jolly old England," Harris said as soon as John got off the phone.

The grim sound of his voice tripped the alarm bells in John's head. "Why is that?"

Harris picked up a piece of paper stuck between two pages in the book and held it out so John could see. It was a folded magazine page filled with photos of old homes in the New Orleans area. One photograph in particular caught his eye. It was of an old Southern manor with gargoyle figures perched on the roof, giving it a touch of Gothic architecture.

"This doesn't mean anything," John argued.

"Not by itself," Harris agreed. He held out the day planner so John could see the page it was opened to. It was the schedule for the next week. Across the top, in large bold handwriting, was written *Find house with chupacabras.*

John keyed another number into his cell phone and waited for his old college roommate to answer the phone.

"Vince, I need a huge favor."

"You already owe me three huge favors," the tired male voice chided on the other end.

"Do me this one and I'll give you my firstborn child."

"Like you'd find anyone willing to have sex with you."

"Yeah, yeah. Look, I need to know if a Jessica Winslow was on a flight yesterday leaving Dulles and arriving somewhere in England. Can you access that information?"

"You know I can. The question is, should I? If the government wanted the average citizen to have access to this information—"

"I wouldn't have to call in favors from my best friend, who happens to work for—"

"If you're not on a secure line, you can stop right there," Vince warned him, his tone no longer teasing.

John heard the sound of fingers flying over the keyboard. Though he tried to be patient, he felt as if he were stuck in a time warp, where his thoughts were racing along in hyperdrive while the rest of the world was moving in slow motion.

Finally, Vince's voice sounded in his ear. "Okay, I checked every flight leaving for England from any airport in a hundred-mile radius of the D.C. area, and there was no Jessica Winslow on any of them. I did, however, find a Jessica Winslow on the 9:00 A.M. flight to New Orleans yesterday."

"Thanks, man. I owe you big-time."

"Yes, you do. And that's the way I like it. You. Owe. Me. It has a nice ring to it, doesn't it?"

About to hang up, an idea came to John. "There is one more fav—"

"I already booked you on the next flight to New Orleans. It leaves tomorrow morning at 9:10 A.M."

"Thanks, I'll pay you back."

"No need. I used your credit card."

John disconnected the call, not wanting to know exactly how Vince had accessed his card number, and turned to see Harris watching him.

"You're going after her?" he asked.

"I am. I hope I'm wrong about this and Brody's not after her." *Maybe I'm the one obsessed with her*, he thought miserably to himself. "But I have to make sure she's okay."

His cell phone rang and he saw by the caller ID that Charles was calling him back.

"I finally reached Gerard," Charles said. "Not only is Jessica not there, but he's not expecting her any time soon."

"I know where she is," John told him. "She went to New Orleans."

"Oh, good." Charles sounded relieved. "I'll call her and tell her to be careful then."

John was confused. "You know how to get in touch with her?"

"Of course. If she's gone to New Orleans, then she's probably staying at our family home."

John couldn't believe his ears. "You have a home down there?"

"Really, it's more of an estate. No one's lived there in years, but I pay a service to keep the place cleaned and operational, just in case."

"Will you give me the address? I'm flying down there. I know she can probably take care of herself, but I'll still feel better if I go."

There was silence on the other end and then Charles spoke, sounding calm but serious. "I'll give you the address tonight, when you stop by."

"Charles, I don't really have time—"

"It's important. Just swing by on your way home."

The admiral's mansion was a good thirty minutes out of his way. John sighed. "Fine. As soon as I'm finished here, I'll swing by." He hung up, wondering what was so important it couldn't be discussed over the phone.

He turned to find Harris watching him. "What?"

"If you're right about Brody, then this could be a very dangerous situation you're heading into."

"True."

"Brody's not like me—he wasn't created by a chupacabra. I created him. Do you realize what that means?" Harris didn't wait for John to answer. "It means that every day, his intelligence deteriorates a little more. The longest I've seen a vampire last is two months. Some don't make it that long. And when their mind starts to go, it goes fast. Then all that's left is a creature with superhuman strength and no capacity for rational thought."

John stared at Harris. "If you're trying to scare me, then you've succeeded. But if you're suggesting that I stay here and let Jessica face this creature by herself, forget it."

"Actually, I was going to suggest that I go—by myself."

"What?"

"I think it would be better if I went, instead of you," Harris elaborated.

"No way. Besides, how are you going to get down there? Fly?" He paused. "Vampires don't really fly, do they?" Suddenly, he wasn't sure.

Harris shook his head. "No, we can't fly. So I'll have to get down there the same way Brody does—on foot. It might take a day or two longer, but I shouldn't be too far behind him. Hell, I might even catch up to him."

"If you do, great. But if you don't, then I want to be down there when he arrives."

Harris shrugged. "Suit yourself."

John grew thoughtful. "Let me give you my cell phone number. You can call me when you get to New Orleans." He paused. "I don't suppose you have a cell phone?"

Harris gave him a look. "What do you think?"

"I think we have a lot to do before tomorrow morning, so let's get started." He looked back at the dead woman's body, new rage and frustration filling him. There was no way he was going to let Brody get his hands on Jessica. Brody would have to kill him first.

John showed up at the Winslow mansion an hour after parting company with Harris. He was perplexed by the strange relationship he was developing with the vampire. They shared a common interest in wanting to find Brody, but beyond that, he didn't know. Vampires were supposed to be evil and yet he didn't get that sense from Harris.

Even more perplexing to him was the relationship Harris had with Mac and Dirk. He wouldn't have thought it possible that vampire hunters could be friends with a vampire—and truth be told, the interaction he'd witnessed the other night wasn't exactly the friendliest. On the other hand, Mac and Dirk hadn't made any effort to kill Harris, so that said something. He just wasn't sure what.

"Come into my study," Charles said after he'd ushered John inside.

As he followed the admiral down the hallway, John wondered exactly what it was the older man wanted to discuss. "Charles, I'm not going to let you talk me out of going."

Charles waved his comment aside as he sat down behind his desk. "I have no intention of trying to talk you out of going, I assure you."

"Then why—"

"The other night," Charles interrupted, "after you

made your big discovery, we dumped a lot of information on you at once. Because it was so much, there were other things we never got around to telling you; things I think you should know. For instance, Mac and Dirk aren't just vampire hunters—they're Night Slayers."

John mentally waved the information aside and sank into the chair opposite Charles. "Vampire hunters, Night Slayers—I don't care what you call them, Charles."

Charles's brows furrowed and he flexed his hands where they rested on the desktop. "Perhaps I'm explaining this badly," he tried again. "What I'm trying to tell you is that Mac and Dirk are especially *equipped* to hunt vampires."

John grew impatient because they were wasting time. "I know. I've seen the sword."

Charles's eyes lit up. "Exactly; the sword is a perfect example. Those are Death Rider swords and in the hands of a Night Slayer, very powerful weapons."

And in *his* hands, a .44 mag was a powerful weapon—what was the man's point?

"Mac and Dirk are not like you and me," Charles continued. "They're changelings."

"Like I said, I don't care what you want to call them—"

"They're not human," Charles interrupted, earning John's undivided attention.

"Excuse me?"

Charles sighed. "They're not human—anymore."

"They're not?" First Jess. Now Charles. John wondered if insanity ran in the Winslow family.

"I understand that you've met Sheldon Harris."

John nodded. "The vampire."

"Okay. Well, the same chupacabra that killed him and

turned him into a vampire also attacked Mac and Dirk. The chupacabra venom is what turns dead humans into vampires. Mac and Dirk were injected with enough venom that had they died, they would have become vampires. Because they didn't die, the chupacabra venom couldn't take over their entire system, so instead, they became changelings—half-human and half-vampire." He paused, giving John time to absorb what he was hearing.

"*Half*-vampire?" *Sure, why not*, John thought, feeling himself slip a little farther through Alice's Looking Glass. If there could be vampires, why couldn't there just as well be half-vampires?

"You might not have noticed the changes in them, but they do share some of the vampire's attributes," Charles continued. "For instance, they are immeasurably stronger than they were before, and they move with almost as much speed as the full vampire."

As Charles talked, John thought back to how fast Mac and Dirk had moved on campus. He hadn't been able to keep up.

"They have incredible hearing," Charles went on. "And their night vision is better than our day vision. Have you ever noticed that sometimes their eyes glow with reddish light?"

An image of Dirk standing at the trunk of John's car, studying the sword, flashed through his mind.

"On the downside," Charles continued, "while they are very energetic during the night, they have a hard time functioning during the day." He paused noticeably, making John wonder what else he was about to hear. "They also have fangs."

John tried to remember if he'd ever seen Dirk's or

Mac's teeth. They didn't smile much and he'd always assumed they lacked a sense of humor, but if they had fangs . . . "Do they drink blood?"

"They only drink the blood of those who willingly give it—and they don't do it often. Unlike vampires, changelings don't need blood to survive, but small doses of it, freely given, can be a powerful source of energy and strength. And that's a critical point—the blood must be freely given. A changeling who takes blood by force will die."

Charles finally stopped speaking and let John digest what he'd heard.

"Thank you for explaining all of that," John said finally. "It was very . . . enlightening. However, I haven't changed my mind. I'm going to New Orleans because I believe Jessica is in danger. If Mac and Dirk would like to come along . . ." He didn't finish the sentence because Charles was shaking his head.

"They can't. Dirk and Beth are on their way to Hawaii. I won't be able to reach them until they land—and then there's the trip back. There's not enough time."

"I understand, but what about Mac or you?"

Charles frowned. "We've got a critical progeny situation here and too many lives at stake for us to leave. I'm afraid you're on your own, so let me give you a few pointers. A gun may slow them down, but it won't kill a vampire unless you shoot their head off, literally. The sword should be your weapon of choice and, barring that, a dagger. Aim for their heart and when you strike, you hit those sons of bitches just as hard as you damn well can. You understand?"

John nodded, feeling much like a soldier under the admiral's command must have felt before going into battle.

"All right. Once they're dead, either cut off their head or leave them out where the sun can turn them into stone—or both. Once the sun converts them, any stiff breeze will disintegrate the stone and turn them to dust. Any questions?"

"No, I think I've got it."

"Good. We'll do our best to get the situation here under control so at least one of us can join you in New Orleans ASAP." He paused, and John thought he saw the admiral struggling to keep his expression carefully schooled. "You take care of Jess, you hear? That kid's been through a lot in her life. She's not as strong as she thinks she is."

John wasn't sure he agreed with Charles's assessment. He thought Jess was a lot stronger than the admiral gave her credit for being, but kept his opinion to himself. "I'll keep her safe, I promise."

Charles nodded. "All right. Let me give you directions to the Winslow Manor."

Moments later, he handed John a piece of paper and then stood to come around the side of the desk, holding out his hand to shake John's. "I'm counting on you, son."

"I won't let you down." He started to leave, but then stopped to turn back to the admiral. "It might be better if you didn't tell Jess I was coming. I have a feeling she won't exactly be thrilled to see me."

Jess sat at the kitchen table of the Winslow Manor studying the vast assortment of equipment and supplies that she'd accumulated over the last two days. There were coils of rope and chain, heavy locks, IV needles and tubing, an assortment of chemicals, and some herbs she'd brought from home. She even had frozen containers of pig's blood sitting in the freezer. There was everything here that she needed to lure and trap a chupacabra of her own.

All she needed now was to find the house pictured on the magazine page. Find the house; find the chupacabra colony. Both were close to the Winslow Manor—she'd learned that much after talking to someone at the magazine's publishing company. And it made sense that the Winslows would have a house close to where the vampires existed. The only reason there weren't Winslows still living there was because all the vampires had presumably been killed generations ago. Jess was about to find out if that status had changed.

Pushing away from the table, she went outside to the old barn. Fortunately, it had been built of sturdy wood that was still in good repair. The sides of the stalls were only about ten feet tall, and she hoped that would be enough to keep a small creature trapped inside.

After double-checking the condition of the wood and testing the strength of the padlocks, she headed back to the main house, satisfied with how everything was going. Her flight coming down had been uneventful. With the Mardi Gras celebrations going on, New Orleans had been a crush of people and activity, but she hadn't stayed to enjoy any of it. Instead, she'd rented a car and driven out to the Winslow Manor, located far enough outside of New Orleans to be considered "in the country," but still close enough to the city that she could enjoy everything the city offered without spending half a day driving to get there.

She'd found the estate well maintained and ready for immediate occupancy. To her further relief, the key she'd taken from her father's desk still unlocked the doors. Starting to feel like a kid who had successfully run away from home, she had been surprised when, last night, Charles had called to chew her out for lying about flying back to England and to warn her about Brody.

For some reason, he thought the vampire was on his way to New Orleans to find her. The idea was absurd, but Charles wouldn't get off the phone until she'd assured him she'd be cautious, and she'd hung up before thinking to ask how he'd known where to find her.

Now, sitting at the kitchen table once again, she checked everything against the list she'd made and found it all accounted for. She glanced at her watch. It would be dark in a couple of hours and she really wanted to get started on her search for the colony, but knew it would be better to start in the morning, after the sun was up.

She was so focused on her train of thought that she jumped when the doorbell rang. Thinking it might be yet another deliveryman, she cast a quick glance over the assortment laid out on the table as she stood up. For the life of her, as she crossed the room to open the front door, she couldn't think what might be missing.

"You!"

Dressed in a gray short-sleeved shirt tucked into charcoal gray jeans and carrying a duffel bag, John Boehler looked like he belonged on the pages of a sports and casual clothing magazine. Without his usual long raincoat, he seemed so much more virile to her. She tried to ignore the sudden rush of her heartbeat.

"Hi ya, princess. It's good to see you, too." He pushed

past her and walked into the foyer before she could stop him. There he paused and, tipping down his sunglasses to peer over the upper rim, scanned the inside of the manor. "Nice place." She followed his gaze to the upper level, visible from below. "This place must have at least a dozen rooms."

"I don't know," she said primly. "I've not counted them."

He smiled at her. "Doesn't matter. One's all I need."

Chapter 9

"Don't be absurd," Jessica spit out as soon as she recovered from her shock. "You are most definitely not staying here."

"Oh, I think I am." He bulldozed past her attempt to block the stairs and took them two at a time to the top.

"In fact, it would probably be best if we shared a room," he began, causing her to nearly trip as she raced after him. He seemed to hone in on her bedroom right away, and she barely had enough time to duck past him and block the doorway before he got there.

"Absolutely not." Arms braced on either side of the doorway, she faced him. For seconds, they stood toe-to-toe, his expression unreadable, and then he gave her a partial smile. "Fine, but later, don't come begging to share my bed. You had your chance."

With an evil grin, he turned and opened the door opposite hers. "This looks nice. I'll stay here."

Jess followed him to the doorway as he walked into the

room and looked around. Finally, he set the duffel bag on the bed.

"What are you doing here?" she asked, exasperated.

"I'm here because I have reason to believe that Brody is on his way down here with the express purpose of coming after you."

Jess stared at him and then gave a bark of laughter. "So you came to what? To protect me? That's awfully sweet of you and absolutely not necessary. I'm sorry you wasted your time. Good-bye."

"Oh, I'm not leaving." He reached up to undo the first button of his shirt. Confused, she watched him undo the next. Slowly, he worked his way down, seemingly oblivious to her standing there. When he began to pull his shirttail out of his pants, she jerked to attention.

"Excuse me! What are you doing?"

"I'm going to take a shower and then change clothes. It'll be dark soon and I'm not sitting outside all night feeling grungy and wearing these. Don't bother showing me the bathroom—I saw it down the hall, thanks." He gave her a lascivious smile as he removed his shirt. "I don't care if you want to stay and watch, but you should know that I'm a staunch believer in turnabout as fair play. If you're gonna watch me now, I get to watch you later."

Jess stared at him, speechless. The minute he'd removed his shirt and she'd seen his surprisingly muscled chest, covered with a thick mat of dark hair, all coherent thought fled. She'd seen men wearing less to the beach, but none of them had ever caused her pulse to race as it did now.

At the sound of a zipper, her heart skipped a beat and

nearly stopped. He was issuing a challenge, testing her nerve—daring her to calmly stand and watch him undress.

She folded her arms across her chest and leaned against the doorframe, knowing he wouldn't dare continue.

Smiling, he hooked his thumbs inside the waist of his jeans and shoved them down.

Shocked, she quickly snapped her eyes shut. Then, emitting a noise that sounded disturbingly like a squeak, she raced back down the stairs.

On legs not quite steady, she walked into the living room and collapsed into the chair. What was she to do? She couldn't share a house with *him.* He didn't even wear underwear. It wouldn't matter if the house were twice the size of Buckingham Palace, there simply wasn't enough room for both of them.

Upstairs, she heard footsteps, followed shortly thereafter by the sound of a door closing and then of running water. John, she surmised, was taking a shower. For some reason, the thought that he was safely occupied for the next few minutes did little to ease the tension building inside her. Try as she might, she could not stop her mind from conjuring the image of him standing nude before her.

She jerked her attention away from the dangerous path it had taken and focused on her plans for the next day. Then she heard the water stop. This was followed a short while later by the sound of his footsteps coming downstairs. Her traitorous heart sped up again. He didn't come into the living room, however, so she stayed where she was.

When she heard the sound of cabinet doors being slammed shut, followed by a clattering of pots and pans, she couldn't help but wonder if he was deliberately trying to make as much noise as he could.

Finally, having listened to as much as she could take, she rose from her seat and headed for the kitchen. As she approached the doorway, she took a deep breath in preparation for the tirade she was about to deliver—only to stop dead in her tracks.

"Don't you ever wear clothes?" she blurted.

Clad only in faded jeans that hugged his body in all the right places, his hair still damp from his shower, he turned when he heard her. A drop of water hanging from a lock of hair caught her eye, and she watched as it dripped onto his broad shoulder where it slowly ran down to his chest. There her eyes followed the mat of dark hair down to washboard abs, and then lower still, where the hair trailed off beneath the waistband of his jeans.

"See something you like?" he taunted.

Feeling indignant, she started to sputter. "Why, I never—"

"Yeah. *That* I can imagine. Well, relax, princess. Your virginal status is safe with me."

Jess gaped at him, hurt despite her effort to ignore the insult. "Why are you tearing my kitchen apart?" she demanded, not making any effort to be polite.

"I'm looking for food."

"Then you can stop making that racket because there isn't any."

He shut the pantry door behind him with a decided click and then turned around so he could lean against the counter. Folding his arms across his chest, he gave her a look. "Are you telling me you had enough time to get all that shit on the table over there but not enough time to pick up some food?"

"Priorities," she managed to say with a saccharine-sweet smile.

"Yeah, well, don't get me started on what I think of your priorities."

Her control snapped. "You know, if you're going to insult me, you can leave. Preferably as soon as possible."

"No, I can't." He pushed away from the counter, looking like a man stuck with an unpleasant chore he couldn't escape. "Do whatever you need to do to get yourself ready. We're going to dinner."

He had to walk past her to leave the kitchen and as he drew near, she crossed her arms and gave him a defiant look. "I'm not hungry."

He stopped and stared down into her face as if daring her to keep up the lie. He was standing too close, and she wanted to escape as much as she wanted to remain where she was. She felt her body sway toward his as if drawn by some magnetic force.

"I guess I lied to you, princess," he said in a voice gone suddenly gruff as he dipped his face closer to hers. "Your virtue isn't safe around me—at all." He closed the remaining space, his lips capturing hers even as his hands stole up her arms and held her tight. He guided her back until she was trapped between the wall and his body. Pure hard male muscle leaned into her and, unable to stop herself, she placed her hands at his waist.

"You are just too damn tempting," he said between attacks of his mouth on hers.

His admission shocked her, and when she opened her

mouth to say something, he took advantage of the opportunity and swept his tongue inside.

He moved then and the evidence of his arousal pressed into her, dragging a groan from deep inside her as she got lost in the sensations he was stirring within her.

As abruptly as the kiss started, it ended, and he loosened his hold on her. She felt dazed, unable to focus her thoughts, rattled by the unmistakable hunger in his eyes.

"Here's the deal, princess. I now have two needs, and by God, I'm going to satisfy one of them. So, either we're going to eat or we're going to fuck. You choose."

Jess stared up at him, having no trouble believing that he'd follow through with his crude promise. What bothered her was just how much she didn't want to go for food.

She hesitated too long, and a slow, wicked grin spread across his lips. He braced one arm against the wall by her head and started to lean toward her. In that instant, she knew she couldn't go through with it. For him, it would be just sex, but she wanted more than that for herself.

"All right," she said, surprising herself at how calm she sounded. "There's a nice Cajun place just up the road."

Eating out became a habit over the next two days, but other than taking their meals together, John kept to himself.

On the third evening following his arrival, John still hadn't heard from Harris—nor had there been any indication that Brody was in the area. He and Jess had eaten at a Mexican restaurant that night and as they pulled into the driveway, John kept his eyes peeled for signs of trouble.

The tension between him and Jess was like static electricity. It couldn't be seen, but when they accidentally touched, they both felt the shock. John knew he was to blame. He hadn't touched her since that first night, but that didn't mean he hadn't thought about doing so—constantly. But it would be a mistake and he knew it. Their personalities blended like oil and water. The last thing he needed was to get physically involved with her.

As these thoughts tumbled about in his head, John followed her to the front door, scrutinizing every shadow along the way, watching for anything that shouldn't be there. Once they were safely inside with the door locked behind them, John felt a slight easing of tension.

As he was about to go double-check the back door, his cell phone rang.

"Boehler here."

"It's Harris."

Finally. "And?"

He heard Harris's sigh, and there was a wealth of communication in what wasn't said.

"How soon will you be here?" he asked after giving Harris the address.

"Five—maybe ten minutes."

"Okay. I'll be ready." He hung up the phone and turned to find Jess staring at him.

"That was my . . . associate." He wasn't sure how to explain Harris to her. "Brody is in the area."

"Good, let him come. We'll take care of him once and for all."

That cocky, self-assured attitude of hers made him so mad, he didn't know whether to shake her or kiss her. "I don't think you understand how dangerous this man—this vampire—is."

"He's no different than any of the other vampires I've

killed," she said defiantly. "Besides, I think your associate is mistaken. It makes no sense that Brody would leave Washington, D.C., to come all the way to New Orleans. And why New Orleans? After Hurricane Katrina, there's nothing here." She paused and waved a hand in the air. "Okay, they're having Mardis Gras, but still, of all the places he could go, why here? It's too far away."

John took a breath and told himself to be calm. These were all legitimate questions. "Wait here. I've got something in my room that might help answer those questions."

He took the stairs two at a time, leaving her standing in the foyer. At the top, he stopped and looked down at her. "Oh, do me a favor, don't answer the door when my associate arrives. I'll get it."

He didn't wait to hear her grumbled response, but hurried into his room to change clothes. Then he grabbed her day planner from his bedside table. He'd held on to it because he wanted to read its contents, arguing that he needed to know what information Brody might have learned from it. The truth, however, was much more self-serving. He was the one who'd wanted to learn more about her. Now, it was time to give it back.

When he started down the stairs Jess was standing in the foyer holding a sword.

"Where the hell did you find that?" he asked, watching her take a few practice slices.

"There is a case full of them in the study," she replied casually. "As I said earlier, I'm fine here by myself."

Just then there was a knock on the door. As he watched Jess turn to answer it, alarm shot through him. "Jess! No!" he shouted, leaping down the six remaining steps as she turned the knob.

He heard her gasp of surprise and grabbed her sword arm just as it went into motion. Wrapping his other arm around her waist, he lifted her off her feet to prevent her from moving. At the same time, he saw Harris, quick as a flash, jump from the front door to about fifty paces back.

"What are you doing?" Jess screamed, kicking at his legs. He winced when the heel of her foot caught his shin, but instead of letting her go, he clutched her tighter, giving her less room to fight.

"It's okay," he said breathlessly, still recovering from his mad race to the door. "She's not going to do anything." Then, still holding a squirming Jess, he stepped back enough to allow Harris room to enter. "You want to come in?"

The vampire declined. "Thanks, but I think I'll wait out here."

"Yeah, okay. I'll be out in a second." He shut the door with his foot and then pulled the sword from Jess's hand before releasing her.

"What are you doing?" she bit out, pinning him with an angry gaze.

"You can decapitate or run through any vampire you want—except that one, understand?"

"No," she stared at him, aghast. "He's a *vampire.*" She made it sound as if Harris were evil incarnate.

"You don't kill that one, understand? He's not like the others." He leaned over and picked up the day planner from where it had fallen on the floor and held it out to her. "Here, I think this belongs to you."

She stared at it, her eyes open wide. He could imagine

the confusion she must have felt. "How'd you get it—I thought I lost it that night Brody . . ."

"Yeah, you did. I found it, along with your jacket and some other stuff, in an abandoned building Brody was using as his lair. You know, the one that had your name written all over it—in blood."

"What?" She sounded dazed and he swore, realizing that Charles hadn't told her everything.

"That's not all." He tried to figure out how to soften the blow of what he was about to tell her and then decided it would be better if she felt the full impact. "There was a woman there as well, dead. She was about your height and build, and had long, dark hair. Basically, she looked like you." He remembered the moment he'd first seen her and had thought it *was* her.

Shutting out the memory, he gestured to the book. "There were a couple of pages missing—specifically for this week. Do you remember what was on those pages? Did you happen to mention coming to New Orleans or the address of this house?"

She gave him a depressed look. "Yes, it was all there."

He saw her glance toward the door, as if finally appreciating the legitimacy of his warning.

"Don't worry," he reassured her. "I'll find Brody and stop him."

Her chin went up in defiance. "You've never even killed a vampire. I'll take care of it. Just you and your vampire friend stay out of my way."

"Jess, Brody isn't just a vampire, he's a psychotic killer who targets women. He doesn't want to kill you, he wants to rape you and then torture you because that gives him a sense of power. I've been after him for a long time, but I've always been hampered by the law. That's no longer a problem so when I find him, I *am* going to kill him, but I don't need you running around out there where I have to worry about you or where you can get in the way. Stay in here."

She stared at him in disgust. "Brody will probably slip right past you and your vampire friend."

"Well, if he does, then you'll get a chance to show us what a hotshot vampire hunter you are." He handed her the sword and then started for the door, feeling her glare burning a hole in his back.

"Just so you know," she said after he had the door open and was about to step out, "I'm killing any vampire that comes through that door, got it? So you might want to tell your friend that."

John glanced over at Harris, still standing far from the house. "I think he knows."

He pulled his Smith & Wesson from his holster and checked the cylinder.

"That's not going to help you much," she commented, following him to the doorway. "You should take a sword."

He almost smiled at the note of concern that slipped into her voice. Maybe she really did care about him. "I have extra bullets," he replied, placing the gun back in its holster. Mac said it took a lot of bullets to kill a vampire, so he'd remembered to bring extra ammunition. Looking at her now, seeing the worry behind her defiant glare, he couldn't resist her. Before he could stop himself, he cupped the back of her head with his hand and leaned forward, delivering a searing kiss, which, God help him, she returned. "Stay inside and lock the door after I leave," he said huskily—and then he walked out, leaving her standing there with a bewildered, lost expression on her face.

"Looks like you have your hands full," Harris said, moving out of the shadows where John could see him.

John grimaced. "Nothing I can't handle."

"Right."

He thought he saw Harris smile, but the movement was so slight, it was hard to be sure. He was about to tell the vampire to mind his own business when a shift in the shadows caught his attention. "Behind you," he warned, drawing his gun.

"No, don't shoot." Harris moved into his line of fire. "It's only Lucy."

"You brought a date?" John asked in total disbelief.

Harris scowled at him. "Not exactly." The shadows shifted and a figure stepped out.

"Holy shit." John stumbled back from the five-foot-tall gargoyle-looking creature. "What the hell?"

"I guess you've never seen a chupacabra?" Harris asked as calmly as if he were asking if John had ever tried a beignet.

John swallowed hard and stared at the large hind legs the creature was balanced on, the talon-sharp three-toed claws, the large oval red eyes and almost feline-shaped round head. Sweat broke out along his forehead as he realized that this was the kind of creature that had killed Harris and made Mac and Dirk changelings. "No. I think I'd have remembered seeing something like this."

Harris chuckled. "Yeah, chupacabras certainly leave an impression." He shrugged. "I thought maybe you'd seen Gem."

"Gem?"

"The young creature that Mac's wife is taking care of? Lucy here is her mother."

John only heard the first part of what Harris said. "There's a creature like this at the admiral's house?"

"She's much smaller. Still a baby, really. She and Lucy were found together in the Amazon jungle."

"So how come Lucy's with you and not with the admiral and her baby?"

"It's a long story, but the short version is that she was severely mistreated by one of the vampires she created, and now she tends to avoid anything that resembles a human. I think she must be okay with Lanie Knight caring for Gem because I think if she wasn't then there's not much that would have stopped her from getting her baby back. But Gem seems happy where she is, so Lucy goes by to visit a couple of times a week. I usually go with her, but not always."

"And you call her Lucy because?"

"It's stupid, really," Harris said, looking suddenly embarrassed. "Sometimes she'll show up at my lair and I'll have no idea where she's been or what she's been up to, which is strange since we share this psychic link. When she sees me, she gives me a look of such total innocence that I know it's a cover. I end up feeling like Ricky Ricardo. You know? *'Lucy, you have some 'splaining to do.'* " He shrugged. "The name sort of stuck."

John stared at the creature, who stared back at him. "What's she doing here?"

Harris looked affronted. "I'm not leaving her in D.C. all alone."

The chupacabra stepped closer, and it took a tremendous effort on John's part not to shy away from her when she leaned close, like she was smelling him. Then, apparently satisfied, she stepped away and moved off into the night, disappearing once again.

"Where's she going?"

"I don't know," Harris admitted. "I'm not her owner; she's not my pet."

"Aren't you worried that she'll get lost?"

"No, I—" Harris stopped, cocking his head to one side. "Brody's in the area. Let's get settled."

He led the way to a spot near the corner of the manor where the trees and bushes provided excellent cover, while still giving them a clear view of at least two sides of the mansion. The night was clear, and light filtering down from the full moon made it possible to see.

"The most logical point to approach the mansion is from that direction." Harris pointed, echoing John's thoughts. "I think we'll see him before he even knows we're here."

John agreed and, used to long stakeouts, settled in to wait. It was nice to have company, even that of a vampire. Without the luxury of conversation, part of John's mind wandered to Jessica. The woman bothered him in more ways than one and kissing her sure as hell hadn't helped.

Very gently, he felt Harris's hand touch his arm. Then Harris pointed to the left rear corner of the mansion. At first the shifting in the shadows was hard to make out, but slowly the dark form of a man became visible. *Brody.*

He neared the front of the house, moving fast. John was concerned that if they didn't go after him soon, it might be too late. Just then, Harris took off.

With superhuman speed, he crossed the yard, with John racing after him as fast as he could pump his legs. Up ahead, Brody froze. When he saw them, he turned and raced off into the night. Harris followed with John, at his much slower human speed, falling far behind.

They disappeared into the woods, and it soon became too dark for John to see. He was forced to slow down and finally to stop altogether.

After catching his breath, he straightened from his bent stance and looked at his surroundings. He was standing near an old cemetery.

Like most New Orleans cemeteries, the graves were aboveground, and the place was ornate with an abundance of statuary. It was a perfect place to hide, he thought, moving toward it.

Gripping his gun a little more tightly, he entered the cemetery and began working his way systematically through it, using moonlight to guide his steps. Still, progress was slow, and as he wove his way through the tombs, he couldn't shake the feeling that he was being watched.

Common sense told him he should stop and return to the mansion—wait for Harris to return; but the old need to bring Brody to justice spurred him on. He moved down the next row of headstones, stepping around a statue that bore an uncanny resemblance to Harris's chupacabra, except the statue had huge, batlike wings. Briefly, John wondered if the sculptor who created this work might have seen the real creatures at one time, but then he dismissed the thought as he focused his attention once more on his task. If he didn't pay attention, Brody could step—

A movement off to the side caught his attention. John whirled and found himself facing the statue he'd just passed, eyes now glowing with a spooky crimson light and very much alive.

John brought his gun up to fire, but before he could, a huge, talon-tipped claw knocked the gun from his hand, sending it sailing into the night.

Jerked from his paralysis, John scrambled back, but the creature's huge wings wrapped around him and drew him inexorably closer. John fought against it, but when his fists struck the creature, it was like hitting stone. He was going to die. The realization hit him with such suddenness, all he felt was shock until the searing pain ripped through his neck. Then there was nothing.

Chapter 10

Harris saw Brody disappear around the corner of a house not fifty yards ahead of him and put on a burst of speed. The thrill of the hunt filled him with exhilarated anticipation. Tonight, it would be over. He would correct his mistake before the Progeny was allowed to kill again. All he had to do was turn the corner and—

A bolt of alarm shot through him with such force, he literally stumbled and almost fell. Confused, he slowed his pace, trying to identify the source. The emotion hit him again—alarm mixed with a more primitive, animalistic need to protect. *Lucy.*

Focusing his attention on the link he shared with the chupacabra, Harris received an image. It was distorted, as if he were looking through the bottom of a glass bottle, but he made out the form of a man, lying on the ground. A tall, dark shape loomed over him.

It took Harris only a second to realize that the detective

was in trouble, with only Lucy standing between him and death.

There was a momentary flash of regret that Brody would escape again, but there was no question in Harris's mind about what he should do. Thinking he recognized some of the distorted background from the cemetery he'd passed a short distance back, he hurriedly retraced his steps.

As soon as he reached the place, he saw them. Lucy stood over John, her blazing red gaze focused on the creature she faced. Her mouth was open so far her fangs protruded like weapons, and she emitted guttural, hissing noises, warning the other creature back. Despite its larger size, it seemed to obey.

Moving forward slowly, Harris studied the other creature. It was also a chupacabra, but it stood a good foot taller than Lucy, with slightly longer fangs. Its coloring was also different: while Lucy was of a medium-gray coloring, this creature was a dark charcoal black.

Harris wasn't sure if he would have been able to see it if it hadn't been for his night vision. There was one last difference between the creature and Lucy—this one had a set of batlike wings that were so large, Harris thought its wingspan must be at least fifteen feet.

It took Harris only seconds to notice all this as he drew within a few feet of John's prone body on the ground. He was still too far away, though, to tell if John was alive or dead. In either event, Harris couldn't leave him here. If he was alive, he needed to get help. And if John was dead . . . he didn't relish the thought of staking the detective. He wouldn't be so bold as to claim they were friends, but Harris had enough respect for the man that he wouldn't condemn John to the same life he was forced to endure; he wouldn't allow the detective to become a vampire.

As he wondered how he might retrieve the body, Lucy, who had been facing off with the creature, moved forward, keeping herself between Harris and the winged chupacabra. The larger creature growled when Harris inched forward, but didn't try to attack him. Feeling like this was as good a chance as he was going to get, Harris went for the body.

Jessica was exhausted. She badly wanted to soak in a steaming hot bath and then collapse into bed. Unfortunately, she was a bundle of nerves and much too agitated to relax. She wished John would come back soon and berated herself for not sneaking out after he left in order to follow him. She couldn't believe he'd willingly gone out with a vampire. If the creature attacked him, John would be dead before he realized he was in danger.

She'd killed plenty of vampires in her time; knew how silently they could move—and how quickly. She tested the weight of the sword in her hand once more as she glanced at the clock on the wall. It was late—or early, depending on whether you were thinking in terms of the night or day. She estimated the sun would be up in about three hours. Surely, John would be walking through the door any minute now.

A noise outside caught her attention and she stopped pacing long enough to listen. She heard it again and felt her blood run cold. Whoever it was knew her name. She moved closer, trying to make out the words.

"Jessica! John's hurt. He needs help."

It was a trap, she told herself even as she hurried to the

window to peer out. Standing less than five feet away, the vampire from earlier stood holding John's limp body in his arms. From where she stood, she could see that John's throat and shirt were covered with blood and his complexion had grown much too pale.

"Open the damn door before it's too late," the vampire growled. "He's dying."

Gripping her sword more tightly and hoping she wasn't making a fatal mistake, she yanked open the door. She barely had time to step out of the way before the vampire entered.

"Where?"

"The couch." Still gripping her sword with one hand, she gestured to the living room with the other. "What did you do to him?"

"Other than bring him here, nothing," the vampire said, gently laying John down. She gestured with the sword for him to move back, out of the way, and then bent over John. He looked so pale, her heart clenched at the thought that he might die. She pressed her fingers against his throat.

"He's got a pulse," Harris told her. "But it's faint."

"If you didn't do this, who did? Brody?"

"No. It was a chupacabra, I think. Over in the cemetery."

Despite her fear for John, Jess felt a spurt of excitement. There were chupacabras close by.

"He lost a lot of blood," the vampire continued, coming up behind her, standing just a little too close for comfort.

"I should call an ambulance," Jess said, hurrying to the phone. Before she could punch in a single number, however, the vampire was beside her, snatching the phone away.

"What the hell are you doing?" She leaped back, raising her sword defensively. Immediately, the vampire was on the other side of the room, the cordless phone still clutched in his hand.

"I have other phones," she informed him, backing toward her purse where her cell phone was resting.

"Just stop and think," he implored her. "If you call an ambulance, they're going to want to know what happened to him. What are you going to tell them? That he was attacked by a wild animal? They'll have animal control and game wardens out here so fast, we won't have a chance of hiding the chupacabras from them. How many humans do you think they'll kill before it's all over? There'll be vampires all over the place—and they'll be so hungry, there won't be enough humans to feed them or hunters to kill them. Is that what you want?"

Jess let herself consider the scenario Harris described; vampires, like a plague, spreading across the nation, all because she called an ambulance to save John's life.

She glanced at him now, lying pale and lifeless on the couch. "I don't care," she said resolutely. "I'm not going to let him die."

"I don't want him to die either," he said so gravely that, for a second, Jess actually believed he cared. "He needs a transfusion," he continued. "I can get blood and bring it back."

Jess's eyes opened wide in horror. "I'm not going to let you kill innocent people to bring him blood."

The vampire gave her a disgusted look. "I meant from a blood bank."

"You can't just walk in and ask for blood," she argued,

but the vampire wasn't listening. He was headed for the front door.

"Try to keep him alive until I get back," he said. "And stay alert. Brody is still out there. I'll leave Lucy on guard out front, as added precaution."

"Who the bloody hell is Lucy? Another vampire?" She was feeling inundated with the undead.

"She's a chupacabra."

Before she could learn more, he disappeared, leaving her alone in the living room, clutching the sword in her hand with John's still body lying on the couch.

As she hurried to the bathroom for a wet cloth and medical supplies, she found herself feeling grateful the vampire could move so quickly. He would be back shortly. She wasn't sure how she knew it, but she did.

She carried her supplies back to the couch. John hadn't moved, so she knelt by his side and fought a wave of dizziness at the sight of all that blood. She had to be strong, she chastised herself, for John's sake, because she couldn't let him die. Gritting her teeth, she stroked the hair from his face. "I don't know if you can hear me," she said. "But you have to fight, John, like you've never fought for anything before. You can't give up. Please, don't give up."

She steeled herself and slowly wiped away the blood using the cloth she'd brought. The twin holes where the chupacabra's fangs had pierced him seemed unusually large, reminding her that she'd never borne witness to a fresh chupa bite before. Had Mac's and Dirk's wounds looked like this?

Thinking of the changelings made her realize that even if John lived, his life wouldn't be the same. He'd be like Mac and Dirk—a changeling. Her knowledge of changelings was limited to what she'd read in old family texts and the stories her father had relayed to her from Charles regarding Mac and Dirk.

At that moment, John jerked. Alarmed, Jess placed her hand on his chest, trying to calm him. His heart pounded erratically as it labored to pump what little blood he had throughout his body. Jess feared he was on the verge of having a heart attack.

She remembered the legend of changelings and how, if they consumed freely given blood, it would imbibe them with great recuperative powers. Would giving John some of her blood now do the same thing for him?

Another convulsion had her reaching for the rubber tourniquet, syringe, and needle.

She moved to the living room table and with practiced ease, used one hand to wrap the tourniquet around the upper portion of her other arm. Actually drawing the blood one-handed would be a little trickier, but it wouldn't be the first time she'd done it.

Resting her outstretched arm on top of the table, she used her free hand to smack the inside of her elbow until a vein rose to the surface. Then she grabbed the syringe, popped off the top and, taking a breath, let it out slowly and applied enough pressure on the needle that the tip penetrated her skin and entered the vein.

A ringing in her ears started as she watched blood appear at the bottom of the syringe. She forced herself to relax and pulled back on the plunger. Balancing the syringe on her arm, she let it go long enough to pull off the tourniquet and then watched the syringe fill with blood.

"I give this blood freely." She said the words aloud, wanting whatever mythos was involved to know that this was a gift of life she was giving John. At least, she hoped it was.

Pulling the syringe from her arm, she pressed a ball of cotton against the injection site and bent her arm to hold it in place. She kept the pressure on for only a moment, because that was all the time John had. Then she carried the syringe over to him and knelt on the floor.

Then she hesitated. Did she inject the blood into his mouth to be ingested? Or inject it into a vein? She didn't know. The vampires and changelings bit their victims, but were they really drinking the blood? Or was it being sucked through their fangs, which she knew to be hollow, and then into their bloodstreams?

She decided to do both. Digging through the container of medical supplies, she found a pair of scissors and used it to cut open the sleeve of his shirt, exposing his arm. Fortunately, John's veins were large and visible.

Holding the syringe upright, she depressed the plunger, expelling the air trapped in the tube. When she was satisfied that the syringe was ready, she selected a vein and injected him. "Come on, John. Take this blood, freely given, and live, damn it."

She emptied the syringe halfway and then pulled it out. Careful not to depress the plunger, she popped off the needle and then shot the rest of it into his mouth, forcing him to swallow it, all the while fighting to keep down the contents of her stomach. *Please let this be the right thing to do,* she intoned silently.

When John's body jerked, she forgot all her other thoughts and fell to her knees at his side. Her blood was working its way through his system and when his body spasmed again, she placed her hands on his chest, trying to quiet him. It didn't work; he was dying, and Jess didn't know what to do.

Tears of frustration and grief sprang to her eyes. She tried to remember any helpful medical knowledge she'd ever learned, only to come up blank. All she could do was hold him, hoping the convulsions would stop.

"Oh, John," she pleaded, so filled with despair that her head fell to his chest. "I was trying to help. I'm so sorry. Please, please don't die."

She felt something touch her hair and realized that John's fingers had closed about several strands. She lifted her head enough to see his face. His eyes remained closed and he seemed oblivious to what he was doing, yet the convulsions began to weaken and after a few minutes, he was lying peacefully once more.

Then the door to the mansion burst open and the vampire was stepping inside, kicking the door shut behind him.

"Where the hell have you been?" she shouted, jumping to her feet to help him unload the bags of blood in his arms.

"I ran into a few problems," he muttered, not bothering to spare her a look as he pulled IV tubing and needles from his pockets and hooked them up to the first bag.

"What kind of problems?" She was almost afraid to ask.

"Vampires."

"Here?" It was surprising news and yet it was the reason she'd come down here.

"Yeah. They smelled the blood on me. I didn't think

you'd appreciate my leading them back here, so I had to lose them."

By now, he had the transfusion ready to go and looked to her for help positioning John's arm. When he saw the bandage on her arm where she'd drawn the blood, he cocked an eyebrow in question.

"I was afraid he was dying," she explained. "So I gave him some of my blood."

He seemed impressed, but didn't say anything. Instead, he focused on finding a vein in John's arm. When he found one, he inserted the needle. Jess marveled at the ease with which he set up the transfusion.

"Looks like you've done this before," she observed.

"I used to be a medic in the Navy," he said, and then as if she needed further explanation, added, "I used to be a SEAL."

Alarm bells started ringing in her head. "You're Sheldon Harris." She said the name like she was testing the sound of it.

He glanced at her sharply. "My reputation precedes me."

"I've heard of you," she confirmed.

He paused what he was doing, a wary expression coming to his eyes. "Mind telling me from whom?"

She wondered where she'd left her sword and tried to look around without actually giving herself away by moving her eyes. "Beth told me that a couple of weeks ago, you saved her and Dirk."

He seemed to relax a little. "I won't take credit for that because technically, it's not true, but I'm not surprised Beth would see it that way. She's a good woman; a good person."

"Yes, she is." She paused for a millisecond. "So is Lanie."

The announcement seemed to deflate him because his hands stilled on the IV tubing and his head seemed to fall forward briefly. "So you heard that story as well." He looked at her then. "I won't make excuses for my role in what happened to her and Mac. It was wrong." He took a deep breath and went back to what he was doing.

When he finished, they waited in silence for the first bag to empty. As far as she was concerned, Harris was capable of both heroic and inhumane acts. Just because he was here helping to save John's life now didn't mean she trusted him. Only time—and his actions—would convince her one way or the other.

When the bag emptied, Harris hooked up a second one. When it was flowing smoothly, he turned to her. "Do you think you can finish this?"

"Yes," she said, realizing that dawn was approaching.

He nodded, gave John a last look, and then walked out the front door. Jess watched him go, wondering what his true nature might be. She'd run into a lot of vampires in her twenty-five years and so far, only one had proven himself worthy of being allowed to live. In her book, Harris had a long way to go before he could even come close to Erik's standard, but saving John's life was one hell of a good start.

Jess watched over John all through the morning, switching out each bag as it emptied and then starting a fresh one. There had only been six bags of type "O," and she prayed that would be enough. When the last bag drained, she pulled out the IV and bandaged his arm.

He seemed to be resting more peacefully now and there was color in his complexion. She wished she'd asked Harris to carry John to the bed where he could have more room, but she hadn't thought of it.

The best she could do now was make him as comfortable as she could, and to do that she'd have to get him out of his bloodied clothes. An image of the way he'd looked earlier, standing in nothing more than his jeans, came to mind and she felt her face heat at the prospect of removing his clothes.

She tried to convince herself that there was nothing sexual about what she was doing, yet her fingers trembled when she cut open his shirt and pulled it off. Next she got a bowl of warm water and a washcloth and slowly bathed him. She took special care to avoid his neck, which she had cleaned and bandaged sometime between the transfusion of bags two and three.

She ran the cloth over his body using long, upward strokes, having heard somewhere that rubbing in an upward direction stimulated circulation and produced positive energy. She didn't know if it was true or not, but figured it couldn't hurt. If she seemed to labor particularly long over the planes of his chest, it was only because she was being thorough and not because he had the sexiest chest she'd ever seen.

When she was finished—when the water had grown too cold for her to continue—she covered him with a blanket. There was nothing more she could do at this point. Exhausted, she took the water and cloth back to the kitchen and threw out his shirt before returning to his side. Then, she let herself collapse into a nearby chair.

She awoke with a start some time later, not sure where

she was or what had awakened her. Then she heard John moan. Immediately concerned, she looked over at him and saw that he was thrashing about on the couch.

"It's okay," she soothed, moving to his side to stroke his head. "Oh, no." She laid her hand across his forehead, pulling it back a second later. He was burning with fever.

Rushing to the kitchen, she refilled her large bowl, with cool water this time, and again grabbed the washcloth. She carried it to his side before going to the bathroom for extra towels. She knew she had to get his fever down.

When she returned to his side, the blanket was once again on the floor. This time, she tossed it into the chair where she'd slept and was about to kneel beside him when she realized he was still wearing his jeans. The bath would be more effective if she wiped his legs as well as his arms.

Since this was not the time for modesty, she quickly undid the snap at the waist and, making the least amount of contact, pulled down the zipper. She stood at the far end of the couch, grabbed hold of the hem of each pants leg and tugged, using her own feet against the couch as leverage.

It took some effort, but finally, after much side-to-side tugging, they slid off. Tossing them to one side, she tried not to notice the black briefs hugging his hips or the contour of all that lay beneath them. She was simply grateful he'd chosen to wear briefs at all.

John's moan brought her attention back to more pressing concerns. Placing the extra towels along his side and beneath his arms and legs to catch the water as it dripped, she wet a cloth and began to bathe him.

For twenty minutes, she stroked his forehead, arms, chest, legs, hands, and feet, trying to reduce his temperature. Eventually, he fell into a peaceful sleep.

Afraid that he might chill, she covered him with the blanket and returned to the kitchen to switch out the water in her bowl. Armed with fresh water and clean towels, she went back to the living room. If his fever spiked again, she wanted to be ready.

She repeated the process three more times over the next several hours. By midafternoon, when his fever spiked a fourth time, his moaning barely woke her from an exhausted sleep. Functioning in a mental fog brought on from sheer fatigue, she knelt by his side, pulled the blanket back, and began bathing him. By now, her actions were routine and she half-dozed as she ran the cloth over the curve of his chest, enjoying the muscled firmness of his pectoral muscles.

When she finished bathing his upper half, she rinsed out the cloth and started at the other end. She ran the cloth across the bottoms of his feet, taking a moment to massage them. Then she stroked the cloth up legs that were strong, well-shaped, and surprisingly hairy. That made her smile because it meant that he wasn't all physical perfection.

She barely noticed that he had stopped moving on the couch as she ran the cloth up first one leg and then the other. She'd reached the top of his legs when her eyes fell on his erection, not that she could have missed it, even in her most exhausted and distracted state of mind.

Horribly embarrassed, her gaze flew to his face, but his eyes were closed and he seemed oblivious to her actions. She concluded that she was witnessing nothing more than a biological reaction to her ministrations and there was absolutely nothing sexual about it—except what lurid imaginings her own mind conjured.

Struggling to ignore it, she worked her way back down his legs and repeated the process. She'd just reached mid-thigh when John suddenly groaned aloud. He sounded as if he was in such pain that Jess tossed the cloth back into the bowl and leaned over him, afraid something was horribly wrong. "John? Can you hear me? Are you hurting?"

She didn't expect an answer, so when his eyes suddenly flew open she lurched back, but didn't get far. Instantly, John's hands were clutching her upper arms, holding her in place.

"You've got one hell of a bedside manner, princess." His voice was scratchy and rough.

Amazed to hear him talking at all, she stared into his eyes, mesmerized at the way they seemed to glow, unaware that he was pulling her down in a slow controlled move. Then he was kissing her, and she had neither the energy nor the desire to pull away.

The minute she hesitated, he deepened the kiss, his lips assaulting hers with gentle insistence until she opened her mouth. At the invitation, his tongue plundered her mouth. An answering hunger rose up inside her and she kissed him back with abandon. She ran her hands up his arms, enjoying the sinewy strength of him as she hadn't allowed herself to do before when she'd bathed him.

There was no longer a need to hold her down. She was barely aware of his hands moving to the front of her shirt until she heard the sound of ripping fabric and felt the cool air touch her skin. Her bra met the same fate as her shirt, then she felt the rough texture of John's hands covering her breasts.

Sensation shot from her breasts straight to the sweet spot between her legs and she shivered with need. Somewhere, a small sane voice screamed at her to stop. She couldn't do this. He shouldn't do this.

John pulled her down again to capture her mouth. The feel of his chest against her bare breasts drove all thought from her, and she kissed him back with enthusiasm.

The sound of the doorbell ringing slowly penetrated the fog of pure emotion whirling around inside her brain. She lifted her head and listened, trying to ignore John, who'd taken her pulling away as an invitation to pay homage to her breasts.

The doorbell sounded again and Jess tried to leverage herself off the couch, but as soon as she tried, John had his arm around her, holding her to him.

"Someone's at the door, John. Let me go."

"No," he growled, kissing his way up her neck. His breathing had grown harder as he opened his mouth and lightly bit at her throat. It sent shivers down her spine even as warning bells went off in her head.

"We shouldn't do this," she tried again, fighting her own reaction to what he was doing to her.

She strengthened her resolve and tried to pull away again, using more force. She thought she'd succeeded when she felt an easing of his grip, but then suddenly, her world tilted and she found herself flat on her back on the floor, her legs spread wide and John on top of her. His hips pressed into her, driving his erection against the juncture of her legs.

Surprised, she looked up into his face. Crimson-lit eyes gazed down at her with a wild intensity. John's breathing now sounded erratic as he held himself so still above her. When he moved, she felt the fullness of him against her own swollen flesh. The pressure sent a bolt of desire shooting through her and she couldn't stop the groan it pulled from her.

It seemed all the invitation he needed. Gripping the waistband of her jeans, he ripped them open.

Chapter 11

The implications of what they were about to do hit Jess with the sobering intensity of a bucket of ice-cold water.

"John, wait . . ."

He covered her mouth with his as he tried to shove her pants down none too gently. What had started as potentially romantic was rapidly turning into something unpleasant and frightening.

Twisting her head, she broke free of John's kiss and tried again to get his attention. "John, please, get off me. I don't want to do this."

He'd moved from her mouth to her neck, and she felt the pressure of his teeth against her skin. It was too early for him to have fangs, but even his going through the motions of biting her was more than she wanted to endure.

She bucked her body, hoping the sudden motion would get his attention, but when he raised his head to look at her, his eyes were burning brightly, and she knew that he was still in the throes of whatever fever had held him all day.

With her pants pulled down past her hips, John reached for her panties and in a single harsh tug, ripped them off her body, leaving her exposed.

A shudder ran through her as fear gripped her. John wasn't himself. She knew this, yet the knowledge offered little comfort at the moment. She lay there feeling helpless. And then that part of her that refused to be a victim took charge, forcing the paralyzing fear to fade.

When John lifted himself up slightly to pull down his briefs, Jess brought her leg up and kicked him in the chest as hard as she could. As he fell back, she pulled herself free and scrambled up, nearly tripping when her feet tangled in her jeans.

She grabbed her sword from the table and swung around to face John, who hadn't moved.

The unnatural light in his eyes faded as he looked around, maybe realizing, for the first time, where it was they were. When he looked at her again, he seemed confused.

"Where . . . what . . ." His voice held the raspy quality of a heavy smoker's and he had to clear it before trying to speak again. "What happened to your clothes?"

She couldn't believe he didn't know, so she said nothing as she watched him closely. She was fairly certain that after what he'd suffered with the fever and the chupacabra attack he didn't have the strength to rush her, but she'd been surprised by his earlier behavior, so she kept her sword raised and ready.

"Jess?" he implored her.

"You . . . got carried away."

She tried to be polite—put a positive spin on it—but he saw through it. "Are you telling me that I did that?" He gestured to her state of undress, and she self-consciously eyed the blanket just beyond her reach. "I almost raped you?" He must have seen the answer in her eyes because he swore and shook his head. "Jess, I . . ." His voice broke and he took a breath before going on. "I'm sorry. I . . ." He suddenly looked ill. "I'm so, so sorry. It won't happen again. I promise."

She flinched at the self-disgust she'd heard in his tone. He seemed genuinely upset. Deciding to take the chance that the man she knew was back in control, she laid the sword on the table and quickly snagged the blanket from the floor so she could wrap it around herself.

Once she was covered, she felt less vulnerable and more able to be sympathetic. "I don't think you knew what you were doing," she assured him. "If I hadn't stopped you, you would have stopped yourself." She wasn't sure if she was trying to convince him or herself with this last statement, so she changed the subject. "You gave us quite a scare last night."

"Us?"

"Yes. Me and Harris."

"You met him?"

"Yes. He brought you back here last night. You had been attacked by a chupacabra." She sounded like she was reporting nothing more exciting than the weather and realized she was suffering from the effects of shock and fatigue working in tandem. She welcomed the mind-numbing effect it was having on her. "Things were spotty for a while. We didn't know if you would pull through."

"Thanks." He still hadn't moved, and she realized he

was doing his best not to frighten her. At least, she assumed that was the reason. "There are some things we should discuss," she began. "Being attacked by a chupacabra means you've been injected with the venom." She wasn't sure the best way to tell him and found herself tripping over the words. "You see, it's the venom that, well . . ."

"I'll become a changeling, like Mac and Dirk."

She stared at him, stunned. "You know about them, then?"

"I don't know that much," he admitted. "But Charles did try to tell me a little about them before I flew down here. I won't pretend to understand what he said."

She nodded her head. "As the name might suggest, you'll experience some changes." It was difficult for her to speak without using her hands, but when she forgot and almost let go of the blanket, she saw his gaze heat up. "We can talk about it later. I think, right now, we could both use a rest." She glanced at the couch. "Do you need help getting to your room? Or are you going to stay down here?"

"I'll be fine."

She nodded, feeling like she was seconds from hitting the proverbial wall. She went to the front door and opened it. On the porch was a package from the hardware store, no doubt containing items she'd forgotten that she'd ordered. Leaving it there, she closed the door and headed upstairs.

John watched her go, then leaned against the couch and put a hand to his face. He rubbed his temples, thinking if he rubbed hard enough, he might wake up and discover that he hadn't almost raped Jess. At the very least, maybe he could rub away the memory of the unshed tears and hurt in her eyes when she'd looked at him.

As he continued to sit there, he noticed that he wasn't feeling right. It wasn't so much that he was in pain—although his neck and throat hurt like a son of a bitch—it was more that he just didn't feel like his old self.

He was beyond tired, which he attributed to the attack, and the light coming in through the front windows seemed unusually bright. He was hungry, but wasn't sure what it was he wanted to eat.

From upstairs, he heard Jess turn on the shower and had to tear his mind away from the thought of Jess standing before him with her clothes ripped to shreds. He'd come down here to protect her, not have sex with her—and certainly not against her will.

He pushed himself to his feet and noticed that he felt a little light-headed, so he angled himself over to the couch and collapsed on it. Closing his eyes, he listened to the sound of running water, letting it lull him into a state of deep relaxation. He must have fallen asleep because when he woke up again, all was quiet upstairs.

He looked around, trying to decide if he had enough energy to go upstairs. The sight of his jeans, lying in a crumpled heap not far off, caused him to realize that he was wearing only his briefs. He stood up, waited for the world to stop spinning, and slowly made his way to them. Picking them up wasn't as taxing as he'd thought, but when he straightened and his gaze fell on the dining room table, he received a shock. Piled on top were several spent bags of blood and IV tubing.

John immediately looked at the inside of his arms and noticed the needle marks where he'd been given a transfusion. Logically, he knew the attack on him had been serious, but seeing the spent bags of blood gave it a harsher reality.

He thought back, trying to recall his last memory from the evening before. He remembered following Harris when he ran after Brody. He'd tried to keep up, but the vampires had moved with incredible speed and John had soon fallen behind.

He remembered stopping at the cemetery to catch his breath, but the events after that were a blank. He tried to recall the chupacabra that attacked him, but could only conjure images of Harris's Lucy. Maybe it was better that he couldn't remember the incident, he thought.

Since he was already standing, he decided to go upstairs. With each passing moment, he felt better, which surprised him given that it had obviously taken six bags of blood to keep him alive.

He paused outside his bedroom, fighting the urge to apologize to Jess once more. He hated to think that he might have frightened her.

Instead of knocking on her door, he went into his room. Tossing his dirty jeans into the corner, he headed for the dresser. Gazing at his reflection in the mirror, he thought he looked worse than he felt. There were several gashes across his chest and back. Someone had closed them with butterfly bandages and the wounds were already healing.

There was another bandage at his neck and he pulled it off. "Holy shit!" He stared at the massive bruising and the two large holes on the side of his throat, suddenly glad that he couldn't remember the details of the attack.

Throwing the soiled bandage into the trash, he stepped out of his room and noticed the bathroom was unoccupied, so he walked down the hall to it. Closing the door, he crossed to the shower and started the water. When it was hot enough, he stepped beneath the water and let the heat seep into his sore muscles.

Finally he got the energy to soap off and when he felt clean, he got out. The shower had revived him enough so that he no longer felt like lying down. He wrapped the towel around his waist, went back to his room, and put on fresh clothes. Then he headed back downstairs.

He assumed that Jess was asleep, so when he entered the living room a minute later, he was surprised to see her.

"I thought you were upstairs," he said, walking into the room.

"I couldn't sleep, so I came down to clean up a bit." Her eyes were guarded as she watched him. "How are you feeling?"

"Not bad, considering."

She nodded and placed the folded blanket she'd been holding on the chair beside her. "That's good."

He didn't like this uncomfortable feeling between them but wasn't sure how to make things better. After a minute, he decided he had to say something—anything. "I'm sorry about earlier. I didn't mean to hurt you—or frighten you. I've never tried to force a woman before. I wouldn't have said it was something I was capable of."

She gave him a hesitant smile. "You're not exactly your old self anymore."

"Well, I'm ashamed of what I did and I wanted you to know how sorry I was." Unable to stand still any longer, he paced the length of the room, stopping when he found himself standing in a beam of sunlight from outside. "Why is this not burning me? Changelings are half-vampire, so shouldn't I be going up in smoke or something?"

"You're not going to burst into flames if you go out in the sun." A small smile touched her lips as she spoke. "I'm sure you've seen Mac and Dirk out during the day."

He thought back. "Not very often."

"That's because the vampire half of you slows down during the day. You'll feel more tired then and will probably want to sleep. I imagine that you'll start to notice the difference even more in a day or two. That's probably when your fangs will come in."

John felt weak all over again. Something of his shock must have shown on his face because Jess took a step toward him, her hand outstretched, ready to help. "Maybe you should sit down?"

He shook his head, preferring to pace. "I'm just having a little trouble dealing with this."

"You'll get used to it."

"Get used to being half-vampire?" He gave her a deprecating look and then paced to the end of the room, stopping only when he reached the wall. "I don't think so. Fuck." He smacked the wall with his open palm. To his surprise, his hand shot all the way through the drywall, sending dust and debris everywhere.

Dumbfounded, he stared at it. Then he felt Jess walk up beside him, looking none too happy.

"This house has been around for over two hundred years," she said in a clipped tone. "Do you think you could adjust to being a changeling with a little less destruction of private property?"

He felt bad, although not as bad as he might have had her tone not been so condescending. "I didn't hit it that hard. Maybe you have termites."

She shot him a look. "We don't have termites. What we have is a changeling who doesn't realize that he's *changed.*"

"Okay, since you seem to know so much, tell me, what else is different about me?"

"Okay." She gestured to the hole in the wall again. "On the *pro* side, you have increased strength—obviously. You can move faster and you have better night vision and more acute hearing. On the *con* side, you're extra sensitive to the light. Something about sunlight makes you tired, whereas the night gives you energy. You'll probably start sleeping all day and be up at night."

He was only half-listening as his mind tried to wrap around the idea that he was a vampire—well, half-vampire. A bloodsucking creature of the . . . "Do I drink blood?"

"Yes, but you don't live off of it. You'll continue to eat regular food, although I believe for the first couple of days, maybe even a week, your diet may tend toward undercooked meat—extremely undercooked—but after a while, it returns to normal, more or less."

"If I don't need blood to survive, then why would I drink it?"

She gave him a funny look. "There are a few times when you might want it—or need it—but only blood that is freely given. There seems to be some truth to the legend that blood freely given will provide a changeling with enhanced energy and recuperative powers."

"You seem to know a lot about this. There must be a lot of changelings over in England."

She shook her head. "No, in fact, to my knowledge, there aren't any."

"None?"

"No. Most of what I know is from what Charles told my father about Mac and Dirk."

One thing didn't make sense still. "Isn't it a bit odd for half-vampires to hunt full vampires?"

She gave him a sharp look. "It makes perfect sense. Vampires aren't human; they're evil. They kill indiscriminately and without conscience. A changeling retains his human morality while sharing the vampire's physical agilities."

"You say vampires are evil, but Harris saved my life, didn't he?"

"Yes—but who knows why. As far as I'm concerned, he's a vampire—and therefore, he's evil."

"And I'm half-vampire. Am I half-evil?"

There was the briefest hesitation, as both of them no doubt remembered the incident on the floor. "No," she said. "That's different."

"Is it?"

"Yes. Now, if you'll excuse me, I'm going to my room. You seem to be doing much better so I believe I'll try to get some sleep after all." She walked out and he let her go. He was tired of arguing.

Over the next two days, they fell into a routine. Jess would wake up each morning just as the sun was coming up. John would come in from standing guard outside the house all night. They would share a meal and exchange very polite, yet limited, conversation. Neither John nor Jess tried to discuss again what had happened on the floor, yet it hung between them like a live electrical wire, sending out sparks of electricity whenever they were together—which wasn't often.

While John slept during the day, Jess would go out and explore the surrounding area for the chupacabra colony. She wanted to ask John where it was, but then he'd want to know why she was interested. She could just imagine what he'd say if he found out she wanted to capture one of the younger creatures.

On the third day, John's diet changed to a preference for extremely rare beef. Jess, anticipating the change, had stocked up on steaks during her last trip into town. She was finding John's metamorphosis fascinating—or at least, that's what she told herself when she found herself staying up later in the evenings and sleeping until noon the next day, just to be with him.

On the fifth day, Jess's scouting of the surrounding area paid off and she found the cemetery where John had been attacked. The aboveground tombs made the gargoyle statues less noticeable, but she knew the minute she saw them that they were day-phase chupacabras. The sheer number of statues left her in awe.

She walked through the front entrance, feeling like she was entering another world. There were enough large oak trees growing that their limbs, heavily draped with Spanish moss, seemed to reach for one another, forming a canopy that allowed only patches of sunlight through to the ground below. At this time of year, when the nights were much cooler than the days, a layer of fog would cover the ground in the early predawn hours. Not one to be easily spooked, she knew that under the full moon this was not someplace she wanted to be alone.

She wondered if the chupacabras sensed the coming of dawn and purposely took up poses around the tombs, in a sense camouflaging themselves, or if they were caught unawares, one moment crossing the cemetery intent on reaching the other side, the next frozen in stone midstep, their journey delayed until dusk.

These thoughts fueled her curiosity and excitement. She wanted to know more about them.

With the sun shining brightly and still hours to go until dusk, there was no chance of them coming to life and attacking her as they had John. Feeling safe, she hurried forward, going from one statue to the next, noticing the various heights and shapes of each creature. She would take exhaustive notes later, but for now it was enough to just look and admire.

The first thing she noticed was that not all of the chupacabras looked alike. There were several consistent shapes, however. There were the ones like Lanie's Gem, with rounded heads, alienlike eyes, and fins running from the top of the head down the center of the back. Then there were others with a more feline-shaped head and muzzle, absent the fins, but with horns on either side of the head or on the tips of their wings.

The wings themselves were something she hadn't expected. Within each physical style of chupacabra, there were winged adults that were larger and heavier than their wingless counterparts. She suspected that these were the males of the species.

She walked up to one of the winged statues in the cemetery. Its dark granitelike surface was cool and slightly rough to the touch. She wondered what his hide would feel like in his "living" phase.

The eyes and fangs were a lighter shade of granite and Jess stepped close, peering into the creature's eyes, wondering if he was aware of her at that very moment. She was so intent on looking that when a shadow passed across the eye, she jumped back. Had the creature blinked?

A gentle breeze lifted her hair and she heard the quiet rustle of tree limbs above. She took a deep breath to quiet her racing heart and decided that she was imagining things. The creature hadn't moved. It was made of stone. What she'd seen had been nothing more than a shadow cast by the tree limbs moving above her.

Feeling calmer, she left the cemetery and returned to the manor, where she collected her camera and a notebook. She briefly considered leaving John a message, telling him where she was, but decided against it. She did not want his interference.

The first thing she did on her return was to study each statue up close and sketch it. There were actually a few statues that she believed to be real masonry, including the large black one. It was behind this one that she finally decided to hide when dusk approached.

The statue was located off to one side of the cemetery, where the iron fence surrounding the graveyard had collapsed. Standing between the statue and the fence, she would be well hidden, as well as have an escape route. If at any time she became nervous about being there with the creatures, she had only to slip over the fence and disappear into the wooded lot next door.

Jess took a few minutes to gather fallen tree limbs that still had enough leaves in order to provide cover.

Getting comfortable in the small space she'd chosen was nearly impossible, but she did the best she could. Kneeling in place, she set her camera down while she arranged the tree limbs so she could see out well enough to take pictures. Then it was just a matter of waiting for the sun to go down.

That seemed to take forever. Jessica started snapping pictures randomly, not wanting to miss a single moment. Then, because she didn't know how quickly the transformation would take, she selected one small creature to focus her attention on and watched him exclusively.

It happened in an instant: one second, she was staring at a statue and the next, a living creature. She was awestruck at the sight and almost forgot to take pictures.

Fascinated, she watched as the small winged chupacabra moved about. When her small subject started to meander out of camera range, Jess pushed herself forward, bracing herself against the leg of the statue to keep from falling forward. She was about to take her next picture when the leg moved!

Frightened, Jess fell back and looked up. Standing above her, skin black as night, was the largest, most terrifying creature she'd ever seen. It stared down at her with eyes that glowed with a crimson light. In a sudden move, his wings snapped open and he flapped them, pounding her with gusts of wind and dirt.

Her camera fell from fingers gone slack and she stared stupidly upward, her mind frozen with terror. Her gaze inevitably sought the two huge fangs protruding from his mouth and she remembered what those fangs had done to John.

She didn't want the same thing to happen to her.

She flinched when the chupacabra opened its mouth, emitting an ear-rending sound that vibrated through her, pulling a similar, primal scream from her own throat. Then its head dipped toward her and she knew the time for praying was over.

Chapter 12

Jess braced for the attack, feeling the chupacabra's warm breath as he lowered his head.

"Jessica!"

John's voice filtered past the shrill static of fear that dominated her senses. A small spark of hope shot through her as she heard his footsteps running toward her.

"Jess, honey, it'll be okay. Nice and easy, walk toward me."

Was he crazy? The chupacabra was ready to strike. Any second now . . .

Another second passed and then another. Almost afraid to move, she dared to look up. The creature was watching her, but no longer seemed intent on ripping out her throat.

"Move slowly," John urged.

Encouraged, she took a step toward his voice. Her attention was so focused on the creature that when a hand grabbed her arm, she nearly jumped out of her skin.

Then John was there, pulling her a safe distance away and running his hands over her as if he were looking for injuries. "Are you all right? You're not hurt anywhere, are you?"

"No, no. I'm fine." Her voice was shaky, and his obvious concern for her was unexpected and touching.

"What the hell were you doing?" he growled, bringing the warm moment to a screeching halt.

She pulled herself from his hands, needing the space. "I was doing research, if you must know."

"You almost got yourself killed."

He was right, so rather than argue with him, she remained silent.

"I would think you, of all people, would be more cautious around chupacabras at night," he continued.

That rankled a bit. "What do you mean, me of all people?"

"I mean someone who hates vampires as much as you do," he said in a quieter, more reasonable tone of voice. "Are you trying to become one?"

"Well, he didn't attack," she pointed out lamely. "So, I'm fine."

He growled. "He didn't attack because I stopped him."

"You?" she scoffed. "How?"

"Apparently there is a psychic link between chupacabras and the vampires and changelings they create."

Jess felt herself pale at the revelation, not of the link—which she'd known about—but at the discovery that this was the creature that had attacked John. She'd had a first-hand demonstration of just how terrifying the creature could be.

"Harris told me about the link the other night," John

continued. "So I've been learning how to use it. When I woke up this evening with a distorted image of you in my head, it didn't take me long to figure out I was seeing you through the chupacabra's eyes. I got here as fast as I could." His grip tightened painfully on her arm. "Don't ever sneak out here again by yourself, do you understand?"

She'd never seen him that angry before and could only nod. He studied her face with obvious distrust and then pulled her along with him as he walked out of the cemetery.

"My camera," she protested, looking back to where it lay too close to the chupacabra standing there, watching them closely.

"Leave it. We'll get it later," John said without slowing his pace.

Once they moved beyond the wrought-iron fencing, they stopped and looked back. The male creature had trailed after them, staying between them and the rest of the colony. Protecting the others, Jessica thought, as the alpha male of the colony would do. She made a mental note to write that bit of information down in her journal and then wondered if that would be her final entry. After all, she couldn't study the creatures if every time she got close they tried to attack. What she needed was some way to control them—or some*one* to control them.

Wondering how best to approach the subject with John, she was distracted by Harris's sudden appearance. She watched John turn to greet the vampire, wanting to trust the vampire but not yet sure about him. He might still reveal his true nature. If John were lucky, the revelation would only leave him disappointed—and not dead.

Determined to keep an eye on the vampire, she pasted

a blank expression on her face and turned to face him—then felt her jaw fall open in surprise when she saw the creature beside him. It was a wingless chupacabra.

After staring for what must have been several seconds, she forced her attention back to Harris and was immediately repulsed. There was blood on the front collar of his shirt. Her fingers itched for the sword she'd left behind at the manor.

"You shouldn't be out," he said, eyeing her before turning back to John. "Brody is still in the area."

Jessica shot him a defiant look. "I'm not afraid of a vampire."

"You should be," he countered.

"Harris is right," John interrupted before she could argue. "It's too dangerous. Let's go back to the manor."

The three made the ten-minute walk to the mansion in complete silence. Once they arrived, Jessica headed up the front steps. From behind, she felt John's gaze on her and knew he was staying with Harris.

It bothered her that he didn't come with her. She wanted to think it was because she didn't want him getting too close to the vampire, although a small part of her thought it might be because she simply didn't like him spending time away from her. With a glance back at the pair, she stepped inside and tried to pretend that she didn't care.

"Okay," John relented the next evening. "I'll make a deal with you. If you promise not to go anywhere alone, I'll try my link with the alpha male. We'll see if I can convince him that we're not there to hurt the colony."

They'd been arguing in the living room ever since he'd come back from patrolling with Harris and found her packing food and water into a backpack. He'd wanted to know where she was going and so she'd told him the truth. When he'd tried to talk her out of returning to the cemetery, she'd remained stubborn. He'd finally realized that she was doing this with or without his help.

"Thank you," she said, fighting unsuccessfully to keep the smile from her face.

"You're welcome." He tried to sound grumpy, but she just kept smiling until he no longer seemed able to resist and actually smiled back.

"Oh," she said, surprised. "When did your fangs come in?"

He ran a finger over the two elongated canines. "The old teeth fell out yesterday and these came in while I slept."

"Have there been any other changes?" she asked, wondering if he'd noticed a thirst for blood. "Have you had any uncontrollable urges?"

"Uncontrollable urges?"

She didn't move away when he stepped closer, but she found herself suddenly very wary of him.

"No urges I can't control," he continued in a slightly husky voice. "At least, none up until now." He brushed the back of his fingers down her cheek.

"I was talking about blood," she quickly amended, sounding flustered. "Have you felt the need to consume . . . what do you mean, up until now?"

He stepped closer, invading her personal space. "Some things are just too hard to fight, even for me." He leaned forward and touched his lips to hers. Soft and gentle, the kiss was meant to tease and entice; a temptation she couldn't resist.

As if sensing her need, his kiss grew more demanding. Clutching his shoulders, she eagerly returned it.

Just as she was losing herself totally, she felt a sharp prick of pain on her lip and jerked back, her hand instinctively moving to her mouth.

"What's the matter?" John sounded disoriented and confused. A drop of her blood colored the outside of his lips and as she watched, he licked it away. She read his surprise and then horror as easily as if it were written across his face. He had liked the taste of her blood and that bothered him—a lot.

"I'm sorry," he muttered, backing away from her so quickly that she thought he might hurt himself in his haste to get away.

"It's just a nick." She dabbed at her lip, not knowing whether she was more disturbed by the reminder of his half-vampire status or disappointed that the kiss had ended. She didn't like the implications of either. She stepped away from him as she fought to clear her thoughts, making a show of picking up her backpack as if nothing had happened between them. "We should probably go to the cemetery now."

His expression was unreadable as he nodded. "Okay. Let me get something from my room and then we'll go."

She watched him walk out of the living room, unable to fight the worry and despondency that filled her.

John went to his room and retrieved his S&W. He'd left his Airweight in the rental car and didn't want to go get it. He felt that the .44 mag, along with the old sword Jess had found in the house, would be enough. He knew that his gun wasn't as effective as that sword, but it was still his weapon of choice.

Going back downstairs, he stopped at the front door. Not really sure what he was doing, he opened up his senses, trying to extend them as far as possible. He was shocked when the noises that had previously been part of the general background din separated into individual sounds and came into sharp focus. He heard the scurrying of small creatures in the underbrush and the movement of the tree limbs swaying in the gentle night breeze. Then he heard something that wasn't normal. He focused on it, trying to figure out what it was. He had the impression of something large moving toward the house.

Instantly alert, he listened more intently, attempting to gauge the distance of this possible threat.

"John, it's Harris."

He heard the vampire call out and relaxed a bit. "Be right out," he said in a normal tone of voice, knowing the vampire would hear him as well.

Then he turned to face Jess, standing at the entrance to the foyer. "Time to go. Harris is waiting outside."

"What's he doing here?" She didn't sound happy.

"I thought it would be better if he and Lucy went with us to the cemetery."

"Why?"

"Because he's had more time to develop his link with Lucy and I thought that might come in handy. Since you insist on studying the entire colony, I'm trying to avoid a situation where the chupacabras attack us because I misread the link."

Her disapproval was written clearly across her face. He knew they were in for an argument that he really didn't want to have right then, so he played his trump card. "Fine. I'll ask him to leave and we'll stay in tonight." He reached for the door handle and had started to turn the knob when she stopped him.

"Fine," she mimicked him. "He can come, but I don't like it."

"You know, he hasn't done anything to hurt you. I don't know why you can't accept that he's a decent guy."

"Maybe," she said frostily, "it's because he's not a 'guy.' He's a vampire and vampires are—unpredictable."

"Harris only kills when he can't steal blood from a blood bank or hospital," he defended. "And his victims are criminals who have committed fairly heinous crimes."

"So you believe it's okay to kill criminals in cold blood, just not law-abiding citizens." She gave him a disapproving look. "You must be a huge asset to the American justice system."

"I'm not going to argue with you about this, Jess. Get your stuff if you want to go; otherwise, stay here." He opened the door and walked out, leaving her to stare after him.

Her remark had struck home, though he didn't want to admit it. She'd raised the same moral issue he'd been grappling with from the beginning. There were many shades of gray involved with the issue of Harris killing criminals, and his own seeming support of it was something he'd thought about long and hard. Hearing the same thing from her made it seem much more black and white—not that he liked the answer any better.

"Aren't they fascinating?" Jessica asked John hours later as she gazed at the chupacabras through her night-vision goggles. They were alone while Harris patrolled the area.

"Have you always wanted to study chupacabras?" he asked her.

"No, it's really only been since I saw the photo in the magazine." A faint blush stained her cheeks and he saw it only because his own vision had undergone a change.

"If you grew up hunting vampires, there's bound to be a colony close to your home."

"Lately, there haven't been as many vampires either, so maybe the chupacabras have moved on, but growing up, we killed five or six vampires a week."

John was stunned. "I had no idea it was so many. And you used swords to kill them?"

"Mostly, although our successful encounters were more a result of strategy than physical strength. Strategy—and vampire toxins."

"You mean like Holy Water?" He wasn't entirely joking when he asked the question, wondering how much wisdom really lay in the Hollywood horror films.

She gave him an indulgent smile. "I think the Holy Water only works on creatures who have been damned by God. That's not really the case here."

"I beg to differ," a voice said from behind them, causing them both to turn around. Harris stood there, Lucy by his side. "If this is not God's curse, then I don't know what is."

"The state of vampirism is the result of being injected with too much of the chupacabra venom," she pointed out. "The problem is that the venom seems to affect some in more negative ways than others." If that was the case, then what about the changelings who were also injected with the venom? She cast a sideways glance at John. Did she honestly think he would turn evil?

It wasn't a line of thought she wanted to pursue, so she ran her gaze across the open expanse of the cemetery. Through the goggles, the chupacabras and the landscape were cast in an eerie green light. In a far corner, she watched as several of the smaller creatures played and it made her smile. As mysterious as they were, it was nice to see that some things—like children playing—were universal.

She watched them for a few more minutes before training the goggles on another area. Near the young creatures were several of the wingless adult females. They reminded Jess of the human mothers she'd seen from time to time at the park, clustered together talking as they watched their children play.

Wondering where the adult males were, she swung her goggles in a wider arc until she saw several of them standing farther away. Enthralled with watching the three groups, she didn't at first notice the one creature off to the side by itself. It didn't have wings so Jess suspected it was a female. Her abdomen was heavily distended and she looked miserable. Jess took a closer look.

"John, do you see that chupacabra over to the right, beside the tombstone marked LeBlanc?"

The conversation behind her stopped as both men turned to see what she was referring to.

"I see her," John replied after a moment.

"I think she's pregnant," Jess said in awe, hardly daring to believe her luck. What a great opportunity this was. She hoped to be able to witness the birthing. "I wonder when she's due."

"I'm getting an impression of worry or concern from Diablo," John added. "Like he expects her to deliver any day now."

Jess let the information sink in. She would come to the cemetery every night, she vowed, just so she wouldn't miss the event when it started.

Feeling better about her plan, the rest of what John said sank in and she turned to him in surprise. "Diablo?"

He smiled, but looked embarrassed. "The chupacabra that attacked me. He's the head of the colony."

"You named him *Diablo*?"

"Actually, I named him *Diablo Negro.*" He said the name using a campy Mexican accent and then shrugged.

Off to the side, she heard Harris laugh. John scowled at the vampire, one eyebrow raised. "I sure as hell hope *you're* not making fun of *my* naming convention?"

That raised her curiosity. "What did you name your chupacabra?"

Before he could answer, they heard a distant cry from above. Looking up, Jess saw something dark flicker across the face of the full moon before disappearing from sight against the night sky. "What was that?" She turned to John, hoping he'd seen it too. Both he and Harris were still watching it, whatever it was.

"He looks hurt," John observed. "You see how erratically he's flying?"

"I can't tell if his wing is injured or if it's something else," Harris said. "Whatever it is, I don't think he's going to make a safe landing."

Jess raised her night-vision goggles and searched the sky.

"We should probably move." John took her arm and

pulled her farther off to the side just as a rush of movement came from inside the cemetery.

Four large winged chupacabras beat their wings as they ran a few paces and then lifted into the sky. Jess followed their flight as long as she could.

"What's happening?" she asked.

"It's a male chupacabra—I don't know if he's dead or unconscious, but he just stopped flying. Those four who just took off caught him midfall. They're bringing him down now."

Finally, she spotted the four chupacabras, their wings beating in tandem as they carried the fifth between them.

As soon as they landed, the five were immediately surrounded by the other chupacabras. Jess looked to John and Harris to see if they were as eager as she to see what was going on.

She was surprised to see that he and Harris seemed locked into some kind of staring contest. Then Harris nodded once and walked off.

"Where's he going?" Jess asked.

"From what we're picking up on the psychic link, it sounds like this chupacabra was being held captive by a group of humans—or vampires. That's the part that's a little confusing. Harris thought he recognized one of the chupacabra's images of a building. He's going to check it out. "Come on," John continued. "I want to take a closer look."

The other chupacabras were too concerned about their injured member to pay much attention to the two humans as they moved among them. In fact, Jess was surprised when the creatures actually moved aside to give them a better view. Then seconds later, she wished they hadn't been so accommodating.

The injured chupacabra sat on the ground, leaning heavily against a raised tombstone, with his eyes closed and head fallen forward. His breathing was loud and raspy, and while the wing closest to the tombstone was folded against his body, the outer one lay at an awkward angle, as if it were broken. Jess was amazed he'd even been able to fly and wondered if it was possible to set the wing so it could heal properly.

Her attention traveled over his body, and she noticed he was covered with a shiny substance that was hard to identify through her goggles. Then she noticed the hundreds of striations across his hide and realized what they were—long strips of torn flesh that could only have been the result of harsh, repeated whippings. She knew, then, that the shiny liquid covering him was blood.

The creature moved slightly and the clanking of chain drew her attention to the metal cuff still attached to his leg. The thick links hanging from the cuff were testament to a desperate struggle for survival and escape. The thought that anyone could treat another creature so cruelly made her mad. Even when she hunted vampires, she strove to make her kills quick and clean.

At that moment, there was a notable change in the male's breathing as a shudder ran through him. Jess cast a questioning glance at John, who simply shook his head. There was nothing they could do.

Then a strange silence filled the night and Jess realized the chupacabra had drawn his last breath. She gazed upon his lifeless body and as she watched, the texture of his skin began to harden. Within a matter of seconds, though it was the middle of the night, the chupacabra turned to stone and Jess knew that when the sun went down tomorrow evening, he would not turn back.

If only she'd been able to do something to help him. Perhaps with time and more research . . .

When John took her by the hand to lead her away, she didn't resist. This time, as they walked through the cemetery, she took another look at the statues she passed. What she had previously assumed were actual stone carvings, she now knew to be dead chupacabras.

Jess woke up late in the afternoon of the next day still depressed over the death of the chupacabra. She had learned a lot in that one evening and was busy entering her observations into her journal as she waited for the coffee to finish brewing.

Intent on her train of thought, she jumped when she heard a noise behind her.

"Do you have to be so loud?" she growled as John came to stand beside her.

"Hello, sunshine," he replied in a caustic tone. "Aren't we in a good mood?" He reached past her into the cabinet to take down a coffee mug. To her dismay, he pulled the carafe off the warming plate before the coffee was finished brewing and poured himself a cup.

"Hey, what are you doing?" she cried, jumping to her feet to snatch a paper towel, anticipating coffee running everywhere. He looked at her like she was crazy and casually put the carafe back on the dry warming plate.

"It's got an automatic shutoff," he pointed out before raising the cup to his mouth and taking a drink. Then he winked at her. "You should have some. Might put you in a better mood."

"Ugh," she growled again, reaching for the coffee and pouring a cup for herself. "What are you doing up so early, anyway? It's only three o'clock."

He took a sip of the hot beverage and let it work its way down his throat. "I need to run into town," he said after he swallowed. "I want to follow up with the local authorities. See if they've noticed any unusual deaths lately. Also, in case I haven't been fired, I should check in with my department back home. When this is all over, it might be nice to have a job to go back to."

"How long will you be gone?"

"Hopefully just a couple of hours," he said, running a hand down his face. Despite the way he sounded, she knew he had to be exhausted. She watched him walk over to the window and look out without wincing too much. The skies were overcast with the promise of rain, making it look prematurely dark. He might not even need his sunglasses, she thought.

"Why don't you come with me?" John surprised her by asking.

"Into the New Orleans police station? During Mardi Gras? I don't think so, thanks. I'll stay here and go over my notes."

"All right. I won't be gone long." He rose and poured himself another cup of coffee to take with him. "Do me a favor and be careful, okay?"

She gave him that look that said she'd been fighting vampires a lot longer than he had and knew how to take care of herself. He apparently got the message because she saw a faint smile touch his mouth before he left the kitchen.

Twenty minutes later, Jess watched him go and felt the loss of his absence more acutely than she wanted to admit. She'd gotten used to having him around. Knowing that it would do her no good to sit around and regret not having gone with him, she topped off her coffee and returned to her bedroom, where she had notes spread across the bed.

Her goal was to put together the most comprehensive volume on chupacabras that she could. It would never be a text available to the public, but that wasn't important to her.

Picking up her pen and notebook, she started to write out her thoughts and impressions. About forty minutes into her work, she remembered the plantation house from the magazine. In the excitement of finding the colony at the cemetery, she'd forgotten about the old manor. Was it possible that there were two chupacabra colonies in the area—the one at the cemetery and a second one at the plantation home? It seemed unlikely, which meant the home had to be near.

Now, suddenly consumed with curiosity, she put down her pen and notebook and stood up. She had to find out.

She glanced outside. It was still cloudy and gray, but there was enough light outside for her to see, which meant she could do a little exploring before the sun went down.

Focused on her plan, she left the mansion and made the short hike to the cemetery. In the fading light, it seemed more ominous than ever. The chupacabras, looking like Gothic statues, stood frozen among the massive tombs. Unable to resist the temptation, she walked among them, dwarfed by their size and grateful that sunset was still hours away.

She headed to the far end of the lot and found the back gate. The area here was overgrown, but now that she was standing there, she noticed a faded path leading off into the tangled undergrowth. She followed it through the woods and stopped when she reached the end of the trail to look around. She was standing on the edge of a backyard lawn that sloped upward to a large, worn house whose once-white exterior had suffered the ravages of time and neglect.

It was a stately home, Jess thought, and her gaze quickly traveled to the roof. She struggled to make out the various shapes and couldn't help but smile when, through the gloom, she spotted the chupacabra sitting on the corner.

After finding the first one the others were easier to see, and soon she'd spotted six forms along the roof's edge. She hurried forward, wanting to take a better look. The neglect became more apparent as she drew closer, and by the time she'd walked around to the front, she knew that she'd found the house from the magazine.

Excitement welled up inside her. She could tell the place was vacant and wondered, as she hurried up the front porch steps, if there was any chance at all that the door might be unlocked.

The outer screen door hung at a slight angle from loosened hinges. She pulled it open carefully, not wanting to break it, and noticed a "For Sale" sign propped at the base of the door, where it had obviously fallen.

She was mildly curious about the price of the house. Not that she was interested in purchasing it, she quickly told herself. She knocked on the inner door and waited, almost holding her breath. After getting no response, she concluded it was empty.

Gripping the doorknob, she turned it. To her surprise, it opened easily.

When she pushed open the door, she saw where the frame had been gouged. It was almost as if someone had shoved the door open while the dead bolt was still thrown.

It would have taken a great deal of strength to force the door open—and she couldn't understand why anyone would do it.

Stepping into the foyer, she saw that the place was mostly unfurnished, but that was all she could see. There was very little light coming in through the windows. It would be difficult to explore the house without a flashlight, but curiosity drove her on.

To the left of the entry was the formal living room, and she went over to the doorway to peek inside. Here, again, the only light available was the little bit coming in behind her, through the open front door. She wished she could see more and noticed that the windows in the room were heavily draped. Knowing the outside of the windows weren't boarded, she pulled open the drapes to let in more light.

Then she turned around to inspect the room.

For several seconds, her mind refused to accept what was before her. When it did, her blood ran cold.

The room looked much the way John had described the one in D.C.; she saw her name was scrawled across the walls in blood. She could barely breathe. Even more distressing were the two bodies—male and female—lying in opposite corners of the room. They were clearly dead, and Jess had no doubt that Brody had been here.

As she wondered what she should do, a faint stirring sound drifted to her from elsewhere in the house. It suddenly occurred to her that Brody might still be here; that this might even be his new lair.

Worse yet, while she'd been busy exploring, the sun had been setting. When the sound from the back of the house came again, she didn't wait around to see what it was.

She raced out the front door, not stopping until she reached the bottom of the hill where the woods started. Then she made the mistake of looking back. There, at the back door, stood a blond figure that she knew must be Brody. She turned and raced through the woods, heedless of the thorny bushes and tree limbs tearing at her clothes and skin.

The sound of something crashing through the woods after her sent fear spiking through her. Logic told her she couldn't outrun a vampire; fear and a sense of self-preservation told her to try.

She burst out of the woods and into the cemetery without slowing. She ran past the tombstones without a second glance and was almost to the other side when she was struck from behind. She hit the ground with such force that the air was knocked out of her.

Gasping for breath, she felt like a boneless rag doll when Brody ruthlessly flipped her onto her back. Then his weight settled on top of her and she found herself staring up into a pair of gleaming red eyes.

"Hello, Jessica." Brody drew out her name, hissing like a snake. "I've been thinking about you."

It was a scene from her past—like her nightmares. She

was pinned to the ground while death stared her in the face. She heard a pathetic mewling noise, and a detached part of her brain told her it was coming from her. She didn't want to die this way—she didn't want to die at all.

Finally gathering her wits enough to fight, she pummeled at the vampire with her fists, but Brody easily caught them and pinned her hands between her body and his knees as he straddled her. Never had she felt more helpless in all her life.

He gave her an evil twisted smile that promised a long and torturous death. When he leaned over and sank his teeth into her neck, Jess almost welcomed the pain. It gave her something other than her fear to focus on. And then, gradually, even the pain began to fade, and her eyes drifted closed.

Chapter 13

As John headed for the cemetery, he told himself that he was overreacting. After all, as she so often reminded him, Jess was an experienced vampire hunter. She could take care of herself.

The argument did nothing to lessen the sense of foreboding he'd had since he left New Orleans to return home. As the cemetery came into view, he hurried a little faster. He should have known she wouldn't stay inside the mansion as he'd asked, and her willingness to put herself at risk infuriated him. So much so that if she was still alive, he'd probably kill her himself; he was so angry with her.

Not sure what he'd do if she wasn't here, he looked around and saw a sight that frightened him as nothing else ever had.

Near the back of the cemetery, he saw Brody hunched over something close to the ground.

Moving faster than he thought possible, John raced toward the vampire, fury, rage, and fear for Jess driving him. As soon as he was close enough, he launched himself at Brody, who had been too absorbed in drinking Jess's blood to have noticed him. The force of the tackle carried both men several feet off to the side and before Brody could recover, John was up and hitting the vampire just as hard as he could. He pounded away at Brody's face, wanting to pulverize it until there was nothing recognizable left.

John hadn't counted on Brody being stronger now, too. Just when John thought he had the upper hand, Brody turned the tables on him, hitting him in the jaw and knocking him off balance.

Both Brody and John scrambled to their feet and squared off. About to launch another attack, John was caught off guard by Brody's smile as he swiped blood off his chin with a finger and then put the finger in his mouth to suck it clean.

"What are you going to do, John?" he sneered. "Her life's blood is draining into the ground. She'll be dead soon if you don't do something to help. Of course, maybe you'll get lucky and kill me. Then again, maybe you won't."

John spared a glance at Jess, and all he saw was her blood. There was no decision to make as he raced to her side, letting Brody escape into the woods.

Scooping her up into his arms, he thought she looked to be at death's door. Strands of hair were plastered to the sides of her face, and her neck and shirt were covered in blood. Determined to race back to the house with her in his arms, he'd only taken a step or two when he felt her hand against his cheek.

"John?"

"It's okay, honey. I have you. I'm going to take you to the hospital."

"Brody?"

John inwardly winced. "Don't worry about him. You're the one who matters most right now."

"No," she cried, though it sounded more like a croak. "I'm fine . . . looks worse than it is."

It had started to rain, and as some of the blood around her neck rinsed away, John saw that the wounds weren't as serious as he'd first thought. Maybe she wasn't going to die.

His relief was so great that he didn't even care that Brody had played him. Jess was what mattered most to him now.

"Let's get you home," he said, still carrying her in his arms. It rained the entire long walk back to the mansion. They were good and soaked by the time they reached it. Jess's lips had turned blue and she was shivering.

He took her directly upstairs to the bathroom and set her down, pleased to see that she was able to stand on her own.

"You need to get out of these clothes," he ordered as he turned on the faucets of the shower. Her teeth chattered so hard he was afraid she might break a tooth; her hands were shaking so badly that she couldn't undo the buttons of her shirt. He went to her and gently shoved her hands aside. Then, with a deft touch, he undid the buttons for her. As the shirt fell open, his gaze strayed to the bra beneath, which, because it was soaking wet, left nothing to the imagination.

Ignoring his body's reaction, he focused on the waistband of her jeans as he undid them. She stood as docile as a child and he wondered if in her state of delayed shock, she was even aware of what he was doing. Taking her firmly by the shoulders, he turned her away from him and slid her shirt down her arms. He tossed it into the corner of the room. Next, he tugged off her jeans, watching as they slid down long, shapely legs to pool around her feet. Her panties had come down with the jeans, and his gaze caressed the contours of her back, waist, and hips.

She wasn't model thin, but to his eyes she was beauty and perfection, even with her skin dimpled from the cold. Already skirting the cliff's edge of his self-restraint, he didn't even try to help her off with her bra. Instead, he pushed her toward the tub, leaned past her long enough to check the temperature of the water, careful not to let his gaze stray, and then pulled up the knob that turned on the shower. With a gentle shove, she stepped into the tub. When the shower door was safely closed between them, he drew his first easy breath.

Knowing she'd need a robe, he'd started to walk out when the sound of the shower door opening behind him made him stop. He knew he shouldn't turn around, but like a moth drawn to a flame, he couldn't resist.

She was nothing more than a flesh-toned blur behind the opaque glass, but as he watched, her arm appeared through the opening, the sheer bra dangling from her hand. Mesmerized by the translucent material, he stared at it, recalling with agonizing detail how she'd looked in it. Then her fingers opened and the bra fell to the floor.

He couldn't take any more. He hurried from the bathroom, nearly strangling on his muffled groan.

Jessica let the hot water beat at her, its heat seeping into her very core. She waited for it to dissipate the bone-deep chill residing there, afraid that it never would.

She kept her eyes closed until she was sure most of the blood had washed down the drain. Having John find her passed out in the shower would be her final humiliation. Some vampire hunter she was. She'd almost gotten herself killed.

She quickly cut off the direction of that thought. She hadn't died. John had saved her.

Saved her. Carried her back. Undressed her. A blush heated her cheeks and she let her head fall forward under the stream of water, wondering how she was ever going to face him again. Maybe she would just stay under the shower until she drowned.

Quite some time later, her fingers and toes pruned from too long in the water, she stepped out of the shower and saw that John had brought in her robe. She quickly dried off and put it on, luxuriating in the feel of the plush terry cloth wrapped around her.

She ran a comb through her hair and, knowing she couldn't hide forever, opened the bathroom door. A clinking sound from the kitchen was followed by the unmistakable aroma of chicken noodle soup. Almost of their own accord, her feet carried her downstairs to the kitchen, where she found John standing over the stove, stirring a pot. He'd combed his hair, but it had fallen in a tousle about his head, and he'd changed out of his wet clothes into a fresh pair of jeans and a sweatshirt.

"Smells good," she said, her voice still sounding a little raw.

John turned at the sound. "I made you some—" He hesitated when he saw her, and his eyes briefly glowed as they raked over her.

"I'm sorry." Feeling self-conscious, she pulled the

robe closed a little more tightly as she turned to leave. "I should have put on clothes before coming down."

"No, you're fine." He crossed the kitchen and took her by the arm, leading her to the table. "Really," he assured her when she gave him a questioning look. "Here, I just made you some soup. Do you feel like eating?"

She managed a wobbly smile. "Maybe a small amount?"

He took down a bowl, filled it with soup and brought it to her along with a spoon. Then he stood over her while she tasted it.

"It's good."

"It's canned." He sounded like he was apologizing for not making it from scratch.

She looked up to reassure him it was fine and made the mistake of looking into his eyes. His gaze nearly scorched her and she forgot what she was going to say.

"Look, I think I owe you an apology," he finally said, interrupting the awkward silence that had fallen between them. He shook his head. "You've got balls, I'll give you that."

She wasn't sure where that comment had come from. "What do you mean?"

"I don't think I could let a vampire suck on me like that—even if I had drunk whatever that tea is that you drink. Anyway, I wanted to apologize for rushing in like that. I saw him on you and just reacted. I'm sorry if I ruined your plan. Hopefully, he got enough of that toxin in your blood that he's already history."

"I didn't drink the tea."

He stared at her, looking confused. "Excuse me?"

"I said I didn't drink the tea. I don't have any of the plant in tea form—it's all in concentrate. And I couldn't take any from Charles because then he'd know I wasn't returning home. I was afraid he'd try to stop me." She hurried through her explanation, willing him to understand. He stared at her, his eyes practically shooting sparks of fire. She didn't think he felt lust this time.

"Are you telling me that you went out there with no protection?" He spoke slowly and distinctly. "After I expressly told you not to go out?" He leaned over her until his face was inches from hers. "Do you have any idea how close you came to getting yourself killed?" He was nearly shouting as he leaned over the table, bracing himself on his clenched fists.

"The sun was still up," she tried to explain. "I wanted to find the house in the magazine, and I did. It's just on the other side of the cemetery. And the chupacabras are there on the roof, just like they were in the picture."

John barely let her finish. "I don't give a good goddamn about any house or chupacabras. I do, however, give a damn about you, although why I should, I don't know. You obviously don't give a damn about yourself." He grabbed her by the upper arms and hauled her to her feet, holding her so she couldn't move. "Don't you ever do something like that again, do you hear me?"

"I won't. I—"

The rest of her words were cut off when he pulled her close and covered her mouth with his. He might have meant the kiss to be punishing, but the instant his lips touched hers, Jessica felt herself go up in flames. She kissed him back with an intensity that surprised her.

When he released her arms, she wound them around his neck, pulling him close. Like a cat demanding attention, she rubbed herself against him and was rewarded when she heard his groan. At the juncture of her legs, through the barrier of her robe, she felt his erection press against her.

She couldn't remember ever before having felt this aroused, and knowing he wasn't unaffected made her act with an unfamiliar daring. She tugged at the hem of his sweatshirt until she could run her hands beneath it, stroking the hard planes of his chest.

It wasn't enough—she pulled the sweatshirt up until he took the hint and pulled it off. The minute it was gone, she pressed her lips to his chest, savoring the feel and taste of his skin against her lips and tongue.

He leaned his head back, taking deep breaths as if standing still for her ministrations was costing all his self-control; control she wanted desperately to make him lose. When she reached for the waistband of his jeans, he sucked in a breath. She dared a glance at his face, saw that his jaw was tightly clenched and paused. Had she misjudged his reaction?

At her hesitation, he opened his eyes and gazed at her from the depths of twin blazing infernos.

"God, Jess. You have no idea how bad I want you." Her robe had fallen open and he pushed her away until he held her at arm's length.

It was her turn to stand still as he ran his hands along the tops of her shoulders, pushing back her robe until it fell to the floor, leaving her completely naked. His gaze traveled over her like a physical caress and she shivered beneath it.

Then his hands were on her breasts, gently molding and lifting the twin globes. His thumbs flicked back and forth across her nipples in rapid succession, and Jess felt them tighten into hard buds even as her breasts seemed to swell and grow heavier. He bent and took a nipple into his mouth, playing his tongue across the hard bud as he gently suckled her. Though he was careful not to cut her with his fangs, she felt their tips scrape across her flesh as he took more of her breast into his mouth.

While he worked magic on her breasts, one hand held her still while the other stroked its way down her side and slipped between her legs. He gently manipulated the folds of her swollen flesh and she knew he'd find her moist and ready. He played with her opening, spreading the moisture to ease the entry of first one, and then two, fingers. She clutched at his shoulders as he filled her and couldn't stop the small gasp of pleasure from escaping.

He stepped away briefly then to shed his jeans. When he gathered her to him moments later for another kiss, she felt his hard member pressing into her.

His mouth left hers to trail kisses from the base of her ear to the nape of her neck. "If you don't want this," he whispered hoarsely, "now's the time to tell me. I'll stop. I swear I will."

He paused long enough to look into her eyes, letting his words slowly penetrate the lust-crazed fog of her mind. She knew that he meant what he said. As aroused as he was, he would stop if she asked him to, but the delicious tension building between her legs said she'd be crazy to ask him.

"I want this," she told him, feeling ridiculously shy under the circumstances.

"Then put your arms around my neck." He gave her a lascivious smile and before she could anticipate his next move, he'd grabbed her behind the thighs and literally lifted her off the ground, maneuvering her legs so they went around his hips. She wouldn't have thought he could hold her, but there were advantages to being stronger than the average man and he held her easily.

In this position, with him between her spread legs, she felt open and exposed, especially when she felt his stiff member probe the sensitive flesh between her legs, seeking entrance.

Then, with bated breath, she waited as, with almost excruciating slowness, he filled her. Farther and farther, her body stretched to accommodate him. Suddenly, he stopped and his gaze sought hers, alarm showing in his eyes.

"Jess?" he croaked, the strain of not moving causing his muscles to tremor. "Why didn't you tell me?"

"Because I was afraid if you knew I was a virgin, then you would stop."

"Damn right." He started to ease out of her, but she locked her ankles behind his back, refusing to let him move.

"Jess, I don't have the strength to resist you for long, so you need to let me go."

She felt so self-conscious, she almost couldn't force out the words. "You don't understand. I want my first time to be with you."

He groaned and she held her breath, waiting. She wasn't aware he had moved until she felt the wall against her back. He held her in place with his hips slowly pressing into her as he gazed into her face. "Are you sure?"

"Yes."

He kissed her then and surged forward, breaking through the thin barrier of her maidenhead and capturing her cry with his mouth. He gave her body time to adjust before gradually pulling out. Before she could protest, he pushed into her again.

He repeated this action, each inward stroke causing an exhilarating tension to build deep inside her.

Every nerve in her body sang until she felt ready to explode.

When his fangs scraped against the unmarked side of her neck, the small pain jerked her back to reality. She didn't want him to bite her. The old fear rose with a vengeance, totally destroying the lust she'd felt moments earlier. Now, the only thing she wanted was to be left alone.

"Stop," she told him, using her hands to push at him. He was still buried deep inside her, and being pinned against the wall left her fighting a growing sense of claustrophobia and panic.

John, unaware of the emotions battling inside her, was lost in the moment and continued to drive into her. When she felt his fangs scratch along her neck, she lost all sense of control and panicked.

"John, stop." She shoved at his chest, trying to push him away. "Let me go." Her voice started to break. "Please . . ."

It took a minute for Jess's sobs to break through his passion-drugged mind, but when they did he froze.

"Jess?" He didn't understand what was going on. She seemed desperate to get away from him, so he reluctantly eased himself out of her. With one arm wrapped around her waist to steady her, he released her legs, letting her slide to the floor. Immediately, she stepped away from him.

"I'm sorry," she muttered, searching the floor for her robe.

"Are you all right?" The sudden Dr. Jekyll/Mr. Hyde change in her behavior had him worried.

"I'm sorry. I just realized that I can't do this." She pulled on her robe, and seemed unusually focused on the act of tying the sash, pointedly avoiding his gaze.

John rubbed his face in an effort to wipe away his frustration. "I don't understand. A second ago, you were begging me. Now, suddenly, you've changed your mind?" He was angry and confused—and so ready to finish what they'd started that he ached with need. "At least tell me what's bothering you. Tell me if I did something wrong."

She shook her head a little too quickly. "I'm just—I'm tired and sore from Brody's attack. I'm still feeling a little weak." She briefly looked up and he supposed it was to see if he was buying her explanation. He wasn't.

"Talk to me, Jess. We can't work through this if you don't talk to me. A few minutes ago, you wanted this as badly as I did. What changed?"

She hesitated, but this time, she didn't look away, meeting his gaze and holding it. "You did." Then she walked out, leaving him standing in the kitchen feeling confused, frustrated, and pissed.

Grabbing his clothes, he headed upstairs to the bathroom to take a very long, very cold shower.

Chapter 14

When John woke up, he still felt tired. He assumed it was from the way things had ended with Jess the night before. Climbing out of bed, he dressed and then checked his phone mail. He had two messages.

The first was from Harris, telling him what he'd found at the house where Brody had been staying. John had called him while Jess showered, to fill him in on what had happened. Harris had volunteered to run by and check it out, though neither of them expected Brody to still be there.

The second message was from Charles.

"John, I haven't heard from you, son, and no one answered the phone at the manor when I called. Is everything all right?" John had taken the phone off the hook before going to bed to ensure that both he and Jess got the sleep they needed. He made a mental note now to put it back. "If I haven't heard back from you by eighteen hundred hours, I'm calling the New Orleans authorities while en route to your location."

John checked his watch. It was almost 6:00 P.M. now, so he hurriedly placed a call to the admiral. Mac answered the phone.

"John, you're alive," Mac said, actually sounding relieved. "What's your situation? Have you found Brody?"

"I found him, but he got away." John paused, wondering how best to proceed. "The situation here has changed."

"How so?" He heard the sharp edge to Mac's voice.

"There's a cemetery here that is home to a colony of chupacabras and . . . there was an accident."

There was a pregnant pause before Mac finally spoke—a single word that spoke volumes. "Who?"

"Me."

"I'm sorry. How are you now?"

How was he? Confused? Pissed off? Frustrated? But none of that really had anything to do with nearly being killed by a chupacabra. "I'm fine."

"And Jessica?"

"She's fine, too, for now."

"Brody?"

"I'll take care of him."

"You sure? I can be down there in a couple of hours," Mac offered.

"Did you get your situation there resolved?"

He heard Mac sigh. "No, but it shouldn't be much longer."

"Stay there and finish," John told him. "I've got this." He could practically hear the other man thinking, and so he hurried to reassure him. "I'm a Night Slayer now—isn't that what Charles called you and Dirk? I'll find Brody, and when I do, this time I won't be stopped by a legal technicality." He paused, wondering how to broach his next topic. "There is something you can help me with, though. Tell me what you know about being a changeling—everything—especially how it affects your relationship with Lanie."

"Why would you need to know about me and Lanie . . . oh. You and Jess?" He chuckled. "No shit."

For the next twenty minutes, Mac told him about the enhanced physical abilities that came with being a changeling. Most of them John had already figured out. He'd also known about the fatigue that came with daylight, though Mac seemed unable to explain the reason for it. He remembered the chupacabras he'd seen during the day and images of his internal organs and blood thickening as if they were trying to turn to stone filled his head.

Mac also told him about taking blood. "It has to be freely given," Mac warned him. "You should never take it by force."

"Not that I would," John said, "but why?"

"To be honest, I don't exactly know. There's a lot of this that can be explained by science and logic. Hell, probably all of it can. I was a pilot in my other life, not a scientist. All I know is that getting blood that is freely offered is like getting a boost of miracle cure. Not only will it cure what ails you, but you'll be high on life for a while; full of energy; feeling invincible."

"Do you drink blood often?"

"No. Most of the time, it's . . . uh . . . recreational." It took John a moment to realize that he was talking about when he and Lanie made love. "But I found that it keeps me up during the day, so I don't take blood that often anymore."

"Did it bother Lanie? You biting her?"

"No. She said it's different than a vampire's bite."

They talked a few minutes longer and then hung up. That's when John caught the odor of cooking food and realized how hungry he was. He went down to the kitchen, feeling as nervous as a schoolboy facing the parents of his prom date the morning after.

He found Jess standing over the stove and cleared his throat, not wanting to startle her.

"Oh, good morning—or evening, I guess," she stammered, sounding as uncomfortable as he felt. "Are you hungry?" She hurried on. "I made extra food, just in case, you know—" She shrugged. "In case you were hungry."

"Thanks. I *am* hungry." She was wearing ordinary jeans and an oversized button-down shirt, but damn, she looked good. His body remembered all too well holding her, kissing her, being inside her.

Suddenly restless, he crossed to the cabinet and got down plates. "How are you feeling?" He'd meant, how was she feeling after Brody's attack, but as soon as the words left his mouth, he realized he also meant about what happened between them. He needed to know that he hadn't hurt her in any way.

He turned to see her face when she answered. It was the only way to know if she was telling him the truth or not.

"I'm fine—really," she added, sensing he wasn't convinced. "In fact, I feel well enough to go back to the cemetery tonight."

He was shaking his head before she finished. "Not such a good idea. Brody's still out there, though he's no longer using the manor as his lair."

"How do you know?"

"I called Harris last night while you were in the shower and asked him to check it out."

"Harris has a cell phone?" She sounded incredulous.

"I put him on my plan. I figured it was well worth the extra expense to keep in touch with him. Anyway," he said, scowling at her, "back to the point I was making. The house is empty. Now that we know Brody was staying there, he's not likely to go back."

"And the bodies?"

"Bodies? Plural?" He gave her a curious look. "Harris only mentioned one—white male, approximately thirty-five years old, dark hair. He was lying in the formal living room."

Jess was already shaking her head. "No, no. There was a woman there, too. What happened to her?"

"Harris never said anything about a woman."

She glanced at her watch. "We still have about thirty minutes of sunlight. I want to go back and take a look around."

John gave her a long, hard look, but then he nodded. "Okay, let's go."

Carrying both her backpack and the sword for her, they set off for the other house by way of the cemetery. As they passed it, Jess made a cursory search for the pregnant chupacabra, but it was hard to differentiate one creature from the next. When they walked by the spot where the male creature had died the other night, her eyes lingered on his still, granitelike form.

Then they moved into the woods and Jess turned her attention toward the mansion. When it finally came into view, she thought that the place looked warmer and friendlier than it had yesterday under the overcast skies.

Still, when it came time to open the door and go inside, she hesitated. The images of the bodies and her name scrawled across the wall were too fresh in her mind. To her immense relief, John opened the door and went inside first.

Harris hadn't bothered to close the drapes when he left, and there was enough sunlight filtering in through the windows that any lurking vampire would have been turned to stone.

She braced herself to face the bloody writing on the walls and stepped into the formal living room. To her surprise, the walls were clean. She was grudgingly grateful to Harris for that small act of kindness.

It didn't take long to tell the room was empty. She walked the perimeter of it anyway, looking for some evidence that there *had* been another victim.

"The woman's body was right there." She pointed to the corner.

"Were the drapes open or closed when you were here?"

She knew where he was going with his question. "I opened the drapes, and even though it was overcast outside, it wasn't that dark. There were two bodies in this room—one there and one there." She pointed to each corner as if that would make things clearer. "Maybe Harris didn't want to tell you about the female because he's lonely and wants female vampire companionship."

"No, Harris wouldn't do that."

"How do you know?" She wished she could trust Harris like John did, but it still bothered her that he had tried to kill Mac and Lanie.

"I just do."

His blind faith frustrated her, so she walked out of the

room and into the next, wanting to inspect the entire house while John was there with her. She wandered from room to room, flipping on the flashlight she'd brought with her as the sun slowly set outside.

"It was a great old home once, wasn't it?" she said, sounding dreamy as she imagined what it must have looked like a hundred years ago. "I wonder what it would take to fix it up?"

John turned to stare at her. "You're not seriously thinking of buying this place, are you?"

She gave him a defiant look. "Maybe I am." Moving to the States would be a big change—but the chupacabras were here, and she wanted to study them.

Lost in thought, she'd wandered from the sitting room into the kitchen and was casually walking around, running her finger along the countertops, imagining how her things would look in there, when her finger touched something. Shining the beam of her flashlight down, she saw that a business card had been left on the counter.

She picked it up. "This is her!" She stared at the photograph of a dark-haired woman. "Clara Parker, with Southern Bayou Real Estate Agency. She must have been showing the house to the man."

John took the card from her and studied it. "This doesn't prove that the body you saw was her."

"It's her, I know it. They must have come out the other evening to look at the house. Brody woke up and killed them both."

"As far as theories go, it's plausible," John admitted. "But I don't think Harris lied about finding only one body. And where's her car?"

"Her car?"

"Yeah. They didn't walk out here."

"Would Brody have taken it?"

John shrugged. "Hell if I know, but if you're right, then we've got another vampire loose in the area. I wonder how many this makes."

No less than fifty vampires filled the old warehouse. Harris wandered among them, unnoticed in the crowd, hoping to find out as much about them as he could.

It had been sheer luck that he'd found this group. After leaving the cemetery the night before, he'd gone back into New Orleans and wandered the streets until dawn, searching for a vampire but finding none. Tonight, he'd done the same thing, only this time, he'd gotten lucky.

He'd picked up the focused thoughts of another Prime in the area. Luckily for him, the thoughts had revolved around finding the very warehouse he now stood in.

He'd counted fifteen Primes in the group. The rest of the vampires were second- and third-generation Progeny in various stages of regression.

The fact that there were other vampires in the area wasn't a surprise to Harris, but he found the sheer number of them unexpected—and daunting. His first thought had been to call John, but then he thought a little reconnaissance might be beneficial.

"You're new here," a male said as he approached, eyeing him with the intelligence of a Prime.

"Yeah. I'm from out of town," Harris replied, deciding it would be better to stick to the truth as much as possible.

The other man looked surprised. "I didn't know there were any of us outside New Orleans."

"We don't have anywhere near the numbers you have."

The Prime smiled and flashed his fangs. "We've got Hurricane Katrina to thank for that. Those of us who stayed behind when the hurricane hit soon found ourselves starving, with no help coming, so we went hunting for our own food. It was easier to hunt at night, when it wasn't so hot, but even then, most of the livestock had either run off or been killed. Then a couple of us found the gargoyle-looking creatures. We'd never seen anything like them, but starving people aren't too picky, and we were determined to eat. That was our mistake."

He shook his head. "I'm not sure how we managed to sneak up on the two creatures, but we did. Brought them back to camp, still alive—we were going to have us an old-fashioned pig roast. We had the fires lit and were trying to figure out how to kill them when all hell broke loose. The creatures went berserk and started attacking us. And it wasn't just those two. Suddenly, the sky was filled with more of those creatures. In less than twenty minutes, it was all over—literally. We were all dead."

"Two days later, you woke up." Harris made it a statement.

"You got it. Sixteen of us—we all woke up with a gnawing hunger and no idea of what had happened. We turned on each other but soon realized that wasn't going to work. Max Caine—the guy over there with the dark hair and scar along the side of his cheek?—decided we needed to get organized. He's a former inmate. He and a few of his buddies escaped when the prison evacuated for the hurricane."

Harris glanced across the opening to check out the man that the Prime had indicated. His arms were muscular and covered with tattoos. Running down his left cheek was a jagged scar. He was busy talking to several other vampires at the moment, but Harris made a mental note to keep an eye on this one. "So Caine took over?"

"Yep. There were five who tried to stop him, but Caine killed them—I mean, really killed them. He stuck his hand through their chests like he was punching through drywall, and ripped out their hearts." The Prime shrugged. "After that, no one felt like going up against him."

"If Caine killed five of you—that would have left eleven," Harris pointed out. "Yet I count fifteen who were killed by the chu . . . creature."

The other Prime stared at him with surprise. "You seem to know more about this than we do," he said. Harris worried the Prime would start asking a lot of questions or draw attention to him, but he didn't.

"You're right. Not long ago, Caine caught another one of those creatures. He tortured it, trying to break its spirit so it would be easier to control. He used humans to tempt it, but once, when the creature killed a human and Caine saw the guy rise up again as a vampire, he decided to put the creature to use. He tracked down a couple of his escaped prison buddies and had the creature convert them. That's where the rest of the fifteen came from." He paused and gave Harris a serious look. "Caine and his buddies don't care who they kill. I tell you, I just don't know where it's going to end."

Harris wondered that, too. Until Brody was caught, John wouldn't consider leaving Jess unprotected, and Harris didn't think he could handle all these vampires by himself. He and John would have to deal with them later.

* * *

John and Jess returned to the cemetery through the woods with John leading the way and keeping a constant vigil for Brody. It made sense to him that the vampire would look for them here.

As soon as they reached the fence around the cemetery, John scanned the entire area, but saw no sign that Brody or any other vampire was nearby.

"Where do you want to set up?" he asked Jess when she came to stand next to him.

She had the flashlight and sent the beam all around as she seemed to look for something in particular. "Do you see her?" she finally asked.

"Who?"

"The pregnant female. I can't see as well as you—do you see her anywhere?"

John searched the area again. "No, I don't," he finally admitted. "She probably found someplace to hide while she has her baby."

He felt Jess's disappointment and for reasons he didn't want to examine too closely, he wanted to make things right. Stretching out his mind, he sought the link with Diablo. When he had it, he formed an image of the pregnant female in his mind. Almost immediately, he received an image through Diablo's eyes of the female lying on the ground behind the large mausoleum.

"This way," he told Jess, taking her hand to keep her from tripping over anything as he led her to the large building.

The odor of damp earth and mildew hit him as he rounded the side of the structure to the more secluded space behind it. There on the ground, as she had appeared in the image, lay the pregnant chupacabra. One look at her and John knew there was something wrong. Her transformation from stone to flesh was not complete.

"What's wrong with her legs," Jess breathed beside him as she played the beam over the chupacabra. "Oh, my God," she gasped, when the beam hit the juncture of the creature's legs where a small stone chupacabra head could be seen. "She must have gone into labor shortly before dawn and the sun came up before she could finish."

John stared at the sight. "You'd think Mother Nature would have this worked out a little better, wouldn't you?" He moved a little closer and noticed that the edges of the transformation were slowly moving down the body as more of the creature turned to flesh.

"I have a feeling there's more to this than we know," he said. "She looks exhausted; like she's been in labor for days instead of hours. She doesn't even have the energy to change back to her living form. See how long it's taking?"

Jess moved forward and John put out a hand to stop her when she would have continued right up to the creature. "Careful," he said. "This isn't the family pet we're dealing with."

"She's not going to hurt me," Jess told him, pulling from his grasp. "She's in too much pain, aren't you, girl?" Her voice took on a gentle soothing tone as she addressed the creature and slowly moved forward. "It's okay. I'm not going to hurt you."

When she was close enough, she stooped next to the female and ran her hand across her shoulder. "Does the position of the baby's head look funny to you?" she asked him after a second.

He wanted to laugh, because everything about this

situation looked unusual to him. "Yes. No. I don't know, Jess. What the hell is it supposed to look like?"

"I don't know," she admitted. "I don't suppose there's a collective memory on this psychic link you have with Diablo, is there? Something you could tap into to see if this is a typical birth or not?"

"Tell me you're kidding." He looked at her again and saw that she was serious.

"Well?" she asked him a minute later.

"Quiet," he told her. "This isn't as easy as making a phone call, you know. I'm working with a primitive system of communication."

The female was panting harder, and Jess knew she was having a hard time catching her breath. It seemed the more she came alive, the more pain she was in.

Jess laid a hand on the creature's shoulder, hoping to offer comfort.

"Okay," John said finally. "As near as I can tell, the baby should be facedown, not up. That's probably what's causing the problem."

"We have to turn it."

"Excuse me?" John stared at her like she was crazy.

"As soon as the transformation to flesh is complete, the baby needs to be turned. You don't have to do it, I will."

At that moment, the female heaved a huge shudder and Jess saw that it was time. Thankfully, the baby had also come to life and now made a series of small mewling noises as it squirmed. The mother raised herself up as much as she could to peer at her baby before turning pleading eyes on Jess.

Jess sidled down until she was at the female's hip. Then, giving John a final look, she reached out her hand

and placed it on the baby chupacabra's head. It squirmed at her touch and let out a pathetic sound. It was all the encouragement Jess needed.

She ran her hand up along the baby's body and then slowly tried to work her hand inside the mother. She immediately discovered the problem. "The mother's pelvis—if that's what it's called in this case—is too narrow. The baby's stuck."

She pulled her hand away and wiped it on her clothes, uncaring if she ruined them. Her thoughts were focused solely on saving the baby.

A noise penetrated her concentration and she looked up at John in alarm, afraid it might be Brody, but John seemed unconcerned. "It's okay. It's only Diablo."

The big male stepped around the corner and walked over to stand by the female. Jess could have sworn that she saw concern in his eyes as the female let her head drop to the ground, unable to hold it up any longer.

Jess swore under her breath. The mother was dying, and if she died before they got the baby delivered, it would die, too. And for all Jess knew, they were working with seconds, not minutes.

"We have to do something," she told John urgently.

She saw him look up and lock gazes with the alpha male. There was some form of communication taking place and John clenched his jaw more tightly. When he turned back to Jess, his expression was grave.

"What is it?"

"Diablo wants to end her suffering," he told her.

"No! What about her baby?"

He shook his head. "I don't think there's anything we can do for it." He glanced down at the small creature only half delivered. "When the mother dies and turns to stone, the baby will, too."

"No. We need to deliver it. Now." She heard the edge of hysteria in her voice and tried to bring her emotions under control.

"Jess, honey. Mother Nature has decided that this birth shouldn't happen. It's survival of the fittest."

Jess looked at the small creature, struggling to get out on its own. Her heart ached for it. "Look at him, John. He's a fighter. He wants to live. If he can't make it on his own, then I'll take care of him."

John's head jerked up. "What?"

"You heard me. I'll take care of him."

"You don't know what you're suggesting."

"John, please. I'm begging you." She turned to look at him, silently pleading with him to understand.

It seemed like he studied her face forever. Then he swore quietly and turned to look at Diablo. "Okay," he said after several seconds. "Let's see if we can deliver this baby.

She gave him a grateful smile. "Thank you—but how?"

John gave her a sad smile. "There's only one way." Then everything happened at once. The alpha male swooped down and clamped his mouth around the female's neck, holding her in place as her body spasmed briefly and then grew still. In that second, John grabbed the sword and in a movement so precise it could only have been executed by a changeling, he split open the female's abdomen.

Chapter 15

Suddenly, the baby chupacabra burst free and Jessica fell back with the wet, warm, squirming baby landing on her chest. She looked at it and found it staring down at her, its small eyes blinking, no doubt trying to bring this strange new world into focus.

Jessica knew she'd never experienced anything like this before. As she gazed upon the small alien-looking head with its tiny front fangs barely large enough to be seen and small wings that looked like a couple of badly folded umbrellas stuck to its back, a wave of maternal protectiveness welled up inside her.

"Hey," she protested when John plucked the baby off her. "What are you doing?"

"I'm letting his mother see him," he replied tersely, "before she dies."

Instantly regretting her tone, Jess got to her feet. The mother hadn't moved, but other chupacabras were appearing, gathering around, just as they had the other night for the hurt male. Jess even recognized Harris's chupacabra standing nearby.

The baby perched awkwardly by his mother, and she made an effort to caress him with her tongue. She quickly fell back and the baby, perhaps sensing his mother was dying, licked her face instead.

It wasn't fair, Jess thought as a lump lodged in her throat. No child should have to grow up without his—or her—mother. Tears gathered in her eyes as she wondered if she'd made a mistake insisting that they deliver the baby. Its chances for survival without its mother weren't good, and from what little she'd learned from Lanie in their brief chat about Gem, it could be decades before this baby was big enough to fend for himself.

Just then, there was a subtle shift in the atmosphere. Jess didn't know what it was until she looked down and saw that the mother had passed. Gradually, as with the male, her skin hardened and turned to stone.

The process took several minutes, but when it was complete the other chupacabras dispersed into the night, until only Harris's chupacabra and Diablo remained.

Jess stepped forward, resolute in her decision to take care of the baby, when John put out a hand to stop her.

"What?" she asked, confused.

"I know you wanted to take care of him, but it seems there's another option." He gestured to Harris's chupacabra. "This is Lucy. You may have seen her before with Harris, but what you might not know is that this is also Gem's mother. Harris told me that she was forced to give up Gem before she'd finished raising her, and I think she might like having another baby to raise." He looked over at the alpha male. "Diablo will protect him."

When she didn't say anything, he went on. "I know you want to do what's best for the baby, Jess, and I think this is it. Let them care for him. You couldn't have taken him back to England, and if you buy that manor and move here, well, then you'll be able to see him every day."

She didn't like it, but she didn't argue because deep down inside, she knew he was right.

"Come on," he said. "Let's go home." He put his hand at the small of her back and guided her out of the cemetery.

Neither spoke much as they walked. Jess didn't know if John's silence was because he was mad at her for forcing the birth or because, with dawn rapidly approaching, he was tired.

"Are you hungry?" she asked once they reached the mansion. "I could make us something to eat." She wasn't hungry herself, so when he refused her offer, she didn't push.

Together, they went inside and climbed the stairs.

"Good night, Jess."

"Good night." She felt unexpectedly disappointed when he headed straight for his room, though she couldn't blame him. She'd been totally sincere the night before when she'd told him that she wanted her first time to be with him. Every time she was near him, her body hummed in anticipation, and the more time she spent with him, the more she wanted to be with him—half-vampire or not.

What was really bad was that she thought her feelings for him might be more than just physical attraction, and now she'd never get to find out because she'd pushed him away. She'd rejected him because of her own fears and doubts, not because of anything he'd done.

Tears of self-pity welled in her eyes and threatened to spill. Not wanting John to turn and see her crying, she ducked into the bathroom as she passed the open door.

"Jess?"

She hurried to shut the door, imagining him walking back toward her. "I'm in here. I . . . wanted to shower before going to my room."

"Oh. Okay."

She waited, barely breathing as she listened. She heard his footsteps continue down the hall, growing faint. After several seconds of quiet, she turned and started the shower water.

A few minutes later, she stood under a hot shower, letting the water pound her sore muscles even as it warmed her. It felt so good that she was tempted to stand there forever—or at least until she ran out of hot water. As a yawn stole over her, she reluctantly turned off the water and got out to dry off.

When she was ready to go back to her room, she wrapped the towel around her and opened the bathroom door. The hallway was empty and John's door was closed. He was probably already fast asleep, she thought.

Burying the disappointment, she went to her room and opened the door.

Her name, scrawled across the far wall in blood, was the first thing to jump out at her. Then the rest of the room came into focus. The sheets and mattress of the bed were sliced to shreds. Her clothes were scattered about the room, and the dresser drawers stood open with handfuls of her bras and panties spilling out. Even from where she stood, she saw a bloody handprint. An image of Brody holding her clothes to his nose, as he had her jacket, flashed through her head. Feeling sick, she had to look away. That was when she saw the small animal carcass at the base of the wall, tossed there after its blood had been used to write her name.

At that moment, the sheers over the window billowed as if someone stood behind them and fear, raw and primitive, took over. She screamed and raced from the room, straight into John's arms. "Jess? What's the matter?"

"He was here," she gasped, trying to catch her breath. "Brody was in my room."

He started for the door, but she held on to him. "No, don't go in there. He might still be there."

"I fucking hope so," he snarled as he pulled her arms from around his waist and pushed her toward his room. "Go inside and lock the door."

"No, John," she pleaded. "I don't want to be alone."

"I'll be right back." He pushed her into the room and she was left staring at the door when he pulled it closed after him.

Still wearing the towel, she wrapped her arms around herself, unable to move from the spot. Brody's single-minded pursuit of her was unlike anything she'd experienced before. If it had simply been a matter of him hunting her, she could have understood that. She'd hunted enough vampires to occasionally have one come after her, but this was different. If Brody ever caught her, she had no doubt that he'd kill her, but it was what he'd do to her first that terrified her. Brody was a twisted, demented creature.

She seemed to wait forever, in that one spot, but finally the door to the room opened and John walked in.

"You were supposed to lock this," he chastised her as

she rushed forward and threw herself into his arms. They closed around her and held her tightly. "It's okay," he said, speaking into her hair as he dipped his head close to hers. "You're not hurt, are you?"

"No." Her eyes were closed and she spoke into his chest because she didn't want to move. "But he was in my room."

"I know, that son of a bitch, but he's gone now. I checked everywhere. And he won't come back while the sun is up."

He held her for a long time before setting her away from him so he could look into her face. His heated gaze raked over her and she finally remembered that she was wearing only a towel.

"Let's get you some clothes," he offered, his voice sounding a little rough.

They both glanced in the direction of her room. "I'm not putting on anything that he's touched."

"No, no. Of course not." John sounded like he wasn't sure what to do. Then he walked over to his duffel bag, sitting on the floor by the dresser, and dug through the contents. Finally he pulled out one of his T-shirts. "Here, you can wear this," he said, handing it to her.

She took it and then waited for him to turn around so she could slip it on. "Thank you," she said when she was finished. "You can turn back around."

He did, but from the way he looked at her, she felt more exposed than she had a few minutes earlier wearing just the towel. He looked away, with effort it seemed, and crossed the room to the undisturbed bed. As she watched, he pulled back the covers. "You can sleep here tonight."

She moved to the side of the bed because he seemed to expect her to, but she was fairly certain she wouldn't be sleeping any time soon. Her nerves were strung tight and fear stole her dignity. "Will you stay with me?" When he seemed uncertain, she rushed on. "I don't want to be alone."

"I don't think that's such a good idea."

A feeling of complete mortification washed over her. "Of course. I'm sorry." She took a step back, knowing she was mumbling to fill the awkward silence. "I shouldn't have asked."

She backed away, so rattled that she couldn't seem to put two thoughts together.

"Jess—"

"No, please," she interrupted, holding up her hand to stop him. She gave a self-mocking half laugh. "This is rather embarrassing." She backed up a few more steps and he followed after her. She wanted to run away, but found that she'd backed up too far and the bed now blocked her escape.

"Jess—" He tried to speak again.

"No, really, I understand," she insisted, knowing she sounded bitter. She opened her mouth but snapped it shut again, not wanting to make an even bigger fool of herself.

"What do you think you understand?" John asked, standing before her so he filled her field of vision, his masculinity teasing her unfairly.

"That you're no longer interested because last night I"—she waved a hand, not knowing what the right word was—"I freaked out on you."

He nodded as if agreeing with her description. "You thought I was going to bite you."

"Yes." She breathed out the word in a rush, grateful that he seemed to understand.

"And that scared you."

"Yes."

"Because I'm half-vampire."

"Yes; no." She heaved a sigh. "Yes, but not for the reasons you think. When I was five, I saw my mother killed before my eyes by a vampire. He bit her neck and drained the life from her before coming to do the same to me. If Erik hadn't stopped him, I would have died, too. I still have nightmares about that night, and when I felt your fangs along my neck, I thought you might be getting ready to bite me, and after Brody's attack . . . I got scared."

"You're right to be scared," he told her solemnly. "But not because I might bite you. No matter how badly I might want to, I wouldn't. Not unless you told me it was okay. No, what you should be afraid of is how I feel about you." He rubbed his temple as if his head hurt. "When I'm with you, it's all I can do not to touch you. I want to hold you in my arms so bad, I ache with the need. Standing this close to you, knowing that you have on nothing but *my* shirt—it's killing me. I want to make love to you until we're too exhausted to move, and *then* I want to hold you while we both fall asleep."

His words left her breathless. Encouraged, she reached for him, but he stepped back quickly and her hand fell awkwardly to her side. Frustrated and confused, she looked at him for an explanation.

"Before we start anything, be sure you're willing to finish it because I don't want a repeat of last night. I don't think I could take it."

"I'm sure." Still holding his gaze, she pulled off her T-shirt and let it fall to the floor. "Make love to me, John."

"Damn it, Jess," he choked out in a strangled voice as he grabbed her to him. His mouth came down on hers with such powerful insistence that she instantly erupted into a raging inferno of need and desire.

He kissed her like he wanted to devour her, and she responded just as hungrily. Her arms snaked around his neck as she pressed her body against his. The fabric of his shirt and pants, scraping across sensitized skin, sent chills through her body.

She quickly lost all sense of time and place, aware only of the things John was doing to her; of the sensations he stirred within her. As she tried to ease the tension building deep inside, she was barely aware of John picking her up and laying her on the bed. He stripped off his clothes in a blur of movement, and before she had time to really notice she was alone, he was there with her, nude and fully aroused.

He kissed her again, and the emotional torrent inside her that had started to calm raged out of control once more. Then he stopped kissing her so he could use his mouth and tongue to lick a trail down her throat while his hand found and cupped her breast. He massaged its fullness and then, taking her hardened nipple between his thumb and finger, he rolled it. Sparks of pleasure shot straight through her and she squirmed, wanting more.

When he lowered his head and took her nipple into his mouth, she arched into him. Still it wasn't enough. She ground her hips against his erection until he groaned aloud.

He wedged his knees between her legs, opening them until he was positioned between them. The head of his shaft probed the tender flesh and she raised her hips, inviting him in.

"Now, John," she gasped, the tension inside her demanding what only he could give. "Oh, please," she cried. "I need you—now!"

He plowed into her. She was already wet, and the sensation of him filling her sent short spasms through her body. When he pulled out and slowly entered her again, she thought she'd die from the sheer pleasure of it, aware of his fullness sliding inside her swollen flesh. Their breathing came harder as his tempo increased, carrying them both closer to their release.

Using one arm against the bed to hold his weight, he wrapped the other under her hips to hold her in place as he pumped into her until she came close to shattering.

"Jess?" His question came out on a ragged breath, but she knew that he needed to hear her reassurance.

"Yes, John. Yes." Awash in sensation, she rode the wave of passion until it grew so huge, there was no place left for it to go and it crashed over her, drowning her in a glorious fireburst of emotion. Seconds later, she felt John tense and knew when she heard his guttural cry that he'd found his own release.

As the euphoria slowly faded, John rolled to his side and gathered her into his arms.

"Wow," he said, sounding awed. "That was incredible." He pulled her a little closer.

Already feeling sated and safe in his arms, his words filled her with joy and contentment. She knew that in

John, she'd found what she'd been looking for her entire life. "Good night, John," she whispered. "I love you."

The steady rhythm of his breathing was the only response she got.

John came awake suddenly. There was no gradual lifting of the mental fog that accompanies deep sleep. One moment, he was sound asleep, and the next, he was awake with senses alert—and he was alone.

There was no nagging sense of urgency to which he could attribute his waking, so he stretched his senses outward, trying to see if he could locate Jess. He heard her working in her lab downstairs and felt himself relax. She was okay.

Cracking open an eyelid, he had to cover his eyes to protect them from the sunshine streaming in through the windows. He hadn't realized he'd awakened so much earlier than normal. It was still hours from sunset and yet he felt amazingly good. If he'd taken Jess's blood, he would have attributed the surge of energy to that, but since he hadn't, there could only be one explanation—and that one scared the hell out of him.

John rolled out of bed and looked for his jeans, finding them on the floor near the bed. Next he went to where his jacket hung over a chair and dug out his sunglasses and put them on. The relief to his eyes was immediate and he finished dressing.

After going downstairs, he followed the aroma of freshly brewed coffee to the kitchen and poured himself a cup. Then he went to find Jess.

The workroom door was open and Jess was standing at a table with her back to him, so John let his gaze travel over her, enjoying the view. She was wearing a pair of his sweats, which were too big and hid her shape, but his body knew what lay beneath.

"Good afternoon," he said softly, not wanting to startle her as he walked up behind her. He set his cup on the counter and slipped his arms around her waist, pulling her back against him. He nuzzled her neck, enjoying the scent of her skin, which was a blend of soap and woman.

She smiled, tilting her head to the side to give him better access. "What are you doing up so early? Not that I'm complaining."

"I missed you." As soon as the words left his mouth, he wished he could take them back. The last thing he wanted her to think was that he was a lovesick fool.

She set down whatever it was she'd been holding in her hand and turned in his arms so she could face him. Lifting her arms to drape them around his neck, she gazed up at him with such longing that it took his breath away. He lowered his mouth until his lips captured hers.

Holding her, touching her this way, was like coming home after a very long and lonely journey. If he'd felt this way with his first wife, he never would have gotten a divorce. The feelings he had for Jess ran deeper than any he'd had before, and he was suddenly unclear about the future.

He broke the kiss, but didn't take his arms from around her.

"I like this," he told her.

"Me, too."

He studied her face and saw that she was telling him the truth and his worries faded. "Since I'm awake, how about you and I go upstairs right now?" He winked and dipped his head to nuzzle her neck.

She laughed and he loved the sound of it. "Later. First I want to show you what I've been working on. I made something for you."

"Really?"

"Yes—come see." She stepped out of his embrace, took his hand, and led him to the worktable where she picked up something small and held it out to him.

"Looks like a bullet."

"Not just any bullet." She pointed to it. "I found extra boxes of bullets in your room and thought I'd take a look. When I saw they had hollow tips, I got an idea. See here at the end, I've filled the cavity with a concentrated toxin and dripped candle wax over the end to seal it."

He glanced from the bullet in his hand to the table where several more boxes of bullets sat open. "What's in the toxin?"

"It's a combination of ingredients, the primary one being a concentrated solution of the *fleur de vivre* herb."

"I thought you didn't have any."

"None in tea form. This stuff is too concentrated to ingest."

He nodded. "And one of these will kill a vampire?" He was already imagining the possibilities.

"In theory."

He'd been staring at the bullet, but now looked at her sharply. "In theory?"

She cringed and made a face. "I haven't exactly had a chance to test them yet," she admitted.

"Why not?"

She glared at him. "It's rather difficult to secure a gun in England, in case you hadn't heard about the ban on purchasing and owning guns. Up until now, this has simply been a theory of mine."

John shook his head. "I'm not going after Brody with bullets that might not even work."

"No, I completely agree," she said, stepping away from him and becoming unusually focused on straightening the counter. "We need to test them, which means we'll need a vampire."

"Exactly. And where do you propose we get one?"

She refused to look at him as he drew the obvious conclusion.

"Harris?" John stared at her. "Please tell me you're joking."

"No, I realize it's not the ideal solution. He's been helpful and I don't think he's entirely bad, but I'm not entirely sure he's trustworthy either. After all, he did try to kill Mac and Lanie."

"He also helped Beth and Dirk escape."

"Only because he was counting on Beth doing research for him."

"What are you talking about?"

"She told me how he wanted her to develop a cure for vampirism. When you think about it, he only let her go because it served his purpose. What's to say he's not using you in the same way?"

John felt himself getting angry, but Jess didn't seem to notice. "You're unbelievable, you know that? To actually have the audacity to suggest killing him?"

"He kills people in order to survive. That's not exactly heroic," she said, as if she were explaining an obvious concept to a simpleton.

"He kills *criminals.* People who are human only as a

technicality." His voice grew louder. "But more important, he's a friend of mine."

She threw up her hands. "You're trying to rationalize his murders?"

"I wish all this was more black and white, but it's not. So I have to play by the rules that let me face myself in the mirror each day. In this case, that means letting Harris live because in my book, he's one of the good guys."

A moment of silence followed his statement as she stared at the floor. In a last desperate attempt to save what they had, he reached out to her. "Jess, I'm begging you to understand."

She looked up at him, her eyes filled with unshed tears. "I do understand," she said, leaning forward to kiss him, a gentle touch of her lips against his. It was over before it even started. "I just hope, for your sake, that you're right about him. Now, if you don't mind, I think I need a bit of fresh air—alone."

She started for the door. Though his first instinct was to tell her not to go, he realized he was being unreasonable. It was still daylight outside.

"Do me a favor and don't wander far from the house, okay? And the moment you see the sun going down, you get back inside. I don't think Brody will come back while we're both here, but I could be wrong. Let's not make it easier for him, all right?"

"Yes. Fine."

He watched her walk out of the room, and it took all his control not to go after her.

Jess felt like screaming as she paced the length of the porch, giving vent to her anger and frustration. She was an idiot. She'd gotten up early and like a lovesick fool, sat in bed just gazing down at John while he slept beside her. The mere sight of him called forth the memories of their lovemaking and her heart sped up. It had been all she could do not to rouse him then and there to make love.

But they needed to base their relationship on more than great sex, and something like a difference in viewpoints regarding Harris might be enough to create a chasm so large they could never get over it.

A cool breeze blew across the porch, reminding her that she'd left her jacket inside. There was no way she was going inside to get it. Wrapping her arms about herself, she started walking a leisurely lap around the mansion, hoping the exercise would help her think even as it warmed her. She was just rounding the corner to the front when she heard the sound of a vehicle coming down the driveway.

She waited as a floral delivery van pulled up and stopped in front of her.

The driver rolled down his window and smiled. "Afternoon, ma'am. I have a special delivery for Miss Jessica Winslow?"

"I'm Jessica Winslow," she said, her anger with John vanishing instantly. The flowers had to be from him. No one else had a reason to send her flowers. She didn't know when he'd ordered them—or why—but his thoughtfulness was touching.

"You'll need to sign for them," the driver said, getting out of the van. He opened the side panel of his truck, reached in and pulled out a clipboard. After checking the list, he held it out to her, indicating which line required her signature. "Right there," he said, holding out a pen.

She took the clipboard and signed her name while he returned to the van for her flowers. When she was finished, she walked the clipboard over and stood waiting.

When he turned to take it from her, he was holding an aerosol can in his hand. Bewildered, Jess could only stare as he depressed the nozzle and a fine mist hit her in the face.

Immediately, her eyes began to sting and tears welled up, blinding her so badly she couldn't see. Everything took on the perception of the surreal, and she couldn't tell if hands were actually grabbing her or she was imagining it.

Then her world tilted off kilter.

A humming noise started in her head, getting increasingly louder, almost blocking out the sound of the van's side panel sliding back. She didn't know if she blacked out, but the next thing she knew, she was lying on the cold hard metal of the van's floor, listening to the faint crunch of gravel beneath the tires.

Then her mind completely fogged over and she sank into icy black oblivion.

Chapter 16

John had Jess's mattress wedged partway out the back door when he heard a noise that caused him to stop and listen. He waited a second or two, but it didn't come again.

Unable to ease his worry—and looking for an excuse to be with Jessica again—he shoved the mattress aside and went to the front of the house to find her. He arrived just in time to see a van disappearing down the driveway.

Knowing instantly that Jess was in that van, he raced for his rental car, grateful his keys, wallet, and cell phone were still in his jeans. Within seconds, he was barreling down the gravel drive.

When he reached the road, he stopped, wondering which way they'd gone. It took only a second to notice the traces of dust hanging in the air. John turned into the dust and accelerated, hoping he wasn't too far behind the vehicle because if they turned off the road before he caught up, he'd never know it. He'd never see Jess again—at least, not alive.

It seemed as if he drove for hours, but ten minutes up the road, he caught sight of a van a short distance ahead. He kept his speed constant, wanting to get close enough to get a better look at it, but not wanting to alert the driver.

He saw the floral company logo and phone number on the windowless back door and pulled out his cell phone. Letting the van gain a short lead, he dialed the number of the floral company.

His conversation with the woman on the phone was short and to the point. Yes, they had a van with the license plate number that John recited to her. She was reluctant to give him any more information until he identified himself as a cop. Then she became a fount of information.

The flowers had been purchased with cash the night before, to be delivered to Jessica Winslow. The woman on the phone remembered the transaction because she'd handled it herself. The man who'd paid for the flowers had been blond and good-looking; classy, like he came from money, but there'd been something odd about him. She had a nose for that kind of thing, she explained to him. She couldn't tell him much about the driver of the van. He was new and she'd never worked with him before.

John thanked her and hung up the phone. The blond could only have been Brody, and John kicked himself for underestimating Brody's resourcefulness.

For nearly an hour, John followed the van around New Orleans. In his solitary focus on Jess and her safety, he'd forgotten that the Mardi Gras celebrations were in full swing. Many of the streets were blocked off for this evening's parade and festivities, but the van seemed to know where it was going and John was able to keep it in sight.

Finally, they reached the French Quarter just as the sun began to set. John watched the van turn down a back alley and, not wanting to be too obvious about following it, drove slowly past the alley's entrance. When he did, he saw the men in the van getting out. There were no open parking spots ahead, so he double-parked his car and got out.

Hurrying back to the alley on foot, he looked around the corner and saw that it was empty except for the van. He slowly rounded the corner and headed toward it, approaching from the side. He made sure to stay hidden from the mirrors, just in case anyone had stayed inside.

Hearing no sounds, he moved closer. Thoughts of Jess, bound and gagged—or worse, unconscious and bleeding to death—spurred him to hurry.

Still there was no sound from inside the van. Bracing himself, he reached out and grabbed the door handle, pulling up on it. To his surprise, it was unlocked and at his tug, the van door swung open.

John ducked out of the way, expecting gunfire, but there was nothing. After a second of no sound or movement, he risked a look in the back.

The van was empty.

He conducted a quick visual search, looking for any clue as to where they'd taken her. They couldn't have gone far. John surveyed the buildings around him and noticed that the ones on either side were standing derelict and empty. He listened, hoping to hear something, anything, to help him. From a few blocks away, the sound of music and revelers could be heard. Here in the dark alley, though, it was hard to imagine the party taking place elsewhere.

The sun was a large, sinking orange ball in the sky, but it was dark enough now that John no longer needed his sunglasses. He pulled them off and shoved them into his pocket, then used his cell phone to dial Harris's number. The vampire had not yet risen and John got his voice mail.

"I think they have Jess," he said and quickly explained what had happened and where he was. He hung up, trusting Harris would check his messages at his first opportunity.

Putting his phone away, he picked the building closest to the van as the one to search, reasoning that since the driver didn't know he was being followed, he would logically park close to his final destination. After all, Jess had been taken in broad daylight, which meant her abductors were human. They wouldn't be likely to carry an unconscious victim very far if it wasn't necessary.

John studied the building. In its day, about seventy years ago, he guessed, it had no doubt been the place to live. He could imagine the hustle of busy lives that took place within its walls. The only things there now were the ghosts from the past.

There was a back door to the building less than three feet from the van and when John tried the handle, it opened easily. He went inside and though it was pitch black, he had no trouble seeing.

He stared at the floor, hoping to see footprints on an otherwise dusty and unused floor. No such luck. There had been enough traffic through this door recently that there was no dust to disturb, but that, in itself, was a good sign.

Continuing down the hall, his ears strained to hear every sound, hoping to catch Jess's voice.

There was no basement in this building, like there might have been in a similar building up north, so John started on the ground floor and systematically went into each room.

When he found the stairs, he took them up to the second floor. There, he stopped before he reached the top so he could listen, but heard nothing. He stepped into the corridor and began his search, staying alert for any sign of danger.

He found Jess in the second to last room on the right, lying off to the side, her hands and feet bound with rope and a gag in her mouth. Seeing her like that infuriated him, but what really frightened him was how still she lay. He didn't know if she was alive or dead.

Looking around, he saw that the room was otherwise empty, so he hurried to her side and knelt. Placing two fingers against her neck, he felt for a pulse and breathed a little easier when he noticed the rise and fall of her chest. She was alive—and her pulse was rapid, but strong.

"Jess, honey, can you hear me?" He shook her, wondering what they'd used to knock her out. She stirred slightly at his touch, but didn't open her eyes. He untied the gag and then undid the knots tying her hands and feet together. By the time he finished, she was starting to wake up.

When she finally opened her eyes and looked around, she seemed to have a hard time focusing.

"Jess?"

At the sound of his voice, she jumped and pushed herself away from him, fear clearly written across her face.

"Jess, honey, it's okay. It's me, John."

"John?" Her speech was slurred and she looked all around her. "John, I can't see you. I can't see anything."

At first, he was alarmed, but then he realized the problem. "The room's dark, Jess, that's why you can't see anything. Take my hand." He reached out and took her hand in his. "Come on. We need to get out of here."

He pulled her to her feet, but she had a hard time standing and he had to hold her to keep her from falling.

"I don't feel very good," she mumbled. "I'm so dizzy." She leaned to the side and he had to force her upright, his concern growing.

"Do you remember anything?"

"There was a . . ." Her voice trailed off and she was silent for so long that John wondered if she'd forgotten her train of thought. "A van," she finally said.

"That's right," he prodded her. "A flower van."

She giggled. "No, silly. It wasn't made of flowers."

She sounded almost drunk, and he hoped the drugs they'd used would wear off soon. "Jess, do you remember who was driving the van?"

"A bad man. Three bad men." She sounded like a pouting child. "They hurt me. Stuck me with something."

"Come on," he told her. "We're getting out of here."

He half carried her to the door and then paused briefly to listen before moving out into the hallway.

"Stop," Jess moaned. "I think I'm going to be—"

John turned her away from him and wrapped one arm around her waist to hold her while he used the other to grab a mass of her hair to keep it out of the way as she bent forward and threw up. When she was finished, he pulled her back away from the mess and waited as she rested her head against his chest. She raised a shaky hand to her head and rubbed her forehead, taking deep, steadying breaths. "I'm sorry," she said, sounding more like herself.

"Do you think you can walk?"

"I don't know. Everything is still spinning for me." She kept one hand pressed against the wall as she held herself upright and took a tentative step. While John wouldn't have said she was exactly steady on her feet, she was better. When they reached the steps, he more or less carried her.

Down at the bottom, about to head out the same way he'd come in, John stopped. He'd caught the distinct sound of voices coming from that direction. He put his finger to her lips and waited until she nodded her understanding, then he pulled her quickly down the hall in the other direction.

He located the front door of the building just as a shout and running footsteps told him that they'd been discovered.

Hurrying toward it, he saw as they got closer that it was boarded up from the outside. He let go of Jess's hand and ran full out. Right before he reached the door, he launched himself into the air, flying feetfirst and broke through it with a loud crashing noise.

He looked back and saw Jess standing awkwardly where he'd left her. He hoped the drugs in her system had already hit their peak effectiveness. If not, the amount of running they were about to do would have them pumping through her system in no time, amplifying their effect.

Fortunately, the streets and sidewalks were filled with revelers and the noise of the festivities filled the night. John pulled Jess forward, wanting to get lost in the moving crowd of costumed partiers. A jazz band was playing as its members walked down the street. They were followed by a succession of decorated floats.

John pushed Jess ahead of him as he fought through the crowds, occasionally looking behind him. Aside from the rising level of noise, he was aware of a buzzing in his head and the overwhelming sense of danger closing in on him.

They'd just reached a particularly large group of revelers when John felt the bite of a mosquito on his neck. He swatted at it, annoyed, and didn't give it another thought until his vision started to narrow and cloud over.

He stared ahead of him, at Jess, struggling to push her way through the crowd. He reached out to grab her shoulder, but his hand moved in slow motion and he watched her disappear into the swirling mass of colors.

The ringing in his ears grew louder as his vision faded to black and the noise around him drifted into silence.

Jess fought to keep calm. She didn't know what drugs she'd been given, but they distorted her vision and balance enough that she had a hard time functioning. It was like she was inebriated, which was possibly why no one seemed to notice. She was just one drunk among thousands.

She pushed past someone, feeling the need to hurry, to get away. Her memory was starting to come back, but the images were distorted and confusing. She remembered a van and a huge flower spraying something in her face.

A man ran into her, causing her to stumble. She reached out, trying to grab John's hand for support, only to find herself fanning open air. She looked back. John wasn't there. In fact, he wasn't anywhere.

Panic hit as she looked all around and realized she was alone in a crowd of strangers. Her vision was still fuzzy and she strained to focus on the faces around her because she knew that John wouldn't just leave her. He wouldn't.

She turned around several times, the effort making her dizzy. She stumbled and would have fallen, only there was no room to fall. There were too many people surrounding her. When the costumed merrymakers surged forward, she was carried along with them.

Then, the flash of a face in the crowd caught her attention. She searched again to find it, replaying the image in her mind—glowing red eyes, fangs peeking out from beneath parted lips. A vampire!

She twisted around, searching all the faces. There were too many innocent lives at risk. She had to find it—and kill it.

Then she saw the man in black, walking not too far from her. Something about him seemed wrong and she waited for him to turn her way. When he did, their gazes locked. He smiled and she saw the fangs.

At first, she didn't know what to do. The music was playing so loud, she could hardly think. Around her, everyone's image wavered like they were passing before a funhouse mirror.

Jess knew she had to act. She had the skill and training to kill a vampire, even under the influence of whatever drug she'd been injected with.

A man eating a sausage-on-a-stick stepped up beside her, temporarily blocking her view of the vampire. As she tried to see around him, her gaze fell on the food. As the crowd surged forward, she grabbed the sausage from his hand and disappeared before he could stop her.

When she knew she was safe, she used her fingers to remove the sausage and stared at the sharp stick she was left holding. It wasn't the ideal weapon, but she was short on options.

Now she was ready to do what needed to be done. She

would find the vampire and before she killed him, she would find out what he'd done to John.

Clutching the stick in her hand, she moved into the crowd. Up ahead, she spotted the vampire and moved toward him. She was only a few feet away when he glanced back and saw her. Again, he smiled and she saw the fangs. Surprisingly, he didn't try to run from her, but turned back to whatever he'd been watching earlier.

She moved right up to him and pressed the stick against his back, applying enough pressure to get his attention.

There was a surprised expression on his face when he looked down at her.

"Over there," she said, gesturing to the side with her head.

He nodded and did as she asked. Thankfully, despite how crowded the streets were, no one seemed to pay them any attention and Jess directed the vampire to the nearest alley.

"I don't know what it is you want, lady—," the vampire began, but Jess didn't give him a chance to finish. She kicked the back of his knee and he fell to the ground with a cry.

Before he could do anything, she was on him with the pointed end of the stick pressed painfully into his back. "Where is he?"

"Where is who?" the vampire asked, his faked innocence making Jess furious.

"Listen, you fucking bloodsucker, I want to know what you did with John. Tell me, now."

"Jess," a familiar voice said quietly behind her. She

looked over her shoulder and squinted to bring the face into focus. "Harris!"

"John called me," he said calmly. "He said you were in trouble; that you had been kidnapped."

"Something happened to John. He was with me in the crowd and then he just disappeared. I think this vampire knows something about it."

"No, man, I don't," the vampire said urgently. "You gotta help me. She's nuts."

"Shut up," Jess said, applying more pressure. Blood welled up where the stick punctured the skin, soaking into the fabric of his shirt. Jess told herself to be careful not to stake him before she got the information she wanted.

"Jess, you don't want to hurt him."

"You're wasting your breath," she growled. She dug her knee into the vampire's back a little harder, until he cried out. "Tell me where John is."

"I don't know," the vampire cried. "Please, lady, I'd tell you if I did. I don't even know who John is."

"Jess!" Harris shouted. "You're making a mistake."

Jess snorted in disgust. He'd shown his true colors at last, trying to save one of his own. Well, she'd deal with him next. Knowing she'd get nothing more from the vampire, she raised her hand, gripping the stick as tightly as she could and brought it down—hard.

Chapter 17

Before the stick met flesh, Jess was hit by something powerful that knocked her off the vampire and pinned her to the ground. She immediately began fighting for her life. Whoever attacked her, though, was stronger and faster. Too soon, the stake was ripped from her fist and she was forcibly subdued.

Fighting the panic at being rendered so helpless, she glared up at her attacker and saw Harris holding her. "I should have known you'd save one of your own," she spit out.

"No," he replied with a patience that sounded forced. "I'm trying to save a *human* life."

She opened her mouth, but he cut her off. "Don't argue with me," he said sharply. "Look at him." Suddenly, he was off and jerking her up to stand beside him, but not releasing her hands. "Look. At. Him," he commanded again. When she refused to cooperate, he shook her until she felt like he'd scrambled her brains.

Too dizzy to disobey, she looked at the other vampire. Slowly, his face came into focus, but instead of the bright red glow of vampire eyes, she saw bloodshot blue eyes, bright from unshed tears and staring at her in terror. Her gaze fell to his mouth, where a pair of plastic vampire fangs dangled, nearly bitten in half. Slowly, reality returned. She had almost killed a human.

The horror of what she'd almost done hit her, paralyzing her with its sheer magnitude until she could hardly breathe, let alone stand.

Harris, as if sensing this, lowered her gently to the ground and walked over to the man.

"I'm sorry, sir. My cousin isn't well." He pulled several of the crisp hundred-dollar bills John had given him earlier from his pocket and held them out to the man. "There's enough here to cover any medical costs as well as a little extra to compensate you for the, uh, inconvenience."

The man, now sensing he had the upper hand, bowed up. "I'm going to have your cousin arrested, and then, I'm dragging her ass to court. This," he said, snatching the bills from Harris's hand, "ain't enough for what I've been through."

Harris agreed, but he didn't have time to negotiate with him because of all the things Jessica had said, crazy as they sounded, the part about John going missing bothered him the most. If there was one thing he knew about John, it was that there was no way he'd have left Jessica alone, especially when she was clearly in a bad way.

He grabbed the man's hand and, using some of his vampire strength, forced the fist closed around the money as he stared into the man's face. His vision bled to red and he watched, with satisfaction, as the other man's eyes widened. Then, in a move too fast for the man to follow,

Harris reached into the man's back pants pocket and pulled out his wallet.

He flipped it open and read the license before closing it and handing it back. "I think my offer is more than generous, don't you agree, Steve Lambkin of 3485 Chisholm Lane?" He gave the man a very unpleasant smile that showed off the tips of his fangs. "But if you're not satisfied, I'll be happy to come to your home, personally, to discuss further—arrangements. Would you like for me to do that, Steve?"

"No, no," Steve said nervously.

Harris nodded. "Okay. Then I guess our business is concluded. You should probably run along."

The man nodded and beat a hasty path out of the alley.

Alone now with a woman who seemed to hate him, Harris turned to look at Jessica where she sat, still stunned. He walked over and squatted beside her, but didn't say anything.

"If you hadn't stopped me, I would have killed that man." Her voice was barely above a whisper. She shivered and rubbed her arms with her hands.

"It was the drugs."

She blew out a breath of air. "We both know that doesn't matter. I almost killed him. If you hadn't stopped me . . ." She looked up at him. "I know you didn't do it for me, but thank you."

"I bet that was hard to say."

She gave him a pensive look. "Not as hard as I would have thought."

So many retorts sprang to Harris's mind, both petty and magnanimous, that he decided to let them all pass. "You said John was with you earlier?"

"Yes. He found me in a building." She looked around. "I'm not sure which one. We escaped into the parade." She rubbed her head. "Things are still a little vague, but one minute, he was behind me, and then the next, he was gone. I tried to look for him, but . . ." She took a deep breath. "I don't think I imagined him, and I know he would never leave me like that. I think something's happened to him, only I don't know what."

"Can you stand?"

"Yes, I think so."

He reached down a hand and after a moment's hesitation, she took it and let him pull her to her feet.

"How will we find him?"

She spoke so softly that Harris wasn't sure if she was talking to him or herself. He answered her anyway. "I guess we'll retrace your escape and maybe search the building where you were held. That might give us some clues. I just think we should get out of here, in case Steve comes back with the police."

She nodded and Harris considered taking her elbow to escort her, but thought better of it. He didn't need to have her cringe from his touch to feel rejected.

They started walking through the crowd and Harris, who had left Lucy back at the chupa colony, sent a probe along their shared link to make sure that the creatures were all right and Brody hadn't been seen in the area.

The response from Lucy shocked him.

He focused on the image she sent and after some effort, it came clear.

"Shit." He reached out and grabbed Jessica by the elbow and steered her away from the crowd of people.

"What's the matter?" she asked.

"I know where John is."

"What?" Her face lit with anxiety. "Where?"

"Brody has him. Back at the cemetery."

John came to slowly, feeling like his entire body was weighed down. The pressure in his head made thinking painful and he was sure that at any moment, his head would split open.

Lying very still, he thought back to the last thing he remembered. The memories returned slowly. He'd found Jess bound in the room. They'd escaped into the Mardi Gras crowd. There'd been so many people, he'd been afraid of getting separated.

Then he remembered the sting in his neck. It hadn't been a mosquito, but a needle. What had they given him, though, to make him feel this bad? Was it the same thing they'd injected into Jessica?

A spasm of pain started low in his abdomen and spread upward. The feeling was so excruciatingly intense that when the darkness enveloped him again, he welcomed it.

"How do you know that's where he is?" Jess asked Harris as they rode in the taxi back to the Winslow mansion. "Is he all right?"

Harris shot a look at the driver before answering her. "Lucy saw men carrying a body in. Diablo sensed it was John, but since John didn't seem distressed, he didn't try to do anything to stop the men."

Jess tried to control her fear. She felt sick to her stomach, but this time, it wasn't the drugs making her ill.

"You need to focus on the facts," Harris told her. "That man in the alley is still alive and you learned a lesson.

Time to move on. As for John, I'm worried about him, too, but I think he's still alive, at least."

"How could you possibly know that?"

"Because Diablo might not know the difference between being asleep and being unconscious, but he knows the difference between being alive and dead. If John was dead, Diablo would know and he would have conveyed that to Lucy who would have shared it with me. So, I feel reasonably certain that John's alive, but unconscious. We just need to get to him before all of that changes."

They continued to ride in silence while Jess fought her instinctive wariness at being in such close quarters with Harris. To take her mind off of it, she replayed the last couple of hours in her head. "It never occurred to me that Brody would hire hu—" She stopped and lowered her voice so the driver wouldn't hear. "Humans to kidnap me during the day."

"I should have warned you and John. I've seen it done before, and Brody certainly had the money to pull it off, but the humans he hired to take you are really the least of our worries."

Something in his voice broke through all Jess's thoughts and brought her to full attention. "What do you mean?"

"From what I picked up from Lucy, John was being carried in by more than one vampire. It would seem that Brody has found help."

The second time John regained consciousness, he felt stronger, though he was still in pain.

He kept his eyes closed, just in case he was being watched, and tried to get as much information about where he was from what he could hear and feel.

He was lying on something cold, hard, and damp, maybe a slab of stone or something similar. The air around him was moist and smelled of earth and mildew. He knew it was night because despite the dull ache saturating his body, there wasn't the fatigue he felt when the sun was up. That meant either only a couple of hours had passed since he'd rescued Jess or an entire day had passed and it was now the next night. He couldn't tell which it was.

He didn't know how long he lay there, listening. He was tempted to open his eyes and get up, try to escape, but some instinct held him back. Time passed slowly. Eventually, he heard voices echoing off the walls, growing louder as they drew nearer.

"Any problems?"

Brody.

"Nah," a second voice said. "Your plan worked as expected. We waited until they left the room and then, just like you told us, made enough noise so that they headed out into the street instead of the alley. Once they came out the front of the building, we followed them into the crowd until we could inject him. There were so many people, he never knew what hit him. Just dropped right there."

"And the woman?" Brody asked.

"She kept on going. I don't think she knew he wasn't behind her."

"Excellent. I'll deal with her later. You brought Boehler's body back as instructed?"

"Yeah. We laid him out on the crypt in the inner chamber."

"And you're quite certain he's dead?"

"Sure thing. There was enough poison in that syringe to kill two humans."

That explained the way he felt, John thought. Brody had somehow hired humans to work for him and they'd tried to kill him. In fact, they thought they *had* killed him, which might be the only bit of luck going his way. Brody didn't know he'd become a changeling. Hell, Brody probably didn't even know what a changeling was, but he was about to find out.

Harris paid the driver and waited until the cab was headed back down the driveway before turning around. "Is there a problem?" he asked Jessica, because she was staring at him so intensely.

She shook herself. "I'm sorry. It just seems strange to see a vampire doing something as mundane as paying for a cab ride. I didn't even know you had money."

He grimaced. "After tonight, I'm about broke."

She looked contrite. "My fault."

He shrugged. "Whatever. I've got to go."

"Wait," she said after he'd taken only a couple of steps. "You're going to the cemetery, aren't you?" She didn't wait for him to answer, but hurried on. "I'm going with you."

"No."

Her eyes lit up with anger. "Fine. Then I'll go by myself." She ran up the steps of the house and Harris hoped she'd changed her mind.

He waited to see if she'd come back outside. About the time he thought she might actually stay inside, the door opened. When she came out, he saw she was carrying a .44 mag in one hand and wore what appeared to be night goggles on her face.

"What the hell?"

"I'm not a complete idiot—despite tonight's earlier incident. I'm going to that cemetery to rescue John, but I'm not going unarmed—or blind."

She came down the porch steps and walked past him, still holding the gun in one hand and shoving extra bullets into her pocket with the other.

"I would think that you, of all people, would know that a gun isn't going to do you much good against a vampire."

"This isn't an ordinary gun," she informed him sweetly, not bothering to look at him as she spoke. "Or, to be more precise, the bullets are not ordinary bullets."

They were crossing the long open pasture that lay between the Winslow mansion and the cemetery. There was enough of a moon out that to Harris, it seemed to be almost as bright as day; not that he'd had occasion to feel the sun on his face in a long time.

"And what's so special about these bullets?"

She jumped when he spoke, letting on that she still wasn't entirely comfortable in his presence. "These are hollow points that I've filled with a deadly vampire toxin."

He wasn't feeling exactly comfortable around her, either. *Vampire toxin?* Part of him felt ill that she had something that actually might kill a vampire; another part worried that, given their situation, what she had might not work.

"Do you even know how to shoot that?" he asked her, pointing to the gun. "The .44 mag's got enough kick to knock you on your as—throw off your aim," he quickly amended.

She didn't bother to look at him when she said, "Oh, I'll manage, thanks."

Well, he thought. *That was reassuring—not.* "So, you mind me asking what's in those bullets?" A thought suddenly occurred to him. "It's not Holy Water, is it, because, I've got to tell you, if it is, it's not going to work."

"Really?" She turned to look at him. "Someone already try that on you?"

"No. If you must know, I went to church the other night. So, you can scratch that off your list of things that will kill vampires."

"Interesting." She sounded distracted and Harris imagined she was making mental notes for future reference. He hoped she lived long enough to have a future. When he saw the cemetery up ahead, he moved in front of her, forcing her to stop.

"Get out of my way, Harris."

"You shouldn't go in there. Give me the gun. I don't even care what's in the bullets. If you say they work, that's good enough for me, but let me go in alone. I promise that I'll find John."

He waited for her answer and noticed that she was staring at the ground instead of him. He thought back over what he'd said and tried to remember at what point she'd stopped looking at him. "You *have* tested the bullets, haven't you?"

She looked up, angry. "No, not technically, but I know they'll work."

"Oh, hell no. We are not testing new ammunition in the heat of battle. You're not going any farther, and don't even bother trying to change my mind. John doesn't have time for us to argue." He walked off, leaving her fuming where she stood.

"You want me to test the bullets?" she asked in a cold tone of voice. "Fine, I'll test them."

He turned around and saw her aiming the gun directly at him. The fact that he could move faster than she could follow him with her eyes never occurred to him. He stood there, frozen, as she pulled the trigger.

Chapter 18

The kick from the gun literally knocked Jess off her feet. She'd never fired a gun before and it was nothing like she'd expected.

Scrambling to get up, she saw Harris standing there, an expression of shock and horror etched across his face. It was almost enough to make her laugh, but she knew he wouldn't appreciate it. But the sight behind him did make her smile.

"It worked," she said triumphantly, running past Harris, who still hadn't moved, to where the vampire she'd shot lay motionless. Afraid to get too close, she stood there, studying the vampire's chest for signs of breathing. There were none.

Her shot had missed the heart, which she'd been aiming for, and entered the lower abdomen, but in her mind, that was an even better test of the toxin. If it could enter the body at any site and still kill, then that was good.

She didn't hear Harris approach, but sensed when he stood beside her.

"Please tell me you were aiming for that vampire all along," he said softly.

"Of course," she replied. "What were you thinking? That I'd shoot you? Don't be ridiculous. I need your help to rescue John. I can't do it all by myself."

He nodded. "Of course. And let me just say that I appreciate you needing my help."

She ignored him and watched as he bent over the body to check for signs of life. "It would appear that your bullets do, in fact, work. Congratulations on a successful field test." He pulled a dagger out from somewhere beneath the dark jacket he wore and stabbed the vampire through the heart as an added precaution. "Also," he added, standing again, "nice shot. How long have you been shooting guns?"

"About five minutes," she answered him. Then she saw his eyes turn to bright, fiery red.

"Five minutes?" he said between gritted teeth.

"I'm from England. There's a gun ban, remember? But hey, it's not like it was hard, right? Come on," she said, starting forward. "Let's go find John."

John felt Brody's presence as soon as he entered the room. It was like an evil stench seeping into all the corners, robbing the room of clean air. As he heard the vampire approach, he kept himself very still and forced himself to relax.

"There he is," a second vampire said.

"My, how the mighty have fallen, eh what, Johnny?" Brody gloated as he walked around. His footsteps stopped and when Brody spoke next, he sounded much closer and John knew the vampire was bending close.

"What was it you said outside the courthouse that day, John? I believe you were going to drag my ass to hell? Well . . ." Brody leaned close enough that John felt rancid breath on his face as he shouted, "Welcome to hell, bitch."

"Thanks," John bit out as he opened his eyes and grabbed a surprised Brody by the throat. One push sent the vampire flying across the room.

He recovered quickly and John had just enough time to get to his feet before Brody was back up and attacking.

"How the fuck did you live?" Brody demanded, getting in a lucky punch that sent John staggering back. He rubbed his jaw and kept moving to stay opposite Brody.

"I had a little accident after I got here," John said conversationally. "I was attacked by one of the chupacabras. You've probably seen them in the cemetery at night. They almost killed me. Instead, I lived and became a changeling." John smiled then, showing Brody his fangs. "All the advantages of being a vampire, without being dead."

John could hear other vampires coming and knew that he needed to take care of Brody soon, before he was grossly outnumbered. He stopped moving and gave Brody a smile. "Time to deliver on that promise I made you . . . bitch."

Outside in the cemetery, Jess looked around, searching for where Brody might have taken John. "I thought you said they were here," she said, glancing at Harris.

"They are," he assured her. "Probably in one of these larger mausoleums." He moved from one building to the next with such speed that he was little more than a dark blur in the night. Jess found it unsettling that he moved that quickly. If Brody . . .

"Here," Harris shouted, breaking her train of thought. He was standing in front of a particularly large mausoleum toward the back of the cemetery. It wasn't the one behind which the baby chupacabra had been delivered, but it was similar.

"Are you sure?" she asked breathlessly, hurrying to catch up to him.

"Whoa." He reached out and gently pushed the barrel of the gun away from him. "You mind not pointing that in my direction? The thought of getting hit by friendly fire makes me nervous. Thanks. Now, I'm going in. You wait here." She gave him a look and he sighed in an all too human fashion. "At least let me go in first—and point the gun down, all right?"

He whirled around and disappeared inside so fast she could well imagine how people centuries ago might have thought that vampires could vanish into thin air.

Holding the gun with both hands, she took a breath and then followed after him.

Stepping through the entry, she found herself in an empty room. Thanks to the night-vision goggles, she saw the small doorway located in the back wall. It had steps leading to a lower level. From where she stood, she couldn't see anything beyond it, but the sounds of fighting were definitely coming from that direction.

She crossed to the doorway and looked inside. Off to the right was another doorway to a third room. She moved toward it and was just able to make out the shapes of men fighting. They moved so quickly that it was hard to tell who was who. Unconsciously, she edged closer, watching for a clean shot and hoping she'd be able to tell the good guys from the bad.

Then, suddenly, hands grabbed her and nails bit into her flesh. There wasn't even time to fire the gun because her captor pulled her in front of him like a shield and held her.

"At last, my sweet," Brody rasped into her ear. As she fought to free herself, she spotted John and Harris, busy fighting other vampires. There was no one to save her.

She raised the gun, hoping to turn and shoot Brody. When he saw what she was trying to do, he grabbed the gun and tried to yank it from her, but Jess refused to let go. Then, to her horror, Brody laid his hand over hers and gripped the gun, moving it until it was pointed right at John.

Then his finger tightened over hers, pressing down on the trigger. She renewed her struggles, but little by little, the trigger went back. She butted Brody with the back of her head, almost knocking herself unconscious, and heard the report of the gun going off. The shot echoed loudly in the room, hurting her ears. Across the room, a body stiffened.

"Oh, God, no," Jess breathed, her gaze locking with Harris's as he fell in slow motion to the floor. Behind her, Brody swore and raised the gun again, aiming once more for John.

Jess screamed as the gun exploded a second time and watched as the vampire John had been fighting was suddenly in front of him to take the bullet.

John released the body and rushed forward. Seeing the cold look of death reflected in his eyes, Jess felt a shiver of fear run down her spine. Brody must have seen it, too, because he pushed Jess into John's path and raced out of the mausoleum.

John caught her before she fell and for a second, their eyes locked. "Move," she said.

John looked confused, but stepped to one side. As soon as he did, Jess pulled a dagger from the sheath strapped to her ankle and threw it at the vampire that had seemingly come out of nowhere. He crumpled to the ground, dead.

Jess dropped her hand to her side, feeling exhausted.

"Are you okay?" John asked hurriedly, gripping her upper arms to hold her still.

"Yes, fine, but—"

"I have to go after Brody," he shouted, already releasing her to run out of the lower chamber.

"No, John, wait!" She didn't wait to see if he'd heard her as she rushed to Harris's side. *Please, let him still be alive*, she chanted over and over in her head.

"Shit." John was suddenly by her side, kneeling over Harris. "It looks like he was shot."

"He was."

"You shot him?"

"Yes, but it was an accident." She felt so guilty. John would never believe she hadn't meant to hurt Harris. "Is he . . . ?"

"How the hell do I tell? Do vampires have a pulse?"

"I think so," Jess said, but she didn't know for sure.

John's jaw was clenched tight as he pressed his fingers against the vampire's throat. After a second, he glanced up at her. "He's still alive. Where's the antidote?"

"There isn't one," she said miserably. "The point wasn't to save the vampires after they were shot."

John raised Harris up and heaved him over his shoulder before standing up. Then he walked out, with Jess following behind him.

"Where are you taking him?"

"Back to the mansion. I can't let him die without at least trying to save his life."

"But Brody?"

"Fuck Brody. Harris needs help, now."

Jess knew better than to argue. Lost in her own abysmal thoughts, her hand strayed to her mother's locket, only to find it wasn't there. She stopped dead in her tracks and felt all around her neck, even patting down her blouse on the chance the clasp had broken and it had slipped inside. Nothing. A faint memory surfaced of something brushing against her hand as she struggled with Brody. It could have been the locket falling.

Not wanting to leave it behind, she called after John to stop but didn't wait to see if he'd heard her before racing back inside the mausoleum.

She still had her night goggles on and made her way to the lower chamber. The bodies of the other vampires lay where they'd fallen, making her feel uneasy. They hadn't been dead long enough for their bodies to grow cold and appeared as bright green blobs in her field of vision.

Jess went first to the spot where Brody had held her and scanned the area thoroughly before widening her search radius, all the while aware of the fact that John hadn't come back to check on her.

She came to the first body and hesitated briefly before carefully stepping over it to continue her search. She reached the second body and stepped over it and searched the farthest corner of the room. It was impossible for the locket to have ended up over there, and yet she refused to leave before checking out all possibilities.

Her search was hurried because knowing that Brody was still out there had her worried. She hadn't brought her sword because she'd had the gun. Now Brody had the gun and she had nothing.

Even she wasn't willing to tempt fate by wasting any more time looking for the locket. She'd simply come back during the day.

Wanting now to catch up to John, she hurried across the room, stepping first over the one slain vampire and then the other. Just as she put her foot down on the other side, however, a hand reached up and grabbed her ankle.

Jessica cried out as she fell to the floor. Throwing her hands out, she managed to break her fall enough to land on her butt, though the vampire still had hold of her ankle. He raised himself up and his mouth twisted into a predatory smile as he snarled and hissed. Before she could do more than scramble back, he was up off the ground and coming for her.

It was her nightmare come to life. Alone with the creature, weaponless, she could only stare in horrified fascination as he came for her.

She prayed for John to rescue her but knew she was on her own. The smell of fear and blood filled her senses, making her want to gag. The vampire was toying with her, moving slowly, letting her know that she had lost. He was going to kill her. In two days, she would be a vampire like him.

Unable to accept her death calmly, she scrambled back and her hands hit a wooden object. As the vampire lunged at her, she raised one end of the piece of wood and braced the other against the floor. The vampire's momentum carried him the rest of the way, and the piece of wood slid into his body with a sickening sound just before he landed on top of her.

Unable to move, Jess held still. After a moment, it was clear to her that the vampire really was dead this time. It took a lot of pushing to work her way out from under the literal dead weight, but she finally managed. Breathless, she got to her feet and then examined her work.

The end of an old wooden torch protruded out the back of the vampire. Looking around, she saw that the room had once been lined with them, although several had fallen. She stared at it for a minute and then looked back down at the creature that had attacked her. She couldn't stop the smile that spread across her face. She had done it. She had killed a vampire. All alone, with no hope of backup and no weapons. Just her and the vampire—and she had won. It was the ultimate test for a vampire slayer and she had passed. It didn't matter that her father hadn't been there to see it, or Kacie, Erik, Charles, or even John. It was enough that she knew it.

Deep down inside, the frightened child inside her drew an easy breath. There would be no more nightmares. She had vanquished the inner demons—but that didn't mean her troubles were over. Harris was dying, and he was one vampire who didn't deserve that fate—at least, not at the hands of a friend.

Jess hurried out of the mausoleum and ran through the cemetery, keeping a wary eye out in case Brody should return. She caught up to John just as he reached the front steps to the mansion.

"Where the hell have you been?" he asked her as she ran up the steps to open the door for him.

"I lost something back in the mausoleum."

"Did you find what you were looking for?"

"Yes, I believe I did." She held the door open for him and then directed him to the small room located under the stairs. There was a cot there and she waited for him to place Harris on it.

"My friend isn't good enough for one of the guest rooms?" he asked her, clearly put out.

She sighed. "It's not like that. This is the only room in the house where the sun won't reach him, but if you'd rather put him in one of the guest rooms, we can try to hang extra blankets over the windows." She started to shut the door.

"Wait. I'm sorry. You're right." He moved into the tiny room. "This is so frustrating," he admitted after getting Harris situated on the cot. "What do we do now? Just wait to see if he lives?"

Jess studied Harris. The bullet had entered his abdomen, close to the same spot that the "test" vampire had been shot. She didn't understand why that vampire had died instantly while Harris remained alive, unless it had something to do with his being a Prime. Maybe the chupacabra venom residing in his cells was potent enough to help him fend off the toxin she'd made.

"I don't know. Maybe we should get the bullet out and try to seal the wound. Also, I think giving him blood might help."

John nodded. "Where's that medical kit you had?"

She hurried to bring him the kit and then left him again

to get damp cloths and dry towels, unsure what they might need.

When she returned, John had already removed Harris's shirt and cleaned the outside of the wound. The torn flesh looked like raw hamburger and turned her stomach. John seemed unfazed by it and took the pair of long, needle-nose tweezers she'd found and started digging around for the bullet.

She prayed it wasn't buried too deep because there was no telling what further damage they were doing in trying to extract it.

After what seemed a long time, Jess heard the dull clink of metal touching metal. A glance at John's face told her that he'd found the bullet. It took several more minutes for him to extract it, but finally, it was out. Both he and Jess heaved a sigh of relief.

John was looking pale and Jess worried he might still be suffering side effects from his experience. Needing to be useful, she threaded a needle with suture and moved to Harris's side.

"What are you doing?" John asked. She hated the censure she heard in his voice.

"I'm going to stitch him closed. We can't leave the wound open like that. You should sit down while I do this. You look like hell."

He glared at her, but didn't get out of her way. "John, I'm trying to help here," she said, exasperated.

"Why should I believe you want to save his life? Less than twenty-four hours ago, you threatened to shoot him. And now here he lies, shot with one of your bullets."

"John, I assure you that if I wanted to kill Harris, I had ample opportunity to do so earlier. I didn't shoot him then, and I bloody well didn't mean to shoot him this time. Now, are you going to let me help try to save his life or shall we continue to argue?"

Reluctantly, it seemed, he moved out of her way so she could kneel beside the body. Taking a deep breath, she distanced herself emotionally from what she was about to do and, grateful that Harris wasn't conscious, started sewing the edges of his skin together.

There were several times when she had to stop and take deep breaths because the sight of blood was making her woozy. At least vampires didn't seem to bleed as much as humans.

Finally, she was done. Her stitching wasn't pretty, but it was effective. The wound was closed and had just about stopped bleeding. She cleaned it once more, patted it dry, and then applied a topical antibiotic before bandaging it. Now came the hard part.

"He needs blood," she told John. "Neither one of us is a great candidate because we've both been dosed with drugs, but I don't see that there are any other options. It's not like we can purchase blood at the local blood bank, so we'll have to hope gifting him our blood will have some influence."

She removed two large syringes, needles, and a tourniquet from the medical kit. Then, she applied the tourniquet around her arm and started flexing it as John looked on.

"Are you sure this will work?"

"No, but it helped you when you were attacked. Maybe it'll do the same thing for him."

"Maybe," John agreed quietly.

As soon as she had a vein exposed, she stuck the needle in.

"What can I do?" John offered.

"Pull back on the plunger, but be careful not to disturb the needle."

He did and at the right moment, she pulled off the tourniquet and watched the syringe fill with her blood. She fought off a wave of dizziness and when the syringe was full, pulled out the needle. Bending her arm to stanch the bleeding, she walked over to Harris.

"Here goes nothing," she said, pulling the needle off and then putting the tip of the syringe against the tip of one of Harris's fangs.

"I give this blood freely," she intoned, remembering when she'd done the same thing for John. How long ago had that been? She squirted just a little blood and watched it get sucked up. Encouraged, she squeezed out a little more and waited until it, too, was sucked up. She repeated the process until she'd emptied the syringe. Afterward, she thought that Harris seemed to be breathing easier.

"I think it's helping," she said to John. "Maybe we should give him more." She started to tie the tourniquet around her arm again, but John stopped her.

"You've already given enough," he told her. "It's my turn."

She nodded and wrapped the tourniquet around his arm instead. Then, taking a fresh needle and syringe, she drew blood. When it was full, she fed it to Harris, who took it as quickly as he had the other.

After she had emptied the syringe, she turned to John. "I don't think we can spare any more blood." He nodded, but continued to stare at her until she felt uncomfortable. "What?"

"Thank you," he said.

"For what?"

"For trying to help me save him. I didn't think you would."

She offered him a tired smile. "It's difficult to admit, but perhaps you're right about Harris. He's not a typical vampire. After all, he not only stopped me from making a grave mistake, he also saved your life. I couldn't have saved you by myself. I realize that now." She fought against the sudden weight of emotion she was feeling. "No, I definitely don't want him to die."

He rubbed the back of his neck in obvious exhaustion. "I guess now we wait and see."

"Why don't you go to bed? I'll stay up and watch over him."

He shook his head. "That's okay. I'll do it."

He didn't trust her, not that she blamed him. She'd tried too many times to kill Harris. If she were in John's shoes, she wouldn't want her help either. She tried to ignore the hurt and disappointment and broached another subject that was bothering her. "What do we do about Brody?"

"Honestly?" he asked. "I don't know."

"But—"

"Jess, we can't solve all the problems tonight. We'll do the best we can. Now, go to bed."

Chapter 19

"Are you sure this is what Harris would have wanted?" Jess asked John two nights later as they walked the last block to St. Magnus Cathedral.

"Yeah, I am. He told me that he came here a couple of times. I think he would have liked knowing we had his memorial service here."

"I'm sorry he's gone, John. I know you two were close."

He gave her a sad smile and squeezed the hand he'd been holding. "Thank you again for working so hard to make these arrangements—and for getting the announcement in the paper. I feel bad because there won't be anyone to mourn his passing."

"That's not true," she said. "I know of at least two who will."

The cathedral was just ahead. As they drew closer, Jess understood why Harris had liked this particular place so much. There was an old-world Gothic charm to the building. It was a massive structure, standing at least three stories tall with a roof that resembled a series of upside-down V's, each adorned with a spire on top. Lit from within, the stained-glass windows were a work of art.

Probably what appealed to Jess the most were the stone gargoyles perched on the roof corners. As far as she could tell, they weren't chupacabras, but actually part of the original architecture. Behind them, the stars shone bright on a cloudless night.

"It's a good night for a service," Jess observed as they reached the church and mounted the steps.

John held the door for her and they went inside. The arrangements for the funeral had taken a day to plan and the casket sitting in front of the altar was largely ceremonial since transporting Harris's body after it turned to stone would have been impractical.

She'd placed the announcement in the paper, even though Harris hadn't known anyone in town, and Jess was surprised to see several people sitting in the pews for the service. She suspected they were there by chance to pray.

She'd called Mac, Dirk, and the others to attend, but hadn't been able to reach them.

She and John walked down the aisle to the casket, stopping before it to share a moment of silence. Then John placed a hand at her back and guided her to the front pew to sit.

The priest appeared to begin the ceremony. When it was over, Jess wondered if, in God's eyes, Harris had redeemed himself. She hoped so.

When John went to speak with the priest afterward, she went with him. They verified the arrangements for the casket's delivery to the cemetery.

"Are you all right?" she asked as they left the church minutes later.

John nodded. "Yes. I just wish I'd had more time to get to know him."

"I'm so sorry," she said. "I'm sorry I ever made those bullets. If I hadn't—"

"Don't," John said, taking her hand and pulling her to a stop outside on the sidewalk. "Don't do that to yourself. You didn't mean to shoot him. I know that—and I think Harris knew that. If you want to blame anyone, blame Brody. He's the one who pulled the trigger."

Jess wiped at her eyes, ineffectively trying to clear them.

John gave her a tender smile. "Hush now. It's time for us to move on. No more tears, okay?"

"Okay," she said through a weepy smile. She reached for her purse to pull out a tissue. "Wonderful," she muttered.

"What's the matter?"

"I forgot my purse in the church."

"Want me to get it for you?"

"No, it won't take but a second." She hurried up the steps and pulled open the door that led to the front foyer. Fortunately, no one had turned off the lights, though the sanctuary was dimmer than it had been during the service.

She hurried down the aisle to the front pew and looked for her purse. It wasn't where she remembered setting it. Confused, she looked around and found it had been moved quite a bit farther down the aisle.

Strange, she thought, going to pick it up. She slipped the strap over her shoulder and had just turned to leave when she stopped short.

"You!"

Brody gave her a smile so evil and predatory that her blood ran cold. "Hello, sweet Jessica. Miss me?"

Jess looked around, desperate for something she could use to defend herself. "I'm surprised to see you here—inside a church." She tried to get him talking. Maybe, if she was gone long enough, John would get worried and come check on her.

"First time," Brody admitted to her. "But rest assured, it won't be my last. I'm sure there are many lonely women to be found here."

His face grew serious. "But right now, I'm only interested in—you."

In a blur of movement, he grabbed her and pulled her against him, her back to his front. She struggled to break free while his fetid breath whisked across the side of her face, making her sick.

"You won't get away with this," she warned. "John is just outside. He'll be here any second, looking for me."

Brody gave an asthmatic, wheezing laugh. "That's what I'm counting on."

At that moment, as if on cue, the door to the sanctuary opened and even before he appeared, John's voice carried to her. "Jess, honey. What's taking so long?" He came to a stop as soon as he saw them. Jess used her eyes to plead with him to be careful.

"Let her go, Brody."

"I don't think so, John." Brody brought up his free hand and she saw that he was holding John's gun with the modified bullets. "Recognize this? Yeah, I thought you might. I took the liberty of testing it myself and whatever is in these bad boys works like a champ on vampires.

That's when I realized that your vampire buddy must not have survived." There was a pause. "I feel bad about that," he said, without sounding the least bit remorseful. "I was aiming for you, Boehler. I realize now that the toxin in these bullets might not hurt you like it does vampires, but tell me, you're not bulletproof, are you?"

Jess watched the frustration on John's face and felt Brody laugh behind her. "That's what I thought. Let's go." He motioned with the gun to the side door that led out of the sanctuary.

With hands raised, John walked in front of them while Jess followed, Brody's arm still pinning her to him. They went through the first door and down a short hallway to a second door that led to an outside courtyard, about the size of two tennis courts. In the center stood a massive oak tree, surrounded by both paved and graveled areas with benches scattered throughout where people could sit and read or relax. Right then it was empty.

Brody motioned them over to the large tree and when they reached it, he shoved Jess forward. John caught her before she fell.

"Please don't," Jess pleaded as he leveled his gun at them.

"Oh, but I must." He pulled the trigger.

John jerked beside her and fell back. Jess could only stare, feeling confused. It took a moment for everything to filter past the shock and then she screamed.

He'd shot John. Just like that. No warning. No nothing. In the dark, she couldn't see where the bullet had hit him, but he wasn't moving. She prayed he wasn't dead and dropped to her knees by his side.

Before she could touch him, Brody grabbed her by the arm and jerked her up.

"Forget it. He's dead."

"You killed him. You killed him." It seemed the only thing she was capable of saying. Her hand flew to her mouth as her mind shut down. John was gone and her life was over. He'd never even known that she loved him. Rage erupted inside her, pushing all other thoughts aside. She turned on Brody, no longer caring if he killed her, and beat at him with fisted hands and feet. "You killed him!" she screamed.

"That was the point," Brody shouted back, using both hands, while still holding the gun in one, to capture her fists. He forced her back against the trunk of the tree and pinned her there. "It never was about you. Writing your name on the walls? Breaking into your bedroom? The attacks? None of that was about you. I've wanted to kill this son of a bitch for a long time. You were just a means to an end." She stared at him in stunned horror and it made him smile. "Don't look so disappointed, angel. Now that he's gone, we can have our fun."

"You know your problem, Brody? You're too quick to assume you've won." A flurry of movement and a resounding click accompanied John's words as he jumped to his feet and pressed the barrel of a gun to Brody's temple.

Brody's eyes opened wide, but he didn't move. "How . . . ?"

"Ever hear of Kevlar, asshole? Too bad they don't make helmets." John gave Brody a nasty smile and pulled the trigger of his gun.

Jess jumped at the sound and watched as Brody's body jerked and then crumpled to the ground. She stared at him, unable to look away, her mind automatically blocking out the details of skull and brain matter sprayed across the courtyard—or the fact that Brody was now missing half of his head.

She felt something damp and sticky all over her face, but refused to think about what it was. Only two things mattered to her at the moment. Brody was dead—and John was alive.

The latter seemed like a miracle too good to be true and she turned as if in slow motion to look at John, needing to reassure herself that he really was standing there.

"I thought you were dead."

"I know," he said gently. "And I'm sorry. I had a feeling he'd try something tonight, so I took precautions."

"But you didn't bother to tell me about it?" She was getting angry. "How come I wasn't wearing Kevlar?"

"He wasn't going to shoot you. That's not his style. You forget, I've studied this man for a long time. I knew that whatever he had planned for you, he'd wait until I was out of the way. I wanted him to think he'd accomplished that so I could catch him off guard."

He seemed almost proud of himself, which just made her even angrier. "What if he'd shot you in the head?"

"He didn't."

She punched him in the chest. "But he could have." He shrugged, as much as saying it was a moot point. She knew that if she thought too much about his cavalier attitude, she'd go nuts, so instead, she focused on what needed to be done next. "We need to stake him—or cut off his head."

"You really think that's necessary?" John gaped at her. "He's not going anywhere."

She tried to imagine the reaction of the priest—or a member of the congregation—walking into the courtyard. Even if they came upon Brody after sunrise, after the body had turned, the stone version of a man with his head blown off would be shocking. "We can't leave him here."

A breeze stirred around them in the courtyard and a shadow at the edge of the roof moved, catching Jess's eye. She turned and saw one of the stone gargoyles rise up on his hind legs. Standing almost six feet tall, he was darker than the night sky around him, but his crimson eyes pierced the black like beacons of impending doom. Diablo beat his wings and the wind he stirred rattled the limbs of the tree and buffeted them below.

Slowly, he rose into the air and for a moment, simply hovered, surveying all below him in the courtyard. Then his gaze found Brody's body and he flew toward them. John grabbed Jess's arm and pulled her back and they both watched as Diablo swooped down and grabbed the body, his sharp claws sinking deep.

Then he rose up into the sky, circling the courtyard, rising a little higher with each circuit until finally he disappeared from view.

"Come on," John said, grabbing her hand and leading her back through the church. They exited the front door and walked across the street, stopping once they were on the other side.

"There." John pointed to something in the sky that Jess couldn't see. She looked more closely and finally spied the white of Brody's shirt, a mere speck that gradually grew larger as Diablo began his descent.

Still well above the highest spire of the church, Diablo opened his claws and released the body.

It plummeted downward, arms and legs flopping against the air rushing past him, looking like a rag doll dropped from a great height. Then there was a sickening crunch as the body landed on the spire and the tip shot through the chest.

Too shocked to form coherent thought, Jess stared in morbid fascination while Diablo landed on the corner of the chapel.

She understood now what would happen. Diablo would sit there all night, watching over the body. In the morning, Diablo and Brody would both turn to stone; Diablo until the next sun set and Brody until the first stiff breeze reduced him to dust and blew him away.

Whether John's bullet had killed Brody or not, by dawn he was dead. The nightmare was over.

"There's no need for us to stay," John said after a while. "Let's go home."

The drive back to the mansion passed in a blur as Jess's mind replayed the events of the evening. She couldn't believe it was all over. Brody was gone, and now there was no reason for John to stick around. The thought of never seeing him again depressed her like nothing else had.

"I need to shower," she mumbled as soon as they arrived. She didn't dare look at him because if she did, she knew she wouldn't be able to hide her emotions. She hurried inside and once she reached the safety of the bathroom, closed the door. She turned on the shower and when the water was hot, stripped out of her blood-spattered clothes and threw them into the wastebasket. She wasn't even interested in trying to salvage them.

Once in the shower, all she could do was stand under the pelting water, too tired to even try to soap off. She let the force of the spray wash away the blood and dirt and troubles. It also washed away the emotional defenses she'd kept erected so long. When the tears came, she couldn't stop them.

"Hey, what's this?" John's voice, gentle and warm, came to her moments later as he opened the shower door and stepped over the side of the tub to join her. He was completely naked and she was so shocked to see him, she wasn't sure how to react.

"I would have asked permission to join you, but I was afraid you'd turn me down," he told her as he pulled her out of the water's stream and gently moved a strand of hair out of her eyes. "I don't think my heart could survive your rejection. I love you too damn much."

He pulled her into his arms, and she couldn't have resisted him even if she'd wanted to. He bent his head, touching his lips to hers, hesitantly, as if he wasn't sure if she'd welcome his kiss. Her emotions already raw and exposed, she wrapped her arms around his neck and returned the kiss, sharing by gesture her love for him, her fear of losing him, and the grief that would come when he left her.

She had no idea if he understood any of what she felt, but when she swept her tongue against his lips in blatant invitation, he opened his mouth and the kiss turned heated. She clung to him almost desperately, branding the feel of him against her lips and body so she would always have it to remember him by.

And he felt so good. She couldn't touch enough of him with her hands; couldn't get close enough to him with her body. She needed him inside her, and it wasn't until she felt the blunt probing of his shaft between her legs that she realized he'd lifted her up so that her legs were wrapped around his waist and her back was against the wall.

He entered her with a single stroke and then lifted her slowly only to drive himself into her again. Water sluiced over them, teasing skin already made hypersensitive by passion.

"Again," she whispered when it seemed he was taking his time. He immediately responded by pulling out and thrusting himself into her. It felt like he was holding back, perhaps afraid that he might hurt her, but she wanted all of him. Everything he had to give. "Harder," she cried when he pulled out of her.

Finally, he seemed to understand and he plowed into her, repeatedly and with such force that all she could do was hold on for dear life. It was exactly what she wanted, what she needed.

The tension rapidly built inside of her until she wanted to scream. Her release loomed just out of reach and still the pressure grew. She knew that all she had to do was surrender to it and it would carry her over the edge into sweet release, but she resisted, wanting to savor each and every moment.

Then she felt John's mouth against her neck, felt the tip of his tongue making swirling motions against her skin, followed by the light scraping of his fangs. When he gently sucked the skin, she felt the pull on her nipples and the tension inside of her increased.

Faster and harder, John drove himself into her until she couldn't hold out any longer and with a breathless cry, she toppled over the edge and rode the wave, barely conscious of John's primal yell as his body stiffened and he spilled his seed into her.

It seemed to take forever to come down off the high of their lovemaking, but eventually, John pulled out of her, holding her to him until she was steady on legs that shook from the intensity of her emotions.

John smiled at her when she looked, almost shyly, up into his face. "Are you all right?"

"Yes. And you?"

"Never better." He picked up a bar of soap and lathered his hands before running them across her shoulders. The feel of his hands on her body felt so good that she couldn't keep her eyes open. She wanted nothing to distract her from the sensation. "What are you doing? Not that I want you to stop," she said as his hands moved to her breasts.

"I didn't get to pay homage to your beautiful body earlier, so I'm making up for it now." He leaned forward and kissed her briefly, before running his hands up along her neck. "I didn't hurt you, did I?"

It was her turn to smile. "No. You didn't even break the skin."

She heard the low rumble of his laugh. "That's not what I meant."

"Oh." She felt her cheeks grow warm. "No, you didn't hurt me there either. In fact, you were . . . it was . . . great."

He turned her around so he could wash her back. "It was better than great." He pulled her against him and the thin layer of soap made their bodies slippery together. His hands came up again to massage her breasts as he dipped his head low enough to speak softly in her ear. "I told you before that I'd never bite you."

"Did you want to?" She was worried that maybe the experience hadn't been as great for him as it had been for her because he'd held back.

"I won't deny that I was tempted, but I don't have to take your blood to be satisfied. There are a thousand ways I want to make love to you and none of them involve taking blood."

"A thousand?" she teased, letting him hear the smile in her voice. "I don't know if I have the energy tonight for more than a hundred or so."

Again, she heard the gentle rumble of his laugh. "Fortunately, we have plenty of time to explore each and every one of those ways." His voice grew very serious. "Hopefully, we'll have a lifetime."

Jess stilled, not sure she'd heard him correctly. "A lifetime?"

"God, I hope so," he said, sounding suddenly vulnerable. He turned her so she was looking up at him. "I meant what I said—I love you. I want to be with you. Marry me. We can work out any differences, overcome any problems, as long as we love one another."

She could hardly believe what she was hearing. "You want to marry me?"

"You sound surprised." He laughed. "Marriage between two people in love is not unheard of, you know. You do love me, don't you?"

She realized then how remiss she'd been in sharing her feelings with him. Wrapping her arms about his neck, she pulled him close and kissed him. "Yes, I love you. With all my heart and all my soul." She thought about all the things she wanted to do with her life. Could she give all that up and move back to Washington, D.C., just to be with John? Yes, she could. "You're all I've ever wanted or needed. Yes, I'll marry you. We can find a nice little house in D.C., start a family—it'll be great."

"Actually, I was kind of hoping you might want to live here in New Orleans."

"What?"

"Yeah, well, you see, I sort of quit my job."

"What?" She knew she sounded like a broken record, but couldn't seem to stop herself.

"I called Gamble up yesterday to check in. Turns out he'd received a phone call from a man claiming to be Brody's killer. He described the Thompson Park murder scene in such explicit detail that Gamble was left with no doubt that he was speaking to the real murderer, which means he no longer considers me a suspect."

"Do you think Harris made that call, before he died?" She felt the pain of his loss stab through her again.

"I think he did. Anyway, after the call, Gamble lifted my suspension and wanted to know when I was coming back to work. I started to give him a date and heard myself resign instead. My heart just isn't in it anymore. Besides, I have a new job."

"You do?"

He smiled. "I'm a Night Slayer."

She cocked her head and gave him a saucy look. "Is that a fact?"

"It is, indeed, a fact."

"Hmmm. New Orleans's very own Night Slayer. But with Brody gone, are there any vampires left to slay?"

He grew serious. "Unfortunately, there are. I didn't have a chance to tell you, but Harris found a whole group—about fifty, and some of them are former convicts. I'm just glad I won't be hunting them all by myself."

She smiled. "That's right, you have *me* to help."

He gave a bark of laughter. "We'll talk about it. I'm not so sure I want the mother of my children out there hunting vampires."

"You can't go out there alone, and besides, I'm not pregnant."

He gave the end of her nose an affectionate flick. "I won't be alone, and you're not pregnant *yet.* I have a feeling that if we don't start using protection soon, that status could change rather quickly—not that I mind at all. I'm looking forward to having children with you."

The admission was so touching, she felt like crying. As if sensing that, John kissed her quickly and then grabbed the bar of soap and washed himself. "I'm going to leave you to wash your hair while there's still hot water. As soon as you're finished, get dressed and come downstairs. There's something I want to show you."

He left before she could ask him for details, so she quickly washed her hair and got out of the shower. With a towel wrapped around her, she hurried to her room and dressed. She combed her hair and though she hated taking the extra time to put on makeup, she found herself wanting to look nice for her fiancé. *Fiancé.* It had a nice sound to it.

As she started down the stairs, she heard the sound of male voices talking. John had company. There was something familiar about the sound of his guest, and she hurried down the stairs.

"Harris!"

The vampire had been sitting and hurriedly got to his feet as she burst into the room, breathless and excited. Not only was he alive, but he looked as vibrant and healthy as he had the night they'd gone into the cemetery to find John.

Overcome with joy and relief, she threw her arms around him, embracing him tightly. "How? I don't understand."

For a second, Harris stood ramrod stiff and then slowly, his arms came up around her. "Does this mean you're glad to see me?"

She stepped back, slightly embarrassed. "Yes, I'm very glad to see you." She gave John a pointed look. "But you told me he died. I made the funeral arrangements."

Harris smiled. "John tells me it was a nice ceremony, too. Thank you."

She glared at both men. "Someone needs to start explaining—now."

"I will," John started. "First, I'm sorry we lied to you, but we felt it was the best thing to do at the time. You see, the blood we gave Harris worked, even more quickly than we could have hoped. Shortly after you went to sleep that night, he woke up and we started talking about what to do about Brody."

Harris took up the explanation. "We knew that over the next couple of weeks, his intelligence would start to deteriorate, so we needed to find him before he lost all sense of reasoning."

"So you set a trap," Jess concluded.

"In a way, it's your fault," John told her.

"How's that?" She wanted to know.

"You're the one who said that the best way to catch vampires is to lure them to you, not go after them."

She slowly smiled. "That's true."

"Given Brody's obsession with you, we knew he wouldn't just leave you alone. In fact, either he or someone he hired was probably watching you at all times, so that's why I had you make the funeral arrangements," John continued. "We wanted Brody to know exactly where we'd be and when. We also wanted him to think he'd been successful in killing Harris."

"He'd feel like he had the advantage," Harris explained. "It would be just you and John."

"But you could have told me," Jess said, feeling a little hurt.

"I'm sorry," John said again. "We needed your actions and reactions to be genuine."

She nodded. "I guess I understand."

"Thank you." John went to her and, putting his arm around her shoulder, pulled her to his side and kissed the side of her head. "I knew you'd understand, but I *am* sorry to have put you through it."

She smiled, unable to tear her gaze from his face. He truly was a very handsome man and she felt so lucky that he loved her.

She was torn from her introspection by the sound of Harris clearing his throat. "I should probably be going," he said, sounding a little embarrassed. "The sun will be coming up shortly."

"Where will you spend the day?" John asked him.

Harris shrugged. "I don't know. I'll find a place."

Jess found she wasn't reassured by that answer. "Harris, if you already have a place where you feel comfortable, that's great, but you're welcome to use that little room under the stairs—at least until we can sunproof one of the other rooms."

"Are you sure?" Harris asked, sounding surprised.

"Of course, I'm sure. It's no trouble, really." She leaned against John and smiled. "In fact, we'd love to have you stay with us for however long you want."

Harris hesitated only a moment and then smiled. "Thanks, I'd like that."

"We'll start work today on one of the other rooms," John told him, "but I have to tell you that with any luck, Jess and I will be moving out in a couple of months."

It was Jess's turn to be surprised and she pulled back enough to look up at him. "We will?"

"Yeah. You see, over the years, instead of spending my money, I invested it. Well, after ten years, I've accumulated quite a nice little nest egg. Yesterday, I withdrew it all and bought a house—the chupacabra house. It'll need a little work, but I thought we could live there after we're married."

Jess couldn't believe it. She grabbed his face and kissed him. "It'll be so wonderful. Thank you, John." She was bubbling over with excitement. "You'll come stay with us, won't you?" she asked Harris.

He gave her a dubious look. "You really want a vampire living in your house?"

"Oh, please." She waved away his comment. "I grew up with a vampire living in my house and you're not nearly the Neanderthal Erik can be."

"I'm just not sure how we'll pay for everything after my savings runs out," John admitted. "It's not like anyone's going to pay us to get rid of vampires they don't even know exist."

Jess smiled. "That won't be a problem."

"It won't?" John asked.

"No. The Winslow Family Trust was set up for this express purpose, so as long as there are evil vampires to slay and good vampires to save, we've got money—and I assure you, it's more than enough to live on for all of us."

"I don't like the idea of living off someone else's money," John told her.

She smiled. "With all those vampires running around? Don't worry—you'll earn every dime, I've no doubt."

"She's probably right," Harris added, sounding worried. "In fact, I'm a little concerned about whether the two of us will be able to handle them."

"You mean, the *three* of us," Jess interjected.

John and Harris exchanged looks. "I'll call Charles tomorrow and brief him on the situation," John said. "If Mac and Dirk have taken care of their situation in D.C., then maybe they can come down and help."

"Sounds good," Harris replied as he stifled a yawn. "If you'll excuse me, I think it's time I retired."

After he left, Jess smiled and took John's hand, pulling him into the kitchen. "We have so many plans to make. I'll make a pot of coffee and we can talk."

She started to walk off, but he tugged on her hand, pulling her off balance. As she started to fall, he swept her up into his arms and headed for the stairs. "I have a better idea. Let's talk later." He carried her up the stairs and into his bedroom, where he placed her on the bed. His eyes glowed with a crimson light, letting her know exactly what he had on his mind.

"Are you sure you feel up to it?" she teased. "After all, it's almost sunup. Maybe you're too tired to make love?"

John gathered her into his arms and kissed her tenderly. Then he nuzzled the side of her neck and whispered in her ear, "I'll never be *that* tired."

About the Author

Robin T. Popp grew up watching *Star Trek* and reading Nancy Drew, Robert Heinlein, Sharon Green, and Piers Anthony. She loved the daring and romantic exploits of heroic characters on grand adventures in otherworldly places. It wasn't long before she wanted to write such tales to share with others. Though she was forced to take a thirty-year detour through the real world—which certainly wasn't without its share of adventures—armed now with two master's degrees, a full-time job, and a family, she has taken the first steps toward realizing her original dream of becoming an author.

Too Close to the Sun, a futuristic romance published in July 2003, was her first novel. *Out of the Night* was her second novel and represents her first foray into another of her favorite alternate realities—the realm of vampires.

Robin lives southwest of Houston, Texas, with her husband, three kids, three dogs, two frogs, one rabbit, and a mortgage. She is living the American dream.

If you hunger for more
Robin T. Popp,

turn this page for a preview of
her next Night Slayer novel

Lord of the Night

available in mass market

Fall 2007.

Chapter 1

The rain shower that swept through Hocksley earlier that evening had soaked the surfaces of the centuries-old storefronts until they glistened like new under the moonlight. The standing puddles cast an eerie glow over the cobblestoned streets that stood as empty and lifeless as the eyes staring up from the severed head that lay in their midst.

In death, Sedrick's face bore little resemblance to the man he'd been in life and Erik Winslow felt the sharp pain of grief stab through him as he stared down at the remains of his friend. It wasn't the first time he'd faced death, nor was this the first friend he'd lost to violence. He'd been born into violent times and had, himself, died violently—four hundred years ago, when a chupacabra attacked him. Just as Sedrick had died—the first time.

This death was different, however. This time, death was permanent.

Summoning the same calm detachment that once bore

him into battle, Erik picked up Sedrick's severed head and placed it gingerly on the headless body lying close by. Slipping his arms beneath it, he was about to lift it when his gaze fell on the thin chain spilling from Sedrick's clenched fist.

He stared at it for a second, unmoving, as the significance of the discovery hit him. This chain, clutched in a death grip, was a possible clue to his friend's killer. Reaching to pry the hand open, Erik felt the hairs along the back of his neck prickle. He was no longer alone.

He stood and moved in front of the newcomer, hoping to block the view of the body before Sedrick's brother got too close.

"Michael," he began, grabbing his friend's arms.

"Where is he?" Michael asked, sounding both worried and guarded. "Where is Sedrick? I heard his cry through the link and then there was silence. I've been searching for him ever since."

His voice trailed to silence as he stared beyond Erik's shoulder. Erik saw the worry and fear in Michael's eyes and gave up looking for an easy way to deliver the news. "Sedrick's dead."

"No." The strangled sound was more like a growl as Michael rushed past him. Erik empathized with his friend's shock at seeing the body and severed head. Michael's pain and rage shot through the psychic link, strong enough that it pierced the barrier Erik kept erected. "Who did this?" Michael growled.

"I don't know. This is how I found him."

"No Prime would dare." Michael turned to glare at him. "I know of only one vampire hunter—"

"Who? Gerard?" Erik asked, not liking how quickly

Michael implicated a member of his family, though as the only hunter in town, it was the obvious conclusion. He shook his head. "No. It's not Gerard. He's been out of town for the last couple of days at a conference."

"Then who did this?"

Erik shook his head, wondering the same thing. He watched Michael's gaze rake over the body of his brother and then fix on the clenched fist at his side.

"What's this?" He bent and forced open the hand. "Military dog tags. American." He stared at them and then handed them to Erik. "Find me this man—this *Edwards, S. Private first-class.* Bring him to me."

"Michael—"

"Bring. Him. To. Me," he demanded. "Or else."

"Or else what?" Erik snapped, starting to lose his temper.

"Or else the pact is off." Michael's eyes glowed with the crimson red of strong emotion and his breathing grew rapid.

"Don't threaten me." Erik didn't like the way Michael was putting this on him.

Michael's face distorted in a mask of rage. "Sedrick is dead. You can't honestly expect me to walk away from this. We both know you didn't, twenty years ago, when your family was attacked and killed. You demanded that Sedrick and I find the killers. You threatened to destroy all of us if we didn't—and because we were your friends, we understood how you felt.

"So we found the killers and though they were Primes—like us—we turned them over and stood aside while you had your bloodbath. Now, it's my turn. I want Sedrick's killer and if I have to go looking for him myself, I don't particularly care how much innocent blood I spill along the way. But I know you do, so that's why I'm charging you with the task."

Erik knew all too well the anger and rage Michael felt, because even though it had been twenty years, he still remembered that night all too vividly. He remembered arriving at the castle to find Lily Winslow and the house servants dead. Only Gerard and the two young girls had still been alive.

He shut out the memory and sighed. Finding Sedrick's killer wouldn't be easy. He had no doubt that the killer was human because Michael was right, no vampire would dare to attack Sedrick. But the prospect of turning a human over to Michael sickened him.

He also knew that if he didn't, Michael, as head of the local lair of vampires, would declare the pact null and void. If that happened, none of the humans in the area would be safe. Was it right to risk all those lives just to save one human? A human who, Erik reminded himself, had killed one of his closest friends. It was hard to feel protective of someone when everything in you wanted to see him pay for his crime.

Making his decision, he met Michael's gaze. "All right. I'll do it."

Michael nodded and then lifted Sedrick's body into his arms. "Don't make me wait too long, Erik. In fact, you have the same amount of time you gave us twenty years ago. You have three nights."

Erik bit back his reply and watched Michael walk off, carrying his brother in his arms.

After he disappeared from view, Erik flipped the dog tags over, looking for anything that might help in his search. He found nothing more than the name, rank and serial number embossed across the front.

Pocketing them, Erik continued down the street. There were things he needed to do before the sun rose, and if he was lucky, he'd come across *Edwards, S.* lurking in some dark shadow before the night was done.

When he finally returned to the Winslow castle, he went directly to his dungeon apartment through the back entrance. He'd had centuries to perfect these living quarters and, short of a large meteor striking the castle, his apartment was impenetrable.

He went down the short hallway to his bedroom where he removed his black leather jacket. Across his back, he wore a shortened sword, which he carefully eased off and hung by its harness over the chair.

Moving about the room, he flexed his arms to ease the tension and aches. He felt old and when he paused to look in the mirror, he expected to see gray hair and a face withered with age. After all, he was four hundred years old. Instead, the same face he saw every morning stared back at him—youthful and, according to several women he'd known, handsome. His dark brown eyes matched the color of his shoulder-length hair, and his features were saved from being too beautiful by a half-moon scar around the outside of his right eye.

He undid the band securing his hair and absently scratched the back of his head. There was a time when he'd been more aware of his appearance; how women seemed attracted to him. Now, there were more important things to worry about in life.

He reached into his pocket and pulled out the dog tags. Tomorrow, he'd start looking for Sedrick's killer. With

Hocksley located in such a remote part of the country, it was unlikely the killer was simply someone passing through. The killer either had to be living here or at least staying in town for a while.

He laid the tags on his dresser and started to undress, moving with a bone-tired weariness brought on by more than the coming of dawn.

Every time someone he cared about died, a piece of his soul died with them. He would have thought that, by now, there was nothing left, and yet the ache of Sedrick's loss told him differently.

Despair filled him as he thought of his life, now measured by the number of loved ones lost rather than the passing of years. The thought of ending it all—meeting the sunrise—flashed through his head with the same intense longing it did every day just before dawn. He could think of no better way to meet his end than by standing on the edge of the cliffs he loved, listening to the ocean's waves crashing below and watching the sunrise. Oh, how he missed seeing the sun and feeling the heat on his face. The misery inside him turned to a physical pain, nearly choking him. He was so tired of living. All he had to do was walk out the door and not stop until he reached the cliff's edge and he could end it all now.

Instead, he crossed the room to his bed and lay down—and waited for sleep to claim him.

The next night, after he woke and sated his hunger with a cup of animal's blood, Erik carried the dog tags to his study and got to work. First, he called Myrtle's, Hocksley's only inn, to see if they had an S. Edwards listed. Of course, that would have been too easy, and there was no guest registered by that name.

Next, he called the hospital in the next town over, on the chance that Sedrick had succeeded in injuring his killer before he died. It was well over an hour's drive away, but was the nearest medical facility. They had no record of a patient by that name, nor had any patient been admitted recently with hard-to-explain cuts, scratches, puncture wounds, or significant blood loss.

Disconnecting the phone call, Erik resigned himself to going back into Hocksley. It seemed that the only way he was going to find Sedrick's killer was to walk the streets.

Donning his sword and jacket, he left the castle and began the downhill hike through the woods. Once he arrived in town, he navigated the streets until he reached the tavern district. There was a time when the residents of Hocksley wouldn't go out after dark, but these days, people seemed to think they were invincible.

As he drew near the tavern, he heard the sound of drunken laughter coming from within. It was the kind of sound that drew vampires—and therefore, a vampire hunter.

Erik selected the building across the street and scaled the outside drainpipe to the rooftop. From there, he could keep an eye on all the activity below.

For an hour or more, all was quiet. When the first drunk patrons stumbled out the door, Erik went on full alert. He didn't have to wait long before a movement below caught his attention. A vampire.

Erik opened himself to the psychic link shared by the vampires and honed in on the one below. As expected, it was a progeny—spawn of a vampire, with degenerating mental capacities and an ever-increasing thirst for blood. It would need to be killed.

About to go after it, a second movement caught his eye. Watching the shadows, he spotted a dark figure as it moved quickly after the progeny. Erik strained to get a better look and saw the sword clutched in the figure's hand.

There was only one reason for anyone to carry a sword with them these days, and that was to hunt vampires. Odds were that this was Sedrick's killer.

Following the figure with his eyes, Erik felt the familiar adrenaline rush of the hunt. Rising, he ran along the top of the roof, keeping himself out of sight from below. When he reached the end of the roof, he didn't even slow down but simply held out his arms for balance and dropped neatly to the cobbled street below, absorbing the shock of impact with his legs.

From up ahead, he heard the muffled sound of running footsteps. He followed the sound to the end of the block and then paused to listen. Noise of a fight drifted to him from the darkened alley beyond, so he continued on. When he reached it, he saw two figures fighting.

The swordsman obviously had skill, but Erik saw right away that he wasn't fighting well enough to win. Drawing his own sword, Erik raced forward, covering the remaining distance in an instant. As the creature turned to face him, he swung his blade and severed the progeny's head from his body. He watched in grim silence as both the head and body fell to the ground.

In his mind, it was Sedrick's head he saw, and anger swept through him, spurring him to leap forward and catch the slayer by surprise.

He shoved the man back against the side of the closest building and trapped him there, one hand pinning the slayer's sword arm against the brick while his other hand gripped the man's throat.

Then Erik caught the faint powdery scent of perfume and took a closer look. A dark knit cap was pulled low over a grease-covered but surprisingly delicate face, and the rounded curves of a feminine form were undeniable.

As he froze with shock, the woman tried once more to free herself from his grip. He was impressed with her strength, but still held her easily. When she raised her leg to knee him in the groin, he twisted his body and took the blow on his thigh instead. The pain was slight, but it did much to remind him of why he held her trapped.

There was no way this woman killed Sedrick. From what he'd witnessed, she wasn't that good. So what was she doing sneaking around Hocksley, hunting vampires? She was going to get herself killed if she didn't stop. What she needed was a good scare.

He moved closer, lowering his head to her neck and drawing her scent deep into his lungs, allowing himself to briefly enjoy the fantasy of holding a woman in his arms. "You're playing a dangerous game, pet. Someone is likely to get hurt."

"If you don't release me this instant, that someone is going to be you."

The voice, more than the words, shook him so badly, it took a minute for his brain to work again. "Kacie? Bloody hell," he swore, unable to stop himself. "When did you get home?"

Instead of answering, she strained against the hands pinning her to the wall. "Get your hands off me."

He laughed at her instead. "Right, so you can run me through with that sword of yours? Not likely."

"I won't run you through," she said between gritted teeth.

"No, probably not, but not because you won't try. Skills a bit rusty, are they? Well, that's to be expected. Not much opportunity to use a sword in the field of accounting, is there?"

She muttered a curse under her breath and shoved against him with her entire body in an attempt to free herself. He almost groaned aloud because little Kacie was all grown up now. "Best you stop that, love, or I might change my mind about letting you go."

"You're not scaring me, Erik. I know you don't feed off humans." Her tone was snide as she glared at him.

He returned the look, staring deeply into her hazel eyes, letting his own take on a reddish glow. "In your case, I'm willing to make an exception."

She opened her mouth, but then bit back whatever she had planned to say and held still.

"That's better," he growled. He took a step back and then, slowly, took his hands away. Though she glared daggers at him, she didn't try to strike him. "I thought you were at school."

"I graduated."

The revelation shook him. "Already?"

"I've been gone six years. How long did you expect it to take?"

"I don't know," he mumbled, trying to see her features beneath the grease paint. He only knew that he wasn't ready for her to be home yet.

He picked up the sweet scent of copper and ran his

gaze over her body until he found the source. "You're hurt." He gently took hold of the arm to get a better look at the cut just above her elbow.

"It's nothing." She tried to pull away as he turned her arm to get a better look.

Reluctantly, he released her. "It's not nothing," he assured her. "It needs stitches. Let's get back to the castle and I'll sew it up."

She gave him a surprised look. "No thanks. I'll go to Doc Turner's and let him do it."

"Doc Turner's dead."

"What?" She looked dazed. "When did that happen?"

"About two years ago."

"Dead dead?"

He felt like rolling his eyes, but didn't. "No one turned him into a vampire. He was eighty-six and died in his sleep."

"I'm sorry to hear that," she mumbled, more to herself than him. Then, lifting her head, she gave him a defiant look. "I'll go to whoever took over his practice."

"No one did."

She looked aghast. "Are you telling me that there's no physician in town?"

Erik enjoyed giving her a nasty smile. "Of course there is. There's the vet, old Hank."

"Fine," she said, lifting her chin in defiance. "Where is he?"

"Let's see, at this hour, we can probably still find him at the pub."

She turned on her heel and started storming off in the direction of the pub, leaving Erik to stare after her, still clutching her sword.

"Forgetting something?"

She turned and he held it out to her, forcing her to walk back for it. When she was close enough, he gripped her uninjured arm above the elbow. "I'm not letting that old boozer mutilate your arm. I'm afraid you're stuck with me doing it."

"I don't want you touching me," she said, trying to pull her arm free.

"Too damn bad. The stink of your blood is filling the night and soon, every vampire in town is going to come sniffing for the source. So, let's go." Still holding her arm, he pushed her to start walking, but she refused to move her feet.

"You can't make me go with you," she challenged him.

The familiar tension crackled in the air between them and his eyes shone a little brighter as he smiled, showing her his fangs. "Want to bet?"

The trek back to the castle was made in silence, but Erik didn't mind. He was too preoccupied with searching the night for the presence of other vampires to make small talk.

"Come sit down," he said once they were inside his apartment. "I'll get the first-aid supplies."

"I told you, I'm fine—"

"Don't argue with me, Kacie. If the wound is left untreated, it's going to get infected."

"I'll clean it myself," she argued, taking a step toward the door leading to the rest of the castle.

"Is that right? You're going to stitch it closed yourself?"

She shot him a scathing look. "I'll use butterfly bandages."

"Those might work for some of the other cuts you have, but not that one on your arm. It's too deep. It needs stitches." He was starting to sound like a broken record, which just added to the irritation he already felt by having her in his apartment like this.

"Have you even fed tonight? I don't really like the idea of letting you near my bloodied arm if you haven't fed."

"I fed. Okay?" Reaching into the cabinet behind him, he took down a bottle of whiskey and poured a healthy amount into a glass and handed it to her. "Drink this. It might not taste great, but it'll help deaden the pain."

She stared at the drink as if she wasn't sure if she should take it, but he stood there patiently and let her make up her mind. Finally, she took the glass from him and raised it to her lips. She hesitated only a second before swallowing the entire contents. She made a face at the initial shock of the drink going down, but recovered quickly.

While he waited for the alcohol to take effect, he took his knife and cut off the sleeve of her shirt, taking special care when peeling it away from the skin. Then, using a soft cloth, he cleaned the wound. When he finished, he sterilized and threaded the needle. Finally, he was ready to start sewing.

Now, it was his turn to hesitate. He'd sewn up a lot of wounds in his time, but this was different. This was Kacie.

"Try to keep your arm relaxed, at least as much as you can," he warned her and then pierced the edge of the wound. Her flinch was accompanied by a quick intake of breath, but she didn't say a word. After that, she impressed the hell out of him by sitting quietly while he worked.

"All done," he said several minutes later after tying off the last stitch.

She studied his work with a critical eye. "Nice job. Thanks."

That surprised him. "You're welcome." The silence between them grew awkward, so he busied himself with putting away the supplies. When he heard her move, he looked over to see her walking across the room, her attention focused on the pictures hanging on the wall. They were the pride of his collection; works by Leonardo, Renoir, Van Gogh, and Rembrandt, to name a few. All were works that the artists themselves had given to him and that remained undiscovered to the rest of the world.

Art was one of his true interests in life, and he liked when he could share that with others. "They're fantastic, aren't they?"

She jumped a little at his question, as if he'd caught her deep in thought. "They're nice."

"Nice?" He couldn't believe he'd heard her correctly. He pointed to one colorful work on the wall. "That's a Monet."

She looked at it. "Yes, very nice."

"They're fantastic," he exclaimed in frustration. "These have been painted by some of the most talented artists the world has ever known."

Her scowl said that she was as exasperated with him as he was with her. "Fine. They're fantastic," she mocked him. "Oooh. Aaaah." She turned her attention back to studying the works on the wall. "Look, I'm just not much into art," she explained, continuing down the hallway. "I . . ." Her words trailed off as she stopped before a landscape painting. "This is a McLaughlin, isn't it?" Her tone had taken on a breathless quality that immediately piqued his curiosity.

"Yes. Are you familiar with his work?"

"I love his work," she admitted. "In fact, I have several of his pictures in my apartment back home—not originals, of course. I can't afford those."

"You're kidding?" He was floored by her admission.

"This one's new to me, though," she went on as if he weren't staring at her stupidly with his mouth hanging open, "but I like it. I feel as if I'm standing there, in the picture, on the edge of the cliff." Her voice took on a distant, dreamy quality. "It's just before dawn. The sun's not up, but you sense it coming. It's that moment when everything grows still . . ." Her words faded off and she glanced at him, clearly embarrassed. "I should go." She turned and went back into the kitchen to retrieve her sword from the table where he'd laid it.

Erik recovered from his shock enough to follow her. "I suspect it's been a long day, between the flight home and then the fight this evening."

"Actually, I got in yesterday."

"Yesterday?" A cold chill crept up his spine. "What time?"

"I don't know—late morning, I suppose. I arrived in Millsburg night before last and tried ringing Dad to come get me, but he never picked up, so I spent the night there and then hired a car to bring me out the next morning. I thought that by now, Dad would have come home. Do you know where he is?"

"Out of town—at a conference," Erik answered absently, already walking down the hall to his office. "Wait here."

He picked up the dog tags lying on top of the desk and

hurried back out to where Kacie stood waiting for him. He held them out to her, hoping his fears were unfounded. "Have you seen these before?"

She gave him a suspicious look as she took them from him. "Where'd you get these?"

"I found them clutched in the hand of a dead vampire." He watched her closely, hoping to see some reaction. "Any idea whose they are?"

She was busy examining the clasp of the chain and barely looked at him. "Yes. They're mine."

"Yours?" It was as bad as he feared, but he had to make sure. "The name on them is Edwards."

"Sam was a close friend of mine. Sam's parents gave them to me after the funeral last week." She turned and started to leave, but he couldn't let her go. Grabbing her arm, he pulled her to a stop, receiving a sharp look. "Not so fast. This is very important. I found these tags clutched in the fist of a dead vampire—did you kill him?"

She glared at him and tried to pull her arm from his grip, but he refused to let her go until he had his answer. "Yes." Her grip on the sword in her free hand changed until she held it up and ready. "Now—let go of my arm before I have to kill another."